Kiss My Boots

Center Point
Large Print

Also by Harper Sloan and available from
Center Point Large Print:

Lost Rider

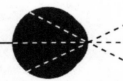

**This Large Print Book carries the
Seal of Approval of N.A.V.H.**

Kiss My Boots

THE COMING HOME SERIES,
BOOK TWO

HARPER SLOAN

CENTER POINT LARGE PRINT
THORNDIKE, MAINE

To my amazingly supportive parents, for teaching me to never give up and to try, try again

Kiss My Boots

1
Quinn

"Middle of a Memory" by Cole Swindell

— ★ —

The aroma of oil and exhaust fumes swirls in the air, mixing and mingling with the scent of metal baking in the strong summer sun. Even with the bays of the garage closed, the shop can't escape the soaring temperatures. Every truck that's brought in gives off waves of fiery heat for what seems like hours while we begin our work.

If you've ever worked under a vehicle that spent any amount of time kicking up rocks on the scorching Texas asphalt, then you know it's about as close to feeling the heat of hell that one chick can take.

And I love every second of it.

Ever since I was a kid, I've been happiest when getting my hands dirty. Most of the girls I knew went to mudholes to find their dirty fun—not me. While they were in the passenger seats of their dads' or brothers' or boyfriends' trucks, laughing and screaming as they bumped along through the holes, I was too busy climbing behind the wheel analyzing each and every move my truck would make—even before I could legally drive, which made my own brothers, Clay and Maverick, insane. But I didn't care. I couldn't get enough of it. I would envision ways to make the truck roar louder, kick up its spray of murky clay and water more powerfully, and take those backwoods trails with a supremacy that even the deepest rut couldn't stop.

Of course, it didn't hurt that while I was growing up, my father had owned the best auto shop around. It was also the only one around, but that didn't mean it wasn't the best. Davis Auto Works has been *the* place for custom auto needs since 1982.

And it's been my haven for longer than I can remember.

"Q! You gotta second, doll?" Tank bellows from somewhere close to the 2017 Dodge Ram I've been working underneath for the last hour.

Taking a second, knowing he can't see me, I close my eyes and take a deep pull of my special brand of calming air. The scent of motor oil, chassis grease, and brake dust trickles through my system and blankets my frazzled nerves instantly.

"What's shakin', cowboy?" I ask with a sigh, pulling myself to my feet. My hands go to the sides of my coveralls to wipe them clean out of habit before I realize I pulled them down after lunch to try and cool off. "Damn," I mutter, peering at the black handprints now adorning my faded denim. "I liked these jeans, too."

"Nothing a little elbow grease can't handle, darlin'."

I look up . . . and up . . . and up, finally meeting the dirt-brown eyes of Miles "Tank" Miller. The man is huge—hence the nickname—and, bless his heart, dumber than a box of rocks. He's a handsome devil, don't get me wrong, but even if he wasn't a complete idiot when it comes to anything other than motors, I wouldn't be interested.

I don't date. Ever.

"What do you need, Tank? I need to get this lift finished before five so I'm not stuck here all dang night."

"Got a real shitter comin' in. Man said he wanted every whistle and toot out there. I ain't sure what that meant though, seein' as he said it ain't even runnin'. Not sure you can put a whistle and toot on a heap of broken metal."

It takes every ounce of sweet southern darlin' I have deep in my soul not to snap at Tank and tell him I can barely understand his broken English, but my brothers didn't raise a rude little bitch.

"Tank, sweetheart, can you be a little more clear for me?" I roll to the tips of my boots and reach up to pat his beard-covered cheek.

He looks down, blinks a few times, and shrugs one meaty shoulder. "Naw."

Patience, Quinn. Patience. "Did you take his number?"

His eyes crinkle as his brow pulls into a frown. "Reckon I might have."

"How about you finish up fine-tuning the suspension system on the Ram for me? I was almost done so there isn't much left, just finishing up with the sway bar. I'll go look for that number. How's that sound?"

"Sure thing, Q. You takin' this baby up nice and high. Chester handlin' the engine on this bad boy?"

I nod, but don't bother answering him since he's already dropped down to disappear under the truck. I walk over to the sink in the corner and wash up with some GOJO. I might love getting my hands dirty working with trucks, but I still enjoy looking like a girl—which means I'm anal about washing often to avoid the perpetual black stains most mechanics have on their hands.

Stepping into the back office, I cringe when I see the mess on my desk. Normally, it's kept in the state of what I lovingly refer to as organized chaos, but all it took was one visit from our resident Tank and it looks like an EF5 tornado blew through.

"Jesus Jones," I mutter, shoulders dropping in frustration. "How the hell am I supposed to find something in this mess?"

"My guess would be clean it up." A familiar sardonic voice laughs from behind me.

"I do clean! Which you know damn well!" Fake annoyance laces my words as I spin around, smiling as I face my eldest brother.

"Let me guess: Tank?" The corner of his mouth tips up as he smirks at me. I can't see his eyes because of the shadow of his cowboy hat, but I imagine the deep hunter green is brighter than usual with a knowing sense of mirth.

"The one and only," I drone.

"I just stopped in to handle payroll. I didn't have everything I needed at the ranch, but I can hang around if you need somethin'."

"Now, Clayton Davis, you keep that up and I might think you enjoy tinkerin' around the garage," I jest, knowing damn well Clay hates working in the shop.

He takes off his hat, placing it on top of the filing cabinet open-side up as any good Texan would, running one hand through his thick black hair. "Funny, Quinny."

"I try, big brother. I know you've got your hands full at the ranch, so don't worry your pretty little head over things here. I've got everything under control."

"I know you do, Q. You could run this place hog-tied and blindfolded. But everything is handled at the ranch. Drew's been one step ahead of me all damn week. It's drivin' me insane."

13

I laugh at the mention of the ranch's foreman, Drew Braden. He's the only man I know who works harder than Clay. He keeps that ranch running with so much pride you would think it was his own family's land—but that's just the type of man he is. He always does say you can tell the measure of a man by how hard he works. He's been around since well before my father died last year, and he's always treated all of us like his children.

"Still workin' like crazy?"

"Ever since Jill told him she was pregnant. You would think at his age he would know how to wrap his shit up, but I have a feelin' Jill knew exactly what she was doin'."

"You make forty-eight sound ancient, Clay." I giggle, pushing some of the papers around, hoping to find some sort of message regarding the call Tank took.

"Shit, Q, I'd be freakin' out too if I was going to be a dad—again—years after my grown kids had already left the house. He's old enough to be *my* dad."

I roll my eyes. "I think that's a stretch, cowboy."

"He had Missy when he was fifteen, Q. And I graduated high school with Missy. Not exaggerating in the least, darlin'."

"Well, even so, that's what happens when you're pushing fifty and get yourself a new bride who probably graduated with your daughter, too."

Clay starts grumbling under his breath about beauty queens, big hair, and gold diggers. Not that I would call Jill a gold digger, but rumor around Pine Oak has it that she married Drew for his money. The man might work at the Davis ranch by choice, but he's never had to work a day in his life, he's *that* loaded. His grandfather's grandfather struck it big in the oil fields years ago, and to this day the Braden family is rolling in money from the investment. Not that Drew acts like it; the man still drives the same truck he had when he was in high school.

Finally spying Tank's near-illegible chicken scratch, I grab the torn scrap of paper and move to sink my tired body into my office chair. Clay heads toward his desk in the corner—much neater than my own—right as I pick up the receiver to dial what I hope are the correct numbers that Tank wrote down.

Then I see the name.

And everything around me washes away, my vision going foggy until memories long since banished start slamming into my head. They're so crystal clear that I feel like I'm the same love-drunk eighteen-year-old all over again.

Nine Years Ago—Beginning of the Summer

"Damn," a husky voice grits out. "It's just not right how hot you look tinkerin' around my truck, darlin'."

I look up from the oil cap I just finished tightening and smile, wide and toothily, before giving him a wink. "Is that why you asked me to change your oil when we both know you're more than capable? You're lucky—I don't normally make house calls."

He reaches up, the material of his T-shirt lifting from his Wranglers, showing off the toned, rock-hard abs and that mouthwatering V at his hips. I let out a squeak when I feel the weight of the hood lift off my hand, looking up to see him gripping it, returning my wink with a smoldering gaze of his own.

"Busted," he whispers, bending down to press his full, smooth lips against mine. The kiss is brief, but the butterflies that take up residence in my stomach whenever he's around pick up their fluttering until I feel like they might fly right out of my mouth.

I move awkwardly out of the way while he slams down the hood on his brand-new Chevy. I busy myself with washing up, making sure to clean my hands thoroughly until not a speck of grease is left on them, even if my pretty manicure is blown to hell. The last thing I hope Tate Montgomery is thinking about is the chipped red polish adorning my nails. His grandparents are out of town at a craft show near Austin and my brothers think I'm at my best friend Leighton's tonight.

We've got more important things to do than hold hands.

Tonight, I hope and pray that Tate makes good on all the promises our heated make-out sessions have been hinting at. I'm ready to give myself to him, pretty red bow intact.

"You hot, darlin'? I didn't think it was that bad since the sun went down, but we can head on in if you want." He points toward his grandparents' house and all I can do is nod. I can see the questions in his eyes, but he doesn't voice them as we make our way inside. "Paw said Gram left a fresh batch of chicken and dumplin's if you're hungry."

He's a few steps ahead—his back now facing me—when he speaks, so I take the time to take a deep fortifying breath before he turns back around. The last damn thing I want is chicken and dumplin's, but how do you tell your kinda-sorta-maybe boyfriend that you would rather he eat you than dumplin's?

"I'm good," I whisper, my heartbeat roaring in my ears. God, Quinn Everly Davis, cowgirl up and take the bull by the horns . . . or the man by the balls, same thing.

"Darlin'?" he questions, heat pooling in his denim-colored eyes.

"Please," I croak, the little badass that usually lives inside me long gone, made weak with hunger that has nothing to do with golden, fried buttermilk biscuits. "Please, Tate. We've been scratchin' this itch for two years now, and every summer you say not yet. Don't make this another summer where you leave without showing me how much you love me."

"Quinn." He sighs, taking off his white Stetson and running a hand through his chocolate waves. "Baby, you know I love you, but this isn't just any other summer. I'm not goin' back home when I leave this time. We're both about to start the next chapter of our lives—you takin' over the auto shop and me startin' at Emory. Georgia is a long way away, and we both know we've never tried long distance for a reason. Not sure that's somethin' I can stomach, finally gettin' to have you completely, only to lose *you*."

His words are all it takes for my temper to snap. "We've never tried the long-distance thing because of you, Tate. Don't put that bullshit on me."

"Not because I didn't want to, and you know it," he growls in return. "Fuck, Quinn, you don't think I've wanted to make you my girl since the first summer my parents shipped me off to Gram and Paw's? You know damn well I have, but it isn't that easy."

"Because I'm not some high-society princess?"

He stomps the few feet between us and curls his fingers around the back of my neck with a touch that is gentle but unmistakably dominant.

18

His thumbs, resting at my chin, give me a gentle push of encouragement to look up at him. I don't even bother fighting him. My head moves, eyes traveling the strong planes and sharp features of his handsome face until I meet his pleading gaze.

"You know I don't give two shits about what they think, Quinn, but until I finish medical school they've got more pull over me than I wish they did."

I sigh, knowing he's right. The Montgomery family holds the purse strings to Tate's future, and that's a hell of a bind. He's had his hopes set on going to an expensive out-of-state school and we both know he wouldn't be able to afford it without their help. I know how much it means to him too—going to Emory University—because it's where his paw attended, so as much as I hate accepting him leaving for a school that far away, I'll support that dream.

The silence ticks on while we hold each other's gaze. I pray that he can see the desperation my love for him makes me feel. The need to get as close as two people physically can is almost unbearable. What I feel—this fire burning deep in my belly—only becomes more powerful the longer I deny what I crave.

He must see something written in the silence around us because in that moment, the deep, dark blue of his irises swirl and light up with understanding. And unmistakable lust.

"You sure about this, Grease?" he questions on a whisper, lips quirking with his nickname for me. He's used it since the first day we met, when I was covered in engine grease.

"I've never been more certain about anything in my life, Starch," I answer, the butterflies picking back up to full speed when his smirk grows into a panty-melting smile at the use of my nickname for him—a standing joke about the high-society world he comes from back home in Dallas.

"Nothing in this world could make me stop lovin' you," he murmurs, his head moving down, closer to me, and before I can reply, his mouth captures mine in a deep kiss. I feel him all the way to my bones with this kiss. He's branding himself into my very soul, and I know without a shadow of doubt I will always feel him there.

There isn't any more talking after that. Moans, grunts, and the sound of bare skin brushing against bare skin, tentatively at first and then more urgently as we move together, are the only things that fill the silence around us. Through the pain of losing my virginity to the only boy I've ever loved, I bask in the beauty of this moment we've been building toward for years, knowing that my life will never be the same. Our future might not be set in stone, but we've come this far with only summers together since we were middle-school age. I have no doubt that we have what it takes to make it through him starting

20

his medical school career and beyond. We're not little kids anymore, confused about how we feel. We're on the cusp of adulthood, old enough to understand our hearts are connected so powerfully, you can almost feel them nestling close together, beating as one.

As one.

Present Day

I gasp when the memory clears, feeling my cheeks wet as I focus back on the paper in my hand. I pray that the name I read wasn't his, but even with the shaking of my hand making the paper vibrate softly, I know it's just wishful thinking.

The Ghost of Heartbreak Past apparently is back in Pine Oak.

Tatum Montgomery.

Jesus Jones.

2
Quinn

"You're Still the One" by Shania Twain

— ★ —

The rest of the day passes in a fog. Memories long since locked away have suddenly slipped free of their confines and infiltrated my mind, filling my brain with bits and pieces of a past I thought I'd left behind. It doesn't matter that I don't *want* to remember them—all it took was one piece of dadgum paper to rip away the metal chains securing those unwanted recollections deep within the depths of my soul. By the time I realize the sun has set and I'm alone in the shop, I've worked myself into a downright tizzy.

On a normal day, I can be hard to handle, but when I'm nursin' a tizzy, whoa boy. Irrational and manic, that's probably the best way to describe me in freak-out mode.

I've found that the best cure for a tizzy is popping open a cold one, so I head to the mini-fridge in my office, pop open a Corona, and perch on my still-messy desk, swinging my legs back and forth as the bitter liquid slides down my throat and brings me instant relief, the first I've felt all day since that piece of paper landed on my desk and shook me to my core.

I hate him for having this power over me.

I hate that I feel the pain of those memories sear through me as if they had happened mere seconds before and not nearly nine godforsaken years earlier.

I hate what he represents in my life.

And most of all, I hate that I care so much.

I'm used to letting those lost parts of my life define the person that I've become. I build a shield out of them, keeping everyone out except a select few, and in the end all it's given me is a whole lotta nothing.

I'm alone.

The story of my life, it seems.

Not alone in the sense that I have no one. I do . . . have some*ones,* that is, but I don't have *someone,* and for a girl who's only ever wanted to feel the love that the other half of your soul can give you—that means a whole lot more than I care to admit.

To be fair, not all the blame for my solitary life can be placed on Tate Montgomery's shoulders, though a big ol' heavy ton of it can. I guess, if I want to be technical about it, a large portion of the emptiness I feel stems from the woman who birthed me. Calling her a mother would be a title she doesn't deserve, but until recently, I would have given anything to have her claim it.

I was too little when she left to have any real memories of her—only the fantasies that I've built around the idea of having a mother—but just because I can't actually recall anything about her doesn't mean that I don't feel her rejection down to my bones. My brothers, God love them, did everything—still do everything—to show me I was loved, but growing up with the father we had. . . . His hate canceled out a lot of what Clay and Maverick tried to give me.

Aside from my brothers, the only other person who I know loves me unconditionally is my best friend, Leighton James. We've known each other our whole lives. Cheered each other on during every single step we took to become the women that we are today. There isn't a single part of my life that her presence hasn't imprinted upon. She is just as much a part of my family as my brothers are, especially now that she's marrying one of them.

If I'm being completely honest with myself, her and Maverick coming together and finally finding their happily-ever-after is playing a big part in this self-pity stew I'm cooking up nice and powerful.

I've avoided finding mine.

I've dissuaded male attention and advancements because I know deep down my heart will only ever belong to one man. It just so happens that he wasn't strong enough to fight for it.

Tate taught me to trust him. Every summer that he spent at his grandparents' ranch only solidified his unrelenting pursuit of me, of us, of our future together. It took him almost four years to convince me of his adoration, his undying love and loyalty. He took a sixteen-year-old girl who had always feared trusting in the very thing he was offering and made her *believe*. For two years we survived on emails, phone calls, and only two months out of the year being spent physically in the same place. That was all it took though. The foundation we built was meant to be everlasting—even if his promises hadn't been.

He taught me trust.

He showed me love.

Then he gave me pain.

So, no . . . all the blame might not be able to fall directly on him, but a large part of it does, and the rest of that dadgum blame only seems to be exacerbated with the unwelcome addition of his memory.

"For fuck's sake," I grumble, angrily swiping at the wetness leaking from my eyes. I look out my office window toward the brightly lit garage floor and contemplate my next move.

That's a lie. I don't think about a dang thing. I drain the last of my beer, grab my purse—a sweet black leather find I got at Coach the other weekend—and make quick work of turning off all the lights that the guys left on when they scattered. Gravel crunches and grinds under my steel-toed-cowboy-booted feet when I spin from the shop door and look down Main Street. It's only seven at night on a Friday, but like clockwork, most of the businesses around are dark and closed for the night. There's only one that I care about, though, and the bright-ass glow spilling from the front windows into the dusk around it makes me quicken my steps.

I hear my name right when I reach for the door to the PieHole, but I'm a woman on a mission. I burst into Leighton's bakery with determination and look for her blond head behind the counter.

"Jesus Christ, Hell-raiser. You got the hounds of hell hot on your heels or somethin'?"

I spin around at the sound of Maverick, my other brother, laughing behind me as he catches up.

"Shut up, Cowboy. I'm in a mood, and right now if you've got a twig and berries between your legs, you're the enemy. Where is my girl?"

Both of his dark brows go up at the clear venom in my tone and he takes just the barest step back. Maverick might be a retired professional bull rider, but I would be willing to bet he'd rather take on a big-ass bull again then deal with a pissed-off female any day.

26

Smart man.

"I'm thinkin' this means I'm not takin' *my* girl out on a date tonight?"

"You're thinkin' right," I confirm, hooking my hand on my hip, just begging him to try and stand in my way.

"Got it. Tell Leigh I'll be at home," he concedes with a sigh, turning and reaching for the door we had both just entered through moments before. With one muddied boot already outside, his body stills and he looks over his shoulder at me. "If you need me, little sister, all you gotta do is holler."

I nod, not trusting the turbulent emotions roaring around inside me enough to actually allow me to speak, but he can see everything in my eyes. Maverick always can. His free hand comes up and he lovingly taps his knuckles against my chin before walking out of the PieHole.

Ignoring the handful of townsfolk still scattered around the room enjoying an evening slice of pie, I walk through the cutout in the counter, past Avonlee, the high school girl Leighton hired to help out part-time, and straight into the kitchen. She's used to me, thankfully, so she doesn't even bat an eye at my boldness. It's always been our way.

"Hey Quinn!" Jana Fox, Leighton's longtime employee and manager of the PieHole, chirps.

I shake my head. "You are *way* too happy, Jana. Seriously, it's just not right."

She waves me off, laughing softly as her gray ringlets dance around her face. I kid you not: the woman is in her fifties and rocks a hairstyle that would rival Shirley Temple's.

"Uh-oh," she says in response, a twinkle in her eye. "You have that look about you, sweet child. Who is he? Don't tell me you didn't learn a thing or two from your brother and Leighton last year. In the meantime, though, while you get your head all screwed on, I just started sellin' those sexy toys that all you youngsters are playin' with if you need some help with your hooha. You really shouldn't let that kinda frustration fester."

"Jana!" Leigh shouts from her office. "Boundaries!"

I let out a laugh that feels like the emotional release I've been cravin' ever since settin' eyes on that damn piece of paper. In addition to being the best bakery manager this side of Texas, Jana also happens to be quite . . . enlightened for a woman of her age. And not shy about lettin' all of us younger ones know it, every chance she gets.

"She thinks I will somehow understand where these invisible lines of hers are if she keeps bellowing that word, but I'm too old to change my ways. Plus, you kids have too many 'boundaries' as it is."

"I'm thinkin' you might have a different

28

understanding of that word, Jana." I laugh sarcastically.

"Oh, hogwash."

I roll my eyes, some of the dark feelings inside of me slinking away in the face of Jana's overwhelming cheer. I ignore the rumble in my stomach when I pass *my* fridge—the special one that Leigh always makes sure is stocked with my favorite pies.

"Oh, shit," Leigh screeches right before we almost collide. I was so busy lusting over a kitchen appliance that I didn't see that she had come to stand in her office doorway, and I almost knocked right into her.

"Got a second?"

"Always," she answers without an ounce of hesitation.

"I sent Maverick away," I confess, pulling her into the office and shutting the door.

"And he let you?"

"He wasn't gonna argue with me."

She laughs softly. "You have to stop threatening his manhood." I narrow my eyes and she holds her hands up. "What? I happen to be quite fond of it."

"There are so many things wrong about that statement. Besides, I didn't threaten his . . . manhood. I just needed my best friend." Thrusting out my hand, I wait for her to hold hers out before unclenching the tight fist I clamped

29

around that stupid piece of paper. I glance at it briefly as it falls into her waiting grasp and see that the ink has started to spider from my sweaty palms, but even so, there's no mistaking the name scratched on it.

Leigh's eyes widen as she reads it. "Oh . . . shit."

I nod. "Yeah. Shit. That 'bout covers it."

She looks up from the paper, holds my gaze for a beat, and then looks back down. "Are you going to call him?"

"Are you going to ask stupid questions?"

"It's not stupid, Q! He called the shop. *The* shop. He might have been gone for a long damn time, but there's no way he forgot who owns *Davis* Auto Works. Even if he really is just looking to get some work done on his shit, he called your shop. You were really upset when he never came back after that summer. Maybe, if anything, you can get some closure with this call."

I feel a little bad knowing that she doesn't understand the whole picture—something I'm reminded of when she plays down the heart-breaking pain I felt when he all but vanished. Of course, that's what happens when you keep things from your best friend.

"There's a good chance he doesn't know it's mine now, you know. The last time I talked to him I had just started working there full-time. For all

30

he knows I don't even live in this town anymore, let alone own my family's shop. Anyway, I think it's past time for closure."

"That's a load of bullshit and we both know it. You guys burned mighty hot that summer, Q. You let it mark you. Hell, you keep letting it mark you, even now, refusing to let yourself get close to a man."

I sigh and drop down to Leigh's "special visitor chair." It's wedged between the wall and a filing cabinet because her office is so small, but I know she keeps it in here for me and me alone.

She moves around her desk and sits, still holding the paper in her hands. "Do you want me to talk you out of calling him or encourage you to do it?" Understanding is written all over her face. I know that either way, she will support me all the way through.

I honestly don't know the answer. "He left me, Leigh. Even though that's what happened at the end of every summer, that last time it was different. We weren't high school kids anymore. He said he would be back, even though he was starting university, with med school to follow. We hadn't ever gone too long without at least checking in with each other when he went home the years before that, but that last summer I give him *all* of me and he just vanishes. I spent a long damn time pinin' after him, making a fool out of myself with desperate attempts to reach him.

I just don't understand how, after all this time, I can possibly handle seeing him again. How does he still have this dadgum power over my feelings, Leigh?"

"I think you know why." She breathes softly.

I don't answer. I just look down at the paper she's pushing toward the edge of her desk—the edge closer to me. She waits, ever the patient one, until I relent and take it. Then she starts pushing the phone on her desk in the same direction. I let out a dramatic sigh, but I turn it to face me. I don't have to put up a brave front, not in front of Leighton: knowing I have her if I fall apart is what made my subconscious mind bring me here to see this through in the first place. Even if she doesn't know just how serious things were between Tate and me, she's giving me what I need: her friendship, love, and support.

Before I can give myself time to chicken out, I pick up the receiver and bring it to my ear, moving my fingers over the numbers written on the paper. If my cell hadn't died earlier, I would be pacing this nervous energy out.

The first ring makes my heart pick up speed, the frantic beat making the hand holding the receiver to my ear shake.

The second ring makes the same galloping heart drop into my stomach.

But it's the voice that I hear in the middle of the

third that makes the rapid beating stop and stall, stealing the breath right from my lungs.

"Tatum Montgomery," a deep, seductive rasp answers. That sound, that tone, matured with age, awakens every single thing—feeling—I had forced myself to forget about him.

My eyes flash to Leighton in panic.

"You got this," she whispers. "You're a hell-raising badass."

"I'm a hell-raising badass," I murmur in confirmation, trying to make myself believe her.

"Excuse me?" the sexy-as-hell disembodied voice asks, now sounding more confused but equally sexy.

I clear my throat.

Close my eyes.

Then pray my heart remembers how to beat after this.

"Starch."

3
Tate

"Vice" by Miranda Lambert

— ★ —

That voice.

Even without hearing that stupid fuckin' nickname come through the line, I would recognize that voice anywhere.

I push back from the restaurant table and give my dinner companion a wave of my hand to let her know I need a moment.

"Grease," I respond, an involuntary smile lifting my lips as I step away, my voice sounding a lot stronger than it should after being knocked off-kilter by her.

"Been a long time, Tate."

Moving through the busy restaurant, I step out into the rain-soaked Atlanta streets. "That it has, Quinn, that it has."

"I'm sorry about your paw. He was a good man."

"I appreciate that. I heard about your old man. I'm sorry for your loss."

"In an effort to make this a little less awkward,

save it, Tate. There isn't a soul around who meant that a year ago and it hasn't changed since. I made my peace with him and our lack of a lovin' relationship before he passed so I don't need your condolences." Her sassy-as-hell temper sparks, and any trace of restraint or attempt at politeness that had previously been in her tone vanishes. "Why did you call the shop?"

I fiddle with some change in my dress pants pocket, look down Peachtree Street, and weigh my words. "Like I told the man I spoke with earlier, I need some work done on an old truck and was callin' to make an appointment."

She laughs, the sound bitter and vile, nothing like the Quinn I used to know. "Are you saying that you, Tatum Montgomery *the Second,* are actually driving something around that doesn't still smell like the showroom floor?"

"It's Paw's old truck," I tell her, ignoring her attempted insult.

I hear her breathing and some whispering in the background, but she doesn't speak right away. I give her time, knowing that she has every right to turn my business away. Hell, she *should* turn my business away.

"Isn't there someone wherever it is you landed that can take care of this for you?"

Wherever I landed. I deserve that, I know I do, but it doesn't make the hurt in her voice sting any less.

"Doesn't make much sense gettin' his truck out here to Georgia only to turn around and drive it back. I don't want those kind of miles on the old beast, and I'd be packin' my bags to head out well before anyone here could finish the work that needs doin'."

"Drive it back where? Head out where, Tate?" The sass is gone now, and, if I'm not mistaken, in its place is something that sounds a whole lot like fear.

Fuck me. I did that to her.

"To Pine Oak, Quinn," I answer, calmly as I can.

"What?" she asks with a quiet gasp.

"Do you have time to work on it?" I ignore her question, hating what I hear in her voice. What my actions must have done to her to put that note of despair in her voice.

"Why would you come back here, Tate? Don't ignore me. I know your grandparents' old place is on the market now, so why would you even need to come back? If you can get all that done from a distance, I'm pretty dang sure you could get the truck done too." She finally stops rambling, the panic in her tone overwhelming the hard-ass sharpness she had been trying for. After a moment of silence, she takes a deep breath. "There isn't anything here for you anymore. You won't find some hotshot medical practice in the middle of nowhere, Texas."

There are so many things I want to say when she finishes speaking. She's wrong—there *is* something in Pine Oak for me. Something I never should have let go to begin with, but I didn't really have a choice. Not like she thinks I had. As much as I loved my paw, his death means that the last string that was held over my head is finally severed.

"Taking over Paw's practice means a whole helluva lot more to me than 'some hotshot' place ever could. As for the rest, well, that's a story for another day."

"Goddammit," she hisses, her voice sounding farther away, and I reckon she pulled the phone away from her face.

"What? Jesus, Q, you look like you're gonna pass out," another voice whispers through the line, muffled and only recognizable as female. I wonder if it's her best friend, Leighton—sounds like it could be her, although older and more mature. Those two were thick as thieves when they were younger, and I reckon they're still right close.

"Quinn?" I ask in concern.

When she finally speaks again, it's in a rush of words, none of which are what I want to hear. "When you get back in town you can call the shop and talk to Barrett or Tank. Barrett would be best, but Tank will still get some kind of message to me. Figure out what you want done and how much you want to spend before you call and save them the trouble of pullin' that outta you. I think it would be in everyone's best interest if you dealt with them and they communicated your wishes to me. I'll do this for you because I respected the hell outta your paw, but I can't *do* this shit *with* you. Not now. Not again. Not *ever*."

I see Ella, my dinner companion, wave at me curiously through the window, and I lift my chin in acknowledgment before giving her my back. "Quinn." I sigh, not ready to let her off the phone but knowing she is too stubborn to listen to reason when she feels backed into a corner. I don't even feel bad about doing it either, not when I know this is my key to getting close to her when I get back. I send a silent prayer of thanks to the gods that Davis Auto is the only game in town, any other potential body shops too fearful of the strong competition the Davis family represents to try their hand at the business. If there was any other shop within a twenty-mile radius of Pine Oak, I know I'd be shit out of luck.

"You have the shop number. I'll let the guys know you'll be in touch. I know this is an entirely foreign concept to you, but this, Tate, is what good-bye sounds like."

Before I can open my mouth and demand her silence so I can say everything I need to say, the call is disconnected and the dial tone is echoing back in my ringing ear.

I pocket my phone and try to ease some of the tension out of my shoulders, replaying the phone call in my mind, hearing her voice, and feeling my body start to come alive for the first time in a long damn while from that alone. I'd stopped believing that I would ever see her again, let alone hear her voice, but now that I have, my body is humming with the reminder of what that husky sound can do to it.

Back then, when I left her for good, I knew I was doing the right thing. It was something I had begrudgingly accepted as each lonely year passed that I longed for her. I would never have gone back, leaving her free to be lost to me forever when another man realized how perfect she is too. Hell, for all I know, that man's already in her life. That was the one update I refused to let my friend Mark, who still lives back in Pine Oak, fill me in on. Ignorance is bliss, and all that.

It took me a while to accept that possibility when I gave in and left her. There were so many days that I wanted to fight the resistance keeping me back and give up everything for her—but it would have been selfish of me to do so knowing it would affect so many others. So I did the only thing I could: I learned to accept the life I was living. I have some good friends in Alpharetta, the town just outside of Atlanta where I live. The position I have in the labor and delivery department at Northside Hospital in Atlanta is challenging and rewarding, just what I always wanted. I date casually, the type of women like the one waiting inside for me to return—even if what I share with Ella isn't special, it's practical. Functional. Satisfying, more or less. Bottom line, I don't do relationships. I feed my body's needs when the loneliness threatens to become too overwhelming, and that's it.

From the outside looking in, I have everything the younger me thought I wanted at this point in my life. I've become the man my parents pushed me to be—a doctor in a top-of-the-line hospital, far away from the private small-town practice I always pictured myself owning. I'm every bit the rich and successful man I appear to be. I could buy the damn world if I felt like I wanted to take it for a spin.

A dry laugh escapes me as I study my reflection in the window. I embody completely the "starch" Quinn and I used to poke fun of. The high-society image that my parents pressed upon me since my boyhood has taken over, when all I ever wanted was nothing more than to pull on some old jeans and get my hands dirty. I've become everything I always resented in my parents growing up, and I might as well be a world away from the only place—and person—that ever made me feel at home.

I wonder how I ever let it get this fucking far.

I reckon I was denying my mind a trip down this path for so long, I didn't even realize how bad things had become. Only difference this time is that I don't have anything standing in my way. My mind is focused on all the things I can fight for now that the worst thing that could happen is rejection. All that's left here in Georgia is a few loose ends to tidy up before I pack up the last eight-plus years and head back to Texas. Like my job.

And Ella.

My eyes roll involuntarily as I think of the situation with Ella and how out of control it's gotten. We aren't even dating. Hell, we were never dating. It was purely two busy people blowing off steam. Two doctors who used each other's bodies instead of going home alone. She said she didn't want anything more and I said I would never want anything more. She caught me each time when I had been letting that lingering loneliness choke me and it worked.

Until it didn't.

Even if I wasn't going back to Pine Oak—finally—this conversation would be happening. I probably would have put it off a few weeks, but once I knew I was going back to Texas an overwhelming sense of urgency hit. The reason I never wanted a relationship since I settled in Georgia was because if I couldn't have it with the one woman I wanted, I didn't want it with anyone, and now that woman is finally on the horizon, waiting for me to return—even if she doesn't know it yet. So I tried to end things with Ella—and then I tried again, and again. The woman just won't take no for an answer. She asked me to dinner tonight, and I begrudgingly agreed on the condition that we at last both come to the same page on our relationship, and where it would finish. Right here, right now, tonight.

But so far, there's been a whole lot of talking on my part and a hell of a lot of eye-fucking on Ella's part.

That's going to end. Now.

With a clear mind and a new fuel of determination rushing through my body, I head back into the restaurant.

"Sorry about that," I tell Ella when I reach our table, picking my napkin off the seat before settling back into the chair across from her, placing it back in my lap. "You ordered wine?" I ask, looking at the two full glasses on the table and the bottle with the expensive French label chilling in a bucket to my right.

"I figured we could relax a little. It's been a long week." She reaches across the table, her small hand about to close around one of mine, but I pull back before she can get purchase.

"I'm on call, Ella," I mumble, pushing the glass closest to me away and picking up my water.

She shrugs, pulling her arm back and winking

before taking a delicate sip of her own wine. "Well, you'll have to cut me off after two, Tatum. Anything more than that and I won't be any good for you tonight."

"Stop, Ella. You know damn well I didn't come out tonight as some sort of prelude to fuckin'. I'm only here for another month before my resignation is effective, but even without me movin' back to Texas, whatever you think is goin' on here isn't. We've talked about this."

Something flashes in her eyes, but it's gone a moment later. Her perfect mask falls back in place. "Oh, Tatum, I understand. Goodness, your accent sure does come back when you're heated. Anyway, I had hoped dinner might lead to a little good-bye fun, but you're right, I'm sorry. You can't blame a girl for trying though, Tatum. I mean, look at you."

I feel one of my brows arch at her continued attempts at flirting, but I ignore it in the hope that she will take a hint. "I'd prefer the remainder of my time here to pass without any more weirdness between us. I'm not goin' to deal with you playin' the role of a jealous girlfriend when you know damn well the time we spent together don't equal a relationship, especially when I made it clear I don't do commitment. We're colleagues and that's all."

She clears her throat. "Of course. I'm sorry. I thought it was just fun and games."

The waiter steps up to the table and sets our plates down and I wave him off with a smile and a nod before addressing Ella again. "Let's finish up our meal and I'll take you home. I appreciate your understandin', Ella, and I apologize if I did something to make you believe this was somethin' it isn't."

She picks up her fork, digging into her salad with a smile. "Nonsense. Let's put it behind us. Water under the bridge and all that. Tell me about this place you're moving to." She holds my gaze as she chews, and I relax now that she clearly understands the line I've drawn in the sand and seems willing to abide by it.

I cut my steak, take a bite, and savor the perfectly cooked meat before telling her all about Pine Oak, not even attempting to hide the excitement in my voice. Ella smiles and nods in all the right places, engaging in the conversation with rapt interest.

In another life—one in which I never knew Quinn Davis existed—Ella is probably the type of woman I would have ended up with. The daughter of two very affluent parents, southern and genteel, beautiful and always perfectly put together no matter where she's going, and intellectually smart and driven.

The perfect woman for a lot of men.

But not for this man.

I live in a world where Quinn Davis very much

exists, erasing any possibility of any other perfect woman existing for me, ever.

My perfect woman is the daughter of a bastard, beautiful, an unpredictable sexy mess no matter where she ends up, and so brilliant and driven that she could race her jacked-up truck in laps around the Ella Fosters of the world.

I'll grovel until my knees have no skin left on them. If I get back and find another man in my place, I'll fight for her regardless. If she forgot how to love me, I'll remind her. Whatever it takes.

No more regrets.

I give Ella a platonic smile over my water glass and signal the waiter for the check. It's time to end this farce I'm stuck living and take back my life—and the woman who has always held my goddamn heart.

4

Quinn

"Love Can Go to Hell" by Brandy Clark

— ★ —

Stupid. *Clink.*
   Infuriating. *Whack.*
Good-for-nothing. *Ping.*

"You keep beating the shit out of that undercarriage and there ain't gonna be shit we can do to put that old beast back together again," Barrett, one of my lead mechanics, jokes gruffly.

"Yeah, well I don't even want to put this old beast back together again anyhow," I snap, pulling myself out from under the truck and standing, stretching out my aching back muscles. I throw my wrench over to the toolbox I had wheeled closer to the side of the truck I was working on, having dragged it over from the other bay in my private section of Davis Auto Works.

"Oh, QD, what did this neglected beauty ever do to you?" Barrett's shoulders shake, a deep rumble of hilarity vibrating from his chest.

Ignoring him, I narrow my eyes and watch him

walk around the old Ford, analyzing it with a critical eye.

"What's the problem, QD? I've never seen you this fired up."

I roll my shoulders and measure my words carefully. Barrett doesn't need me to give him a handful of girl problems. He's got enough of that at home with his middle-school-age daughters.

"Just got a lot on my mind, Ret. I knew this project was coming, but I figured I had some time before I had to deal with it. Last thing I expected was the damn thing showin' up a few days after I got wind about it." Indeed, only several days after I hung up on Tate and wished him good-bye, his paw's damn truck landed in my bay, courtesy of Tank and Ret. Trying to separate the personal from the professional clearly wasn't working for me whatsoever.

"This old man Ford's truck?"

Forgetting my annoyance, I gape at him in shock. "Do you know any other F1's in or around Pine Oak that look like this, Ret? Jesus Jones, everyone and their uncle's brother has been itching to get their hands on this beast for years, but Fisher never wanted anyone to touch it."

"Fisher Ford was always a cranky old geezer," he grumbles. "Knew it was his, just got sick of watchin' you throw your sass around all day. Whatever's got your panties all twisted up, figure it out and stop bringin' down team morale."

47

"Team morale? Janet making you listen to those self-help tapes again?" I laugh.

"That woman's gonna drive me insane, God love her."

"I'm thinkin', Ret, you might already be there." I duck when he tosses a dirty shop rag at my head, laughing again when he starts pouting.

"You keepin' the old flathead in there?"

I shake my head, walking over to look at the old F1's original engine. "The outside of this beast needs love—lots of love—and Fisher might have tried keepin' this baby rollin', but I reckon time got away from him. It's comin' out. I'm pullin' the 329 flathead V-8 outta Bertha instead."

Barrett grunts, the noise a mix of shock and agreement, I'm sure. "Hear what you're sayin', QD, but be a damn shame to see you pull out something you've been workin' your tail off to restore for a solid year now."

"Yeah, well." I sigh, already fed up with the day and mad that it's not even noon yet. "Owner's paying top dollar to fix this up and he said money is no limit, right?"

Barrett nods.

"Well, that's good, because I just so happen to know that the owner of Bertha is askin' well over market value."

Barrett's eyes widen and his big beer belly shakes with hilarity. "Whatever Fisher Ford's grandson did to you must have been terrible."

"What makes you think he did anything to me?" I hedge.

"No woman I know lets that little piece of the devil that lives inside of her out for any other reason, darlin'. You've got it written all over your pretty little face. Just tell me, what did he do to deserve your wrath?"

I roll my eyes. "I swear, you gossip more than Marybeth Perkins after bingo night. You're the one that told him we could start on it right away when I know I told you I wasn't startin' this shit until I was good and ready, so maybe I should be takin' this out on you? You want to continue this blabbermouth session or you wanna help me pull this heap of shit out?"

Barrett's eyes ping from me to the old flathead engine, back and forth, a few times before he gives me a nod. I wait, knowing he's about to open his big mouth again. Two minutes later, he puts his tools down and turns to me, but I just lift my greasy hand and snap out a loud and emphatic no.

We work.

Six long-as-hell hours later, Davis Auto Works is locked up tight and I'm in my baby headed to the ranch. Well, one of my babies. I'm a truck snob, it's true, but I can't seem to part with any of the beauties I bring back to life long after they've been abandoned. My old shrink used to tell me that I was trying to make up for my own issues with abandonment by hunting out these forgotten gems, latching onto them, and pouring all of my love and care into them. I left her practice when she hinted that maybe my "unhealthy" hobbies were doing me more harm than good.

I don't deny I have issues, but I would be hard-pressed to find a single soul in the whole big-ass world who doesn't. I've come a long damn way in working past those dang issues, too; then all it takes is one gusty blast from the past to kick up dust as a harsh reminder that you can polish the past until the wood shines, but the grime always settles back in.

The gates to the Davis ranch hit my vision at the same time a deep rush of air escapes my lips, the discontent I feel echoing around the silent cab. I see Clay's truck parked in his normal spot and pull Harriett, my 1969 Chevrolet C10, in next to his brand-new, offensively shiny, Chevy Silverado . . . that he won't let me touch.

"Didn't expect you home this early," Clay rumbles from his perch on one of the porch's old rocking chairs.

"Cramps," I mumble, shutting Harriett's door *just* a little harder than normal and reminding myself not to stomp as I turn to climb up the porch steps.

"Just because you think I get grossed out by all things menstrual, sugar, I'm not lettin' this drag on anymore. You had 'cramps' two weeks ago when I was doin' payroll at D.A.W. and I might have a dick between my legs, not knowin' much about that shit, but I'm pretty sure they don't last this long."

"You want to compare cycles?" I snap, crossing my arms over my chest.

"Don't start that man-period shit, Quinny. Come tell me what's got you runnin' around like you've got a burr stuck in your ass. You've been avoidin' me."

I don't move. My spine straightens and I lock my knees, defiance written all over my face.

Clay narrows his gaze. "Didn't work when you were seven and wanted a cookie, damn sure ain't gonna work when you're twenty-seven and want to act like a sulkin' brat. I know you ain't talkin' to Leigh, because I asked. She said you've been actin' fine around her. I know you don't want to talk to Maverick because you're still worried he's gonna disappear again if he feels any kind of discord here, which sugar, that's some shit. You know he's settin' down roots God himself couldn't rip up. You got me, babe, and last I checked, I wasn't the worst option."

I deflate instantly, something Clay picks up on, because he drops the legs he had resting on the porch rail, his boots slapping against the wood with a loud bang that makes me jump. He stands to his full height and erases the distance between us, towering over me as always, wrapping me in his comforting arms.

He's been my hero since I was a baby. He stepped up when it became clear the Davis siblings could only count on each other and made sure I was protected, loved, and sheltered. In many ways, he's more of a father to me than my own ever was, and even if I had tried to build that gap with our late father before his death, this special connection would only ever be with Clay.

"I'm a mess, Clay," I whisper softly against his flannel shirt. His arms spasm around me, but he doesn't release his hold.

"Nah, you're not a mess, sugar, just a little dusty."

I smile into his shirt, breathe in the familiar scent of earth and leather, before stepping back to gesture to the row of rocking chairs. "Might as well get cozy for this."

Clay's eyes flicker, but other than that he doesn't give me a clue to what he's thinking.

"Remember Tate Montgomery? Fisher and Emilie Ford's grandson?" I ask after we both settle into our seats. The slow rolling of the wooden rocker gliding against the porch floor dances through the air around us, making me aware of the silence emanating from my big brother.

"Yup," he finally answers, low and menacing.

"He's . . . resurfacin'," I continue, figuring that's a damn good way of explaining his return.

"Meaning? He's comin' to settle out some things his paw left or something a little more . . . indefinite?"

"I would say the former."

Clay hisses a breath through his teeth, the sound harsh and sharp. "That what has you actin' like a lost pup?"

How do I explain to him how I feel? Men don't get this sort of stuff, or at least that's what my experience has taught me. Leigh does, and even though I know she would drop everything for me in an instant, she's got so much going on with her upcoming wedding that the last thing she needs is my bullshit. Which is why I've done my best to put on a good front with her since I called Tate in her office two weeks ago.

"I'm not really sure. I feel like I did back when I realized he really had disappeared without a word. You know we got *close* that last summer. The same hurt I felt then when I would call his number only to find it disconnected is back. I think about how he always said nothin' would keep us from our future—together—only to have him torpedo our relationship himself, and I feel rage. I'm sad that I've lived my whole adult life measurin' every man showin' interest in me against Tate and what he did. Now he's comin' back and the biggest thing I feel is fear because he still has such a powerful hold on me." I take in a gulp of air, feeling oddly close to tears. "I heard his voice on the phone, Clay, and the years just washed away. I have to stay angry. If I don't, I'm terrified I'll give him whatever he wants just to feel the happiness I had with him. That fear turns into an all-consumin' panic when I think, what if he casts his line, gets his hook back in me, then decides I'm not a catch worth keepin' and tosses me back again?"

I glance over at Clay when he stops rocking. His expression is stony, but not angry. I can't quite put my finger on it, but it almost looks as if he's peaceful yet determined.

"What, Clay?"

"Just waiting for you to realize what you just said."

I think back, replaying my words, and then it hits me. The air stalls in my chest and my eyes widen.

"Just because it's been years, sweetheart, doesn't mean feelin's are just gonna vanish. You two always did burn hotter than hell when you were together. Even before I made you sit down and tell me why you were takin' him leavin' so hard, I knew there was somethin' there. Mighta been young, but you were never stupid. What's your gut tellin' you? Think hard, Quinny. Push back that hurt and fear. Really think about what it's tellin' you."

"To run," I whisper.

"Run where?"

"Straight to him."

Clay nods his head slowly, the muscles in his jaw jumping. "Then I guess you need to cowgirl up."

I feel some of the heaviness lift when Clay utters the saying we use between us when we're facing something challenging. *Cowgirl up,* or *cowboy up,* is as good as a dare in our book.

"Easier said than done, big guy."

"It's only as hard as you build it up to be in your mind, Hell-raiser," he stresses, his voice sure and true. "Take it one day at a time. Don't think I haven't heard about him gettin' his paw's old truck into your hands. He sure did move mountains in order to get that done all the way from wherever he is. When he gets back in Pine Oak, sit down and figure out what happened between y'all. After you have all the facts, then I reckon your gut's gonna be talkin' a lot louder."

"For someone dead set on remainin' a bachelor, you sure do know a lot about this kinda stuff." I laugh, pushing through the renewed burst of fear his words settled on me at the thought of sitting down for a chat with Tate.

Clay chuckles. "Blame the Hallmark Channel."

My jaw drops for the barest of seconds before I'm laughing so hard I have to clap my hand over my mouth and calm down to keep from peeing myself. Leave it to Clay, as always, to take the mountain of dread that's been building inside me and level it to the ground.

Maybe he's right, which shouldn't be surprising, since he knows more about how close Tate and I were than anyone else—even Leighton.

All I know is, I can't continue to feel this massive discord inside me. I might not have ever thought this day would come, but it has, and like it or not, it's time for me to pull up my big-girl britches and get back in the saddle of my life.

5

Quinn

"Any Man of Mine" by Shania Twain

— ★ —

Eric Church is blaring through the shop speakers, cranked up loud as hell so I can hear it from the spot I took up outside the back entrance of the bay I'm working in. I have the industrial fans blowing full blast inside, even if they're just pushing oppressing heat around, cooling nothing but at least making it a little more bearable when I step back inside and out of the hot Texas sun.

My coveralls are tied around my waist and my black tank top is rolled up under my sports bra. Thankfully, I can get away with it because I'm not doing much but speed-blasting the rust on the back panels of the F1. I moved outside to ensure I had plenty of open space to run the blaster, but the heat quickly became too much to handle.

The guys around here don't even bat an eye at me, used to me doing what needs to be done to counteract boob sweat. No woman likes boob sweat. Even if the guys were paying attention, my two private work bays are farther away from the hustle and bustle of the main garage floor, so they would have to go way out of the way to do it, and that would mean they weren't working. There isn't anything that chaps my hide more than my guys slacking off on the clock, and they know it. So they take care not to pay me any mind.

Every second of my time at the shop has gone into this baby—whom I've lovingly started calling Homer, because no truck this fine should be without a name. I've fallen in love with it, despite my best efforts to stay cool and detached. No can do. In the years since I took over control of D.A.W. I've stepped back from the day-to-day mechanical needs here. My boys are top-shelf talent, and aside from the customer consultations, I pretty much stick to the design end of our custom auto work. I'm here every day, but not because I have to be. I'm here because I crave it. Taking something like Homer and bringing him or her back to their glory days is my drug of choice. I wouldn't be me without the scent of gasoline and grease emanating from my pores.

Before Tate rammed his way back into my consciousness, I was focusing all my time on another F1—the only other one in this whole dadgum town. Bertha is *my* baby, one that I found at a scrapyard so far past her prime, no one here thought I would be able to find her beauty again—but I did, or I was close . . . until now. Until Homer, I was maybe a week away from firin' Bertha up and hittin' the road.

I pause and stretch to work out some of the kinks in my back and look through the open bay door behind me, seeing her sitting in the next bay over, waiting patiently for me to get back to her. My girl is sweet like that. A part of me regrets making her wait even longer for our date on the open road, but I know she'll forgive me. Well, she'll forgive me when I rebuild another engine for her someday when I finish Homer, since he's taking hers. Sure, I could have found another one for Homer, but when it comes to engines, I won't put just anything in my babies. I all but build them myself, and that kind of labor takes time— time I wasn't willing to give if it meant finishing Homer up before his new owner rolled back in town.

"Am I going to have to drag you away from that damn truck or are you goin' to stop avoidin' me?"

I whip my head around at the shrill voice breaking through my thoughts so fast I lose my footing. Dropping the blaster, my arms windmilling instantly at my sides, I start cursing a solid streak any sailor would be proud of.

I land hard, the sand from the speed blaster prickling the exposed skin at my back, and my elbows digging into the asphalt beneath me. I ignore the pain and glare up at Leighton.

"Don't you give me that look, Quinn Everly Davis! You know damn well you've been avoidin' me."

She doesn't even finish talking before she steps out onto the shop floor and walks over to me, reaching down to offer me a hand up.

"I haven't been avoidin' you, you big jerk. I've been busy workin' on Homer. He isn't gonna put himself back together, you know?"

"Homer?"

I point around me—allllll around me—making sure to indicate all the pieces of Homer that I've slowly been dismantling over the past few weeks that I've had him. Only the shell of him remains at present, but I can already see him taking shape handsomely.

"So, Homer is . . . car parts?" she asks in confusion.

I don't even bother trying to correct Leigh anymore. She's like a dog discovering a squirrel for the first time when I explain what I'm working on. It doesn't offend me, not at all, because I know if she started trying to teach me how to make some of her delicious pies I would be the same way. We can appreciate each other's talents all the same, even without understanding a dang thing about 'em.

"Truck," I deadpan, dusting off my ass before

grabbing the discarded blaster and walking over to my workstation to turn down the music. "Just like Bertha. Same year, too."

"Bertha?" she puzzles.

I lift my arm and point toward my girl, her gleaming black body shining under the shop lights. My skin tingles just looking at her.

"Got it. Kinda," Leigh mumbles.

"You don't, but that's okay, Leigh. I still love you even if you can't tell the difference between a coupe and a sedan."

"A what?"

I laugh, turning to face her. "I wasn't avoidin' you. Promise. Things have just been busy here. I wanted to get as much done on this one as I could before my reprieve is over."

"Do you know when he's gettin' into town?" she questions, knowing instantly what "reprieve" I'm talking about.

"Not a single clue. Ret deals with him when he calls for updates or when I need an approval on another expense. I just do what I need to do to ensure that Fisher's Ford looks like it just rolled off the assembly line and it's 1948 all over again."

Leigh snorts. "Fisher's Ford, that's hilarious. God, he sure was a funny old coot, wasn't he? I bet he never would've dreamt of drivin' anything other than a Ford just for the shits and giggles people got when they said that."

I snicker right along with her. It's been in my head since I started working on it. Fisher Ford and his Ford. Not even sure why I find it so damn funny. "You probably aren't wrong. He was a good man, damn shame about his passin'."

"Ever since Emilie died, he seemed to age daily." She sobers. "I went in for my yearly a few months before he passed and I'm not even sure how he managed to do all his cooter-doc work, his hands were shakin' so badly."

"God, Leigh, you make it sound so disgustin'." I hoot, laughing even harder now.

"Your brother misses you," she tells me, the swift change of subject catching me off guard. "He's worried you're backin' away from him again."

I feel a pang straight through my heart at her words. "Jesus, Leigh. How could he even think that?"

"Probably because the last time you started stayin' away from him for weeks at a time it was right after he told you about your mama. He knows you were hurtin', but I think a big part of him is scared you'll blame him for whatever part he's still convinced he played in her bullshit. Honestly, though, I think he's a little worried you might be gearin' up to ask him to take you to her again," she whispers softly and with care.

"Is he really worried?"

My stomach clenches thinking about her, the

woman who birthed us and abandoned us. When my brother came home king of the rodeo circuit, after being gone for close to a decade, he dropped a massive bomb on Clay and me: not only had our mother cheated on our father, resulting in her pregnancy with Maverick, but she was so mentally gone now from years of whoring and drug use, she wasn't even a shell of herself anymore. She was basically alive physically, but dead mentally. A pill that I still have a hard time swallowing.

I'd reacted emotionally and begged Maverick to take me to see her, which he'd outright refused to do. I was angry at the time, but I know he has his reasons and they're all about doing what's best for me. He figures no good at all will come from my seeing Mama, and I don't disagree. It's taken me almost a whole year to work through my issues with her transgressions and if I'm honest with myself, I haven't even gotten to the heart of those problems, but the last thing I would ever do is blame him. He isn't too far off the mark, though. Part of me does still want to see her, even if it's just to officially close that chapter of my life—the one about a girl who always wished her mama would come back and love her.

"He's just worried about you, Q. So am I. It isn't like you to pull away from us."

"You know exactly what's goin' on with me

right now, Leigh. You could have just told him what was happenin'."

She exhales, the sound hitting my ears even over the noises blasting throughout the shop. "I don't though, Q. You left the PieHole after that call with Tate and then nothin'. You left that night with a smile on your face after we pulled the moonshine out and talked about how you were glad he was comin' back so you could show him what a, and I quote, 'fine-ass bitch' he missed out on. You've never been a good liar, Q, so far as I knew you've been workin' on this grand plan of revenge and using your hot body to get it. It's been three dadgum weeks since that night, and every time I see you, you brush off whatever's up with you as nothin' but work and lack of sleep. Three weeks, Q, and zip on the Tate situation. What gives?"

"That moonshine needs to be buried deep in the earth. It's the devil's brew, I tell you. It does nothin' but make you turn into someone that does and says ridiculous things. When would I ever refer to anyone, let alone myself, as a fine-ass bitch, Leighton James?"

She tosses her head back, her blond locks dancing behind her back and over the delicate straps of her sundress. "You do it all the time, Q!"

I roll my eyes. "Whatever. All joking aside, I've just been workin' through some stuff in my head. It has nothin' to do with Maverick . . . or *her*. I really do want to have as much of Homer done as I can before Tate sets foot back in Pine Oak."

"Since when can't you work things out with me? I get wantin' to have a head start on this truck stuff, but you aren't even talkin' about him comin' back. You just say it's nothin' and then avoid everyone by keepin' yourself at work all the dang time."

She doesn't say all that to make me feel bad. I can tell she's just genuinely confused that I wouldn't go straight to her like I normally do to blab on and on about everything and anything. I guess I haven't been putting on as good of a show as I thought.

"I didn't want to burden you, Leigh. You've got so much goin' on with the wedding plans and Maverick's new students arrivin' on the ranch for the next quarter of trainin'," I tell her honestly, referencing the fledgling training facility that my brother opened when he was forced to stop riding bulls due to his health—the same one that has now become the talk of the rodeo world. "I'm workin' through it, I promise, and Clay helped set my head straight, so it wasn't like I was festerin' in a vat of crushed dreams or anything."

Her eyes heat. "That's bullshit, Quinn! First, I'm never too busy for you. I love you, and you know that. You're my family, and when you're

65

upset, I feel that. Don't shut me out. Second, I love your brother, but there ain't no way on God's green earth that Clay can set your head straight like I can."

"Honestly, Leigh, if you want the truth, I just don't know how to make sense of all this shit swirlin' around in my brain," I tell her on a sigh, pointing at myself with a wave of my hand. "Yeah, I might not have wanted to add to your stress, but I also just don't know how to explain it all. Even to myself."

She looks at me, nothing but compassion and understanding in her gaze. "You remember when your brother came back, Quinn? You remember how *I* was when your brother came back? I think I have a pretty good idea about swirlin' minds. Come to dinner at the ranch tonight and freakin' talk to us."

Her words hit home, their aim true, and I move around my workstation while she gives me the time to get control of the floodgates of my turbulent emotions as they threaten to burst free. The shop is the last damn place I want to have this chat, because I know things are going to get overwhelming once they finally break the hold I have on them, and I'll turn into a blubbering mess. I heave a sigh of acceptance out and give her a nod.

"I know Ret needs to go over the week's parts order before I head out today. Let me finish up and holler at him, and then I'll head out to your place."

She smiles. "Good. I just know Maverick's goin' to want to see for his own eyes that you're okay and not upset with him over whatever he's built up in his head. For such a strong-willed man, he sure does turn into a big baby where his sister is concerned." She winks.

"Help me work through my shit and I promise I'll take care of the big brute. The last thing I want is him thinkin' I'm upset with him for something he didn't actually do."

She laughs, gives me a hug, and takes off after I promise not to be far behind her. It takes me about thirty minutes to make sure I have everything with Homer ready for tomorrow and to tidy up my work area for the day. Ret waves me off, not willing to stop installing a lift on a beautiful new Tahoe to go over the orders, promising to meet with me first thing in the morning before he sends it in. These guys don't need me here, something I'm reminded of daily, but I still like making sure they know I'm never far. I might have built this place up so well it could probably run without me for years, but that doesn't mean I want it to.

With no other way left to kill time, I head out to Harriet and make my way to Leigh and Maverick's ranch, praying that my best friend can help me get through the muddled mess of my mind.

One thing's for sure: it's been close to a month since that first call with Tate, and I know he's due back in Pine Oak any day now. Well, I don't know it for sure, but I can feel it. There's a wicked wind blowin' and it doesn't have shit to do with the stormy weather forecasted. I need to hurry up and figure out exactly how I feel about his return *and* what I want to do about it.

Hell, I don't even know anything about the man he's become. Believe you me, I tried stalking him over the years, but there isn't a hint of him on social media. He could be married with kids by now, for all I know. Or he could be unattached and attainable. Is he even the same young man who disappeared on me? Does his return mean he wants to finish building what we didn't have a chance to complete? My mind races, the thoughts I've been suppressing bombarding me rapidly, but deep down I know he wouldn't have gone so far out of his way to get Homer in to the shop a week after his call if he didn't want to ensure some sort of guaranteed connection between us when he got back. A man that was attached to another woman wouldn't work that hard . . . right?

For all I know, I'm working myself up over nothing, but it's that little nagging voice in my head, whispering behind all the frantic, panicked yells, that tells me I should know better. That I should trust my gut. There's something bigger to the reason he's coming back, I can feel it, and it isn't just because he's taking over Fisher's practice.

Taking over Fisher's practice.

Oh. My. God.

I slam on the brakes and stop dead in the middle of the road that Leigh's drive is off of and stare out the windshield in front of me in horror. Thankfully, no one is traveling behind me.

"Jesus Jones. He's a gyno," I moan into the empty cab. "Tate Montgomery isn't just a doctor. He's a lady doctor."

6
Quinn

"We Should Be Friends" by Miranda Lambert

— ★ —

After my freak-out on the side of the road, I haul ass so fast to Leigh's that I kick up dirt and gravel into the truck bed the whole way down the drive to her house. I'm sure I look like a maniac, but Christ, a girl can only take so much.

Leigh is on the porch watering some of her hanging plants. Or she was, but with my manic arrival, she lets the watering can drop to her side, its contents spilling on the ground as her mouth hangs open in shock, her eyes not leaving my truck as I tear into my usual parking spot so swiftly it feels like the truck might split in two from the momentum.

Half a second later I'm out, slamming the door harder than I ever would and rushing to her. I stop, panting, and sputter, "He's a vagina doctor!" then grab my knees with each hand and lean over to catch my breath, keeping my head tilted so I can see her face.

Her chin tucks toward her chest as her head

jerks at my sudden outburst, and she looks at me like I'm just as crazy as I feel.

"Do you hear me, Leighton? One of the only vagina doctors for miles and miles . . . more miles than I care to drive just to get crotch-violated and my boobs grabbed once a year. Do you know what that means?" I screech, nearly apoplectic with full-blown horror. I straighten from my hunch and pace for a beat before looking back at her and throwing my hands in the air. "Seriously, do you get what this means for me?!"

"Uh, that he might not need to lubricate the speculum before your exam?" she jokes with an awkward giggle that sounds just as forced as it looks.

"That is . . ." I pause to think about it. "Well, actually it's probably true. I mean, if he looks anything like he used to it will be, but that's also beside the point. It means I won't be able to avoid him if things get all gross and awkward. Not unless I want to drive close to an hour away to find a new doctor outside of town. Why couldn't he have been a pediatrician? Or maybe work in geriatrics?"

I can tell Leigh wants to laugh. She rolls back on her bare feet, I'm sure to buy herself some time to squelch the laughter that wants to fly free. I watch as she adjusts the straps of her dress, dusts nonexistent dirt from her front, and then meets my eyes, fully composed.

"Well, I was goin' to ask if you wanted some wine, but I think somethin' a little stronger is in order now."

"If you even think about gettin' that moonshine out, I'll kick your ass," I retort, narrowing my eyes.

Leigh turns, the skirt of her dress twirling around her, and opens the screen door to her and Maverick's house. I see Earl, her big-as-hell Maine coon cat, instantly. It's not like you can miss the big fat beast, but you *really* can't miss him when he's sitting in the middle of the couch, one back leg up in the air while he licks himself. Such a man.

"We've got about two hours before Maverick is done for the day. He's out in the trainin' arena with some of the new cowboys workin' on riding techniques or somethin' like that. All I know is he wasn't wearin' a helmet the last time I went down there, but he made everyone else. Stubborn man knows he can't get another bump on that hard head of his, too. I should warn you, though, he knows you're comin' and wants to see for himself that his sister is okay."

"Is that the warnin' I have to down a few shots and get the hard stuff out of the way before he comes back?"

She giggles. "No. He knows we need some time together. I'm sure he'll be up, especially after that dramatic drive-in, but he's goin' to have dinner with the trainers and the new students tonight. Trey promised me he would keep him busy after that until I let him know it was good to come home."

At the mention of Trey, Maverick's real father's brother, I feel the familiar twinge of emotion I always get when he's around or mentioned. Even though all the shit Maverick found out about our mama while he was gone, especially that Daddy wasn't his biological father, devastated us all, it only served to bring us—Clay, Maverick, me, and even Leigh—closer. We might not have our parents anymore, what with our father having passed away over a year ago and our mama being . . . whatever she is, but Trey arrived and instantly extended his love for his nephew to Clay and me as well.

"Might as well skip the drinks, Leigh. I want a clear head while I get this all out."

She stops on her trek to the kitchen and reverses her steps, following me as I walk into the living room.

I drop down onto her oversize couch and yank off my boots so I can pull my legs under me. Now that I've shed my coveralls back at the shop, my old cutoff shorts aren't offering much warmth in the chilly air-conditioned room.

She starts to talk, but I stop her instantly. "Let me get it out. It's like, every thought I have is pushin' at my mental barriers and if I don't just let them free, I'm going to explode."

"Get it out then, Q. I took a quick twenty-minute power nap, so I'm ready to decipher the ramblin' madness you always spew when you're tryin' to think out loud."

"That was smart," I praise, reaching over to pet Earl now that he's stopped licking his balless self. "So, I should probably admit to you that I kept a lot of the truth from you with how serious things were back then with Tate and me. Don't get mad, I didn't do it because I was hidin' it on purpose."

"What does that mean?" she asks hesitantly.

"The summer Maverick left, Tate's and my friendship got a lot . . . stronger. You were really upset about Mav and, well, I just didn't want to bring it up and make you hurt more, seein' Tate and me together like that. Now before you get mad, I only kept that one summer from you because of everything that happened with Mav. After that, well, it just didn't seem relevant now that summer was over. When he came back the next summer, right after our graduation, I just let you think that was when we finally stopped bein' 'just friends' and hooked up."

"I should probably be mad, but I understand where you were comin' from. That explains why you took his disappearin' so dang hard. I knew you guys had a close friendship for years—he was tighter with you than he was with anyone else in our little group of friends. I thought you

74

had only really been *together* together that one summer, so I figured you missed Tate as a friend more than, you know, you did as a lover."

"Yeah . . ." I exhale, dropping back to rest against the cushions behind me. "Even just calling him my summer lover doesn't sound strong enough of an explanation for what we had. The night he took my virginity, we stayed up for hours talkin' about how we would make it work even with him in college four states away. We had weeks together that summer with our heads stuck in that stupid beautiful cloud, Leigh. Weeks. When he left, I smiled through my tears because he was *so sure* that everything would be okay. And I believed him. Then he was just gone. Even if what we shared that summer didn't mean as much to him as it did to me, *even if,* how did he just give up all those years as friends?"

"You took it hard. I remember. It makes sense now, though. I honestly just thought you were upset about losing the connection you two always had through years of friendship when he came to town. Now though, hell, Q, I'm just as baffled as you are about his abrupt departure."

"I loved him," I admit, my voice full of melancholy. "I loved him so big and bright that the only future I could see was with me at his side. He made me forget the hurt I harbored from my father's verbal lashings. The pain of my mama's abandonment didn't even register anymore. I was *whole,* Leigh. So full inside that it was tippin' over the edges and floodin' everythin' around me in the most beautiful way. Then all I felt was the bone-chillin' loneliness when, just as quickly as that summer passed, I was hollow again."

I hear the tick of a clock behind me mixing with the loud purrs coming from Earl as the silence stretches around us. Me stuck in my memories and Leigh letting me get my thoughts caught up with my mouth. Silently giving me the strength to get it out.

"I want to hate him," I whisper. "I want to hate him so badly that I shake with it. It hasn't been that long, but maybe the last almost nine years have been hard on him too and he's feelin' some karma over leavin' like he did. He was as close to perfect as one man could get back then, but he could roll into Pine Oak baldin' with a giant beer gut. Honestly, though, even if that's how it plays out, I think I'll still feel nothin' but need for him. Each day that's passed in the last few weeks since I called him in your office there's been somethin' growin' inside me that gets stronger with each hour that brings his arrival closer. It's almost as if my soul knows he's comin' back. How stupid is that shit?"

I was zoning out as I rambled, just gazing at a random spot on the wall across the room from me. I laugh dryly thinking about how corny my thoughts sound when voiced out loud and roll my head against the cushion to look at Leigh. I expect her to be holding in laughter at the cheesiness. The last thing I anticipated seeing, though, was tears welling up in her eyes.

"What?" I ask, hesitantly testing the waters, not sure if I like the tingly feeling of trepidation I get with the powerful emotions rolling off of her in heavy waves.

"Do you really want to hear it?" Her voice wobbles, but she composes herself with a small cough.

"I wouldn't have asked if I didn't."

She shifts, turning her body so that she is facing me fully instead of just sitting next to me and looking over. She reaches out, the light catching the diamonds of her engagement ring, and grabs my hand in a strong hold.

"There is only one time in my life I have ever felt that feelin', Quinn, and that was the day your brother came home. I didn't even realize that's what it was until just now. I had just assumed it was just the heaviness of the day he came back." She's talking about my father's funeral. "I get it now, though. That invisible connection only two people meant to be together have was snappin' back in place and pullin' all that slack out of the rope."

"Jesus Jones," I mumble, knowing there is truth to her words even if I'm not ready to admit it to myself just yet.

"Don't fight it. Quinn, promise me that no matter how much you want to, you'll give it a chance to keep pullin' that slack until you two meet in the middle."

"I'm not sure I can make that promise." And I'm not. Really, I'm not.

"You won't have a choice," the deep, rumbling voice of my brother cuts in.

My eyes widen at the same time Leigh's get soft and dreamy.

"I'm not stickin' my head in girl talk, because I don't have the right equipment between my legs to even begin to understand the fucked-up ways y'all twist shit up in your heads, but I'm gonna pretend I have my waders on and muddle my way into the thick of it, got it?"

Maverick must not expect an answer to his question, because he just stomps into the living room and drops his huge frame into the love seat opposite where I'm sitting. I watch him eye Earl with caution, and if it were any other moment, I would laugh that my big, strong brother is still worried the cat might eat him one day.

"The last thing I like thinkin' about is my baby sister being old enough to find the person she's meant to share her days with, but I'm not a stupid man, so I know this day's gonna come whether I want it to or not. You know I fought my own day, Hell-raiser. I fought it so hard that it cost me somethin' fuckin' beautiful for years, and that's not somethin' I want anyone to experience, especially not you. I remember him—Tate, that is. I didn't understand the way he would look at you back then. I reckon I get it now, what he was feelin', because it's the same thing I see in my mirror every mornin' I wake up with Leigh by my side."

"You're readin' a whole lot into somethin' you have no proof of," I argue. "You were hardly around, Maverick."

"I was around enough, Quinny. All it took was one look at the kid and anyone worth a shit saw it."

What the hell am I supposed to do with that?

"You don't have to believe me, darlin'. It really doesn't matter if you do, because in the long run that shit's gonna happen whether you do or not. You'll see that fightin' it is pointless. What's meant to be is gonna be."

"Riddles don't do anything but stir up the mud in the water, Mav," I joke, trying to lighten the heaviness.

"Then get some goggles and learn how to push through the muck."

I roll my eyes with a smile, used to his crazy, confusing logic. It's the kind that makes no sense when he's giving it to you, but slams you in the face with a mighty blow of clarity the second you finally figure it out.

"I know," Leigh exclaims, bouncing excitedly

79

in her seat. Maverick's eyes brighten and crinkle at the edges as he smiles at her. "What you need is a night out, Q! We can make it a family night. Get out and clear your head, then the rest will just fall into place."

"How is that going to help me figure out what to do when Tate comes back to Pine Oak?"

She tilts her head, studying me for a beat before looking over at my brother. My gaze volleys between them as they have some weird-as-hell conversation with their eyes. It almost makes me feel icky to watch.

"Oh, it won't. I just thought it would be fun for us to have family night," she finally says after breaking her gaze away from Maverick's. "It would be nice. We could go to the Dam Bar or somethin'. We haven't been there in a while, and besides, we already know how this is goin' to end between you and Tate."

My brow furrows. "Oh really?" I drone sarcastically.

"Yup."

"You sound mighty sure of yourself." I laugh in disbelief.

Short-lived disbelief, though, because when she opens her mouth next she puts her money where her words are.

"Quinn, babe, you gave him Bertha's engine," she whispers. "You gave him the heart of a vehicle you've been painstakingly breathing

80

life back into for longer than any of your other projects. You think I don't know anythin' about what you do with those trucks, but I pay attention and I know you wouldn't have given Bertha's *heart* to anyone you wouldn't trust your own with."

When she finishes talking there is nothing but silence around us. I see Maverick stand, and I'm vaguely aware of him walking around the coffee table and bending to give Leigh a kiss. Unable to look away from my best friend, I see him out of the corners of my shocked eyes as he gets closer to me before giving me a kiss on the top of my head. His boots echo around the room behind him as he makes his way out the back door of their house, presumably headed back to the mess hall for dinner with everyone like Leigh had said.

Leigh doesn't pay him any mind, her focus completely and wholly on me, nothing but understanding and support in her eyes. Jesus, I didn't give her enough credit if she picked all that up.

"If I take a chance—given that there's even one to take—and let him close to that part of me again, somethin' I haven't let *any* man near since the last time I gave that to Tate, it could end in disaster, Leigh."

"Or . . . it could end in pure magic."

"It could be my destruction," I debate.

"Or it could be your salvation."

My salvation.

I guess that would lead to the question of what exactly I would be being saved from: the life I'm content-ish to live as alone as possible, or the fear I try my hardest not to let rule my world. I don't *want* to give it that kind of power, but it always finds a way to sneak back in.

"You, my best friend, are the strongest woman I know. Maybe its time you stop hidin' behind the wall you've built up around your heart and show Tate Montgomery what a hell-raisin' badass you've become since he saw you last."

I snort, the sound unattractive and loud, right before I choke on the tickle it vibrates up my dry throat. With watering eyes, I laugh through the coughs as I clear my throat. "I'm startin' to think you guys just call me that because you know it's nowhere near the damn truth."

Leigh gets a serious look on her beautiful face and I know I'm in trouble. "I guess you really do need a night out, then, because the Quinn Davis I know never hits the bar without raisin' a little hell. You earned that nickname fair and square, honey."

I scoff under my breath, making a big act out of being put out. "That was *one* time!" I yell with a smile.

"Try every time," she mocks. "This weekend. The Dam Bar. It's happenin'. We can even get all dressed up in all that crap you bought for the girls night we had last summer. Do you still have that purple wig?"

A burst of excitement scatters through my body at the thought. "Do I have it?" I puff in disbelief. "I would never get rid of Lenore."

"It's really weird that you give names to so many things, Quinn."

I shrug, not even giving a single damn about the strange quirks that make me . . . *me*. Now that I'm letting the idea of a night out take root, I really think she's on to something. I can't even remember when the last time we all went out was, and with the long hours I've been spending at the shop working on Homer, I haven't even seen Clay much, and we live in the same, albeit huge, home. The past few weeks we've just been two tired souls crossing paths after long days at work. Maybe she's right and a night with my family—beers flowin', and dancin' with Leigh until my legs fall off—is just what I need to remind myself exactly how far I've come.

I'm not that scared little girl desperate for love anymore. I'm not ruled by the past. Not *any* part of it. Especially not the chunk that houses the memory of the one man that spent every summer for years making me believe that I could trust what my heart tells me. All it took was one stupid phone call to make me remember, and even without knowing what his return means for what we had years ago, I've let him awaken those fears again.

I'll show him. Tate Montgomery isn't going to know what hit him.

"Friday night, Leigh. Make sure that over-protective beast you live with knows that while we're at the Dam Bar, you're mine, and when Lenore and Loretta hit the town, *no man* will stand in our way."

"There's my little hell-raisin' badass!" She jumps from the couch and pulls me to my feet, wrapping me in her slim arms.

We spend an embarrassing amount of time squealing like girls. By the time I leave to head home to the Davis ranch, we've already picked out an outfit from among her "slut clothes"—the very few pieces that I forced her to buy over the years—that will coordinate with the clothes I'm already mentally pulling from my closet back home. It's been a long time since we let the girls out to play. I know it was well before Maverick came home. That thought alone is enough to amp up my excitement. I can't wait to see how he acts when he gets a good look at Leighton in all her Loretta glory.

Most of all, though, I finally feel like myself after spending over three weeks living through the foggy memories of my past. It's out of my system, thankfully before Tate returned, because the last thing I plan on showing him is how deeply I still feel the emptiness his departure left behind.

Nope.

He won't get that. Quinn, the hell-raisin' badass is back, and Tate Montgomery can kiss my boots.

7

Tate

"Get Me Some of That" by Thomas Rhett

— ★ —

Nothing has changed. Everything looks different.

Those are the first two conflicting thoughts to cross my mind as I roll into Pine Oak, thumb tapping against the steering wheel in tempo with the slow classic country music playing in the background. I can see Main Street ahead, and just like the last time I was here, everything is shut down, even though it's just past 8 p.m. Having lived just north of Atlanta since leaving Texas, I'm not used to this . . . stillness, but I find it makes for a very welcome change of pace. I didn't realize just how out of place I had been in Georgia until I got closer to Texas. The stuffy suits I had been wearing for the past few years were left behind, old faded Wranglers and tees, flannels, and casual button-downs taking their place.

It's no secret that I was burned out, and only a little of that had to do with the rut I seemed to have gotten stuck in. It felt like my life was one giant muddin' trail right after the rain. You know that moment when the divots are the deepest and the mud just reaches up, grabs hold of your tires, and won't let go? You could spin those sons of bitches for hours and not get any traction. *That's* where my life had been.

Stuck, spinning for purchase, but getting nowhere despite how much effort I was putting forth.

I hate to admit it, but when my parents called to tell me my paw had passed away, I felt relief. Not because he was gone, but because even in his death he was still saving me. Of course, that relief was short-lived where my parents are concerned. We aren't close, not that we ever were, but they killed any chance of that shit ever happenin' a long time ago. Hell, they didn't even have the decency to tell me about Paw until *after* the fuckin' funeral. I still don't understand it, but I have the feeling a lot of the reason they did that was because they knew I would jump off the path I was on—the one they wanted me to be on—which I did. I had just come home from one of the hardest deliveries I had ever had, having almost lost the mother, and I get that shit from them.

I continue cruising down Main, looking at all the new—and old—businesses. It's shocking how little one place can change so much and yet remain exactly the same. The bakery is new, something my sweet tooth will be happy to visit. The urge to pull into Davis Auto Works when I pass by is so damn strong I almost am not able to keep my truck on the street, my hand twitching to turn into the parking lot. I see the light glowing into the darkness around the building, the only seemingly open business on the street, inviting and taunting me closer, but somehow I manage to keep my trucks' wheels spinnin'.

Just manage, that is.

Fuck. When was the last time I felt this way? The rush of nerves and excitement speeding through my body, feeding some metaphorical, adrenaline-pumpin' erection for life. I don't have one single clue what I'm coming back to Pine Oak to find—aside from the career path I always wanted more than the harried, fast-paced life of a doctor at an overcrowded hospital. I know what I hope to find in addition to that—but will it still be mine for the taking?

Only time will tell.

I reach over and turn up the radio, trying to drown out my thoughts while I take the back roads to my grandparents' old farmhouse. You would never guess I haven't driven these roads since I left to start school in Georgia. Back then I had a raven-haired vixen at my side hootin' and hollerin' for me to go faster so she could hear my tires screech.

God, I miss her.

Missed her since the day I left and haven't stopped since.

The ringing of my phone cuts my thoughts off and I look at the display on my dash to see Ella's name on the caller ID. Swear to God, that woman is on my last nerve. During my final month at work she was fine, abiding by what we'd discussed at the restaurant that night, but the closer it got to my last day, the more she reverted to her overbearing self.

And I've damn just about had enough of it.

"Ella," I answer, my voice sounding monotone and pissed the fuck off. I would ignore her call, like I've been doing all day, but clearly that wasn't enough for her to take a hint and stop.

"Tatum, hello, dear. I just wanted to make sure you were okay."

"I'm fine, Ella. Look, we talked about this last night. I've got somethin' I'm hopin' to build when I get back to Texas, and the last thing I want is her gettin' the wrong idea because you won't leave well enough alone."

"But Tatum," she whines, sniffling. "We had a good thing going. I know you didn't mean it when you said it was over. I just don't want you to make a mistake."

"I'm gonna be real honest with you right now, Ella, and I want this to take root. The only fuckin' mistake I made was ever hookin' up with you. Harsh as fuck, I know, but you can't seem to understand what I'm tellin' you. Stop callin'."

I press the button on my steering wheel to disconnect the call, feeling pissed as fuck.

My mood shifts when I pull into my grandparents'—no, *my*—driveway, a smile creepin' onto my lips when I see Mark Blake waving his arms above his head like an idiot. The glow from the porch light hits him and makes his blond hair look white, shining bright around his shadowed face like a makeshift halo. Mark is one of the only friends I've kept from my summers spent in Pine Oak. He knows all about my past with Quinn, but he also knows why I stayed gone. If anyone has the power to erase the aftereffects of that frustrating-as-fuck call, it's Mark.

"Took you long enough, jackass," he bellows the second I open the door and have my boots in the dirt.

"Took me long enough? How long did you think it would take me to drive from fuckin' Georgia?"

He shrugs, one big shoulder going up, before I see his face split into a wide grin. His hand reaches out to grab mine before he pulls me into a backslappin' hug. "Not sure I ever thought this day would come, Tate. Damn, it's good to see you back in Pine Oak."

I pull away and give my old friend a genuine smile. "You aren't the only one who thought it wouldn't happen," I agree, blowing out a relieved gust of air now that I finally have my boots back on Texas ground. "What's Janie been feedin' you? Last time you came out to see me you weren't this damn big."

He laughs hard, puffing his chest out slightly. "Has nothin' to do with what she's feedin' me, Tate. Reckon you'll figure out once you get set up at the office and all, but we're tryin' to get pregnant. She's got us goin' at it mornin', noon, night, and what feels like every second between. Never thought I'd say this, but fuck, I'm tired of fuckin'."

"Congratulations, Mark, 'bout the baby-makin', not the whole tired-of-fuckin' thing. What's that got to do with you puttin' on a small human's worth of solid muscle though?"

His mouth tips. "Gotta keep up with my woman, so I've been workin' out every second I get. If I ain't at the station or inside my wife, I'm buildin' up my stamina."

I shake my head, not even botherin' to entertain this conversation any longer.

"Anyway, told Janie it wouldn't be right to let you get back to Pine Oak after all this time and not drag you out to celebrate your return. I know you just got in and all, but you got ten minutes to take a piss and grab a sandwich before I take you out. You're damn lucky my wife likes you and made sure to stock your fridge. Janie also said she'd be on call to pick us up later if we got too rowdy, so plan on it bein' a long night."

"Been on the road for close to eleven hours, Mark. Wouldn't be my first choice to go out drinkin' myself under the table."

He straightens and puffs out his chest. I'm a tall man, but Mark is a *motherfuckin'* tall man. He's got a few inches on my six foot three, but he's got close to a hundred pounds to my one-eighty.

I meet his gaze for a minute and try to stare him down; then I give up. "Not gonna let me out of this, are you?"

He shakes his head. "Ever since you headed out yonder, settin' down in Atlanta of all places, I've come to you. I did what you asked, keepin' my eye on Quinn to make sure she was okay, and I respected your wishes when you told me it wasn't my business to butt into that shit between y'all you left hangin', but that was then. Now I'm gonna take my old buddy out, and he's gonna listen to me buttin' in."

I hook my hands on my hips and drop my head to look down at my boots, feelin' tired as hell from my drive. Lifting my gaze, I give him a nod and stretch my road-tired body. "At least let me get my shit inside and make sure I have a clear path to a bed when I end up stumblin' ass-backwards in here later. Hell, for all I know the housekeeping service I hired to make this place livable didn't do their job."

"It's just fine," he says, shock painting his words. "Like I would let some city folks come in here and do that shit. Managed to get some of your paw's shit out before your parents got their stink all over it, came back in when those idiots you hired to fix this place up left and put it back to rights. Well, kinda."

His words cause a sharp pain to slice through my chest. "Fuck, I can't believe they're both gone. I know they understood my distance, but still cuts me up knowin' I won't see them again. Paw seemed lost as hell without Gram, that's the only consolation I feel about him bein' gone—at least he's with her now."

"You're back, Tate. That's all that matters. Shocked the shit outta me when I saw this place go up on the market. Didn't think your parents had it in them. I know your paw would be mighty proud that you stepped in and bought it."

Rage fills me when I think about them tryin' to sell this place. They would have succeeded, too, if I hadn't called to check on things at Paw's old practice a week after he passed. My paw, God love him, was stuck in his ways. He always prayed his daughter—my mother—would come back to her parents. He hated my father. Hated what my father had turned his daughter into, but still he held onto that hope. Which is why he never changed his will. My only guess is that he hoped she would want to come home, eventually.

I guarantee he never thought she would remain the evil bitch she'd turned into, that she'd have a come-to-Jesus moment of some kind. But that moment had never arrived, and the day he died she had this place listed for sale. The same fuckin' day.

I thank my lucky stars for the trust fund my father's parents had set up for me, which they turned over to me when I turned twenty-five. I have more money than I know what to do with now because of them and probably will for the rest of my life, but I also now own the twenty acres of land that my maternal grandparents' home sat on because of it.

And with that land, I've bought back part of my life, too.

It's a damn shame I hadn't been able to get my hands on that money before then, otherwise I would have traveled an entirely different path than the one I had taken.

"Help me get some of this shit inside and then we can head out," I say to Mark, hoisting a bag over my shoulder. Suddenly, a drink sounds like the greatest idea in the world.

An hour later we're pullin' Mark's truck into the crowded gravel parking lot of the Dam Bar, which he claims is still the best bar in town. I didn't feel like pointing out that, as far as I could remember, it was the only bar in town. Pine Oak wasn't exactly a hotbed for partying back in the day, even if we had been old enough to do so legally, and I'm guessin' that hasn't changed much since.

"Are there even this many people who live here?" I ask as we climb down from his jacked-up Ford. I knew without askin' who had done all the work on his truck. A little QD was etched in cursive on one of the back brake lights. Not noticeable to anyone that didn't know to look for it, but that girl wants to mark her creations and always has the back left brake light cover sent off to get etched.

He smirks. "Last time you lived here we'd party down in the fields with whatever beer we could snatch from our houses without gettin' caught. That crew grew up and now this place pretty much fills up all weekend, every weekend."

"You make it sound like everyone I knew back in the day is still here." I laugh. "Last field party I was at had almost the whole damn high school there. No way they're all still here."

"Pine Oak isn't a place you wanna leave, Tate. You know that."

He doesn't wait for me to respond, stompin' through the parking lot and pulling open the door to the bar, sendin' music spillin' into the night air around us. He knew I couldn't contradict him. Pine Oak isn't even where I grew up, but all it took was a few months out of each year for it to be a place I never wanted to leave. I shake my head, not wanting to bring the mood down with the way my thoughts keep wandering back to that shit, pull the old Dallas Cowboys baseball hat I have on a little lower, and follow him into the loud, rowdy bar. With Mark, I know to just go with the flow and hang on for the ride.

Three steps in I'm assaulted by people I instantly recognize, even with the years of maturity on them. Twenty minutes later my own face hurts from smiling so much and my throat is sore from yellin' over the country music blurring through the air, but fuck if I don't feel like this is a welcome-home.

True to Mark's promise, the next few hours pass with us drinking so much beer I get a damn good buzz going on. But no buzz would keep me from feeling her the second she walks into the bar. Even with my back to the door and a bar full of people between us, I know that, just as sure as I'll wake up tomorrow with the world still spinnin', Quinn Davis has arrived.

I can feel it, but I can't see her yet and it's drivin' me crazy. I grab my glass and pour the last half of the cold, bitter brew down my throat. I don't even wait until I'm done swallowing before standing from my stool and looking through the room to find her. The dim lighting and crowded room make it impossible.

I have to force myself to not go rushing off

through the damn room to find her. I've waited this damn long, a little longer won't kill me, especially since I'm not going anywhere this time. And in all honesty, I'm not sure I'm ready to come face-to-face with her. If I see her with another man, I'm about fairly certain I'll turn green with envy, and that mixed with my swirling head wouldn't make for a pretty picture. I'm sure it would be great marketing for Pine Oak's newest—and only—gynecologist to be getting in bar fights his first night in town. Nothing screams, *Trust me with your health, pregnancy, and future* like a drunken bar brawl.

"Gotta piss," I call out to Mark, slapping his shoulder on my way to the back hallway. I take my time, splashing some water on my face, and pausing outside the bathroom to give the room a quick once-over.

And wouldn't you know it, but my eyes collide right with those of the Davis men.

Well, this should be fun.

I lift my chin, acknowledging them, but look away without waiting to see if my salutation is returned, heading back to my spot at the bar with Mark and a few of his friends from the fire station. I signal for another, realizing the second the bartender moves to fill my glass that my spot gives me yet another clear view of Clayton and Maverick Davis. They appear to be alone, but the buzz still crawling across my skin tells me their sister is most likely with them somewhere. They always were a close bunch.

"She's the one in the purple," Mark grunts, leaning his heavy bulk into my side and lifting his hand with a slight tremor toward the open area people are using as a makeshift dance floor. I narrow my eyes to see where he's pointing and almost fall off the fuckin' stool when I see the women he's referring to.

Two scantily clad, sexy-as-hell women wearing bright-ass wigs, one in pink and one in purple. Both attractive with great bodies, but the one he's referring to catches my eye over the other and keeps it. She's got everything a man would ever think of putting on his dream list. Killer body, round ass, full tits, and legs that would look great wrapped around my waist.

"No shit?" I wheeze. Fuckin' wheeze like an old fuckin' man on life support. My eyes remain on her as if I'm in some sort of trance as she rolls her hips to the music, moving in a way that screams, *Good in bed.* I remember with absolute clarity just how good she *is* in bed, getting even better each time we shared that together.

Yeah, Quinn Davis knows how to ride her man almost as well as she could ride a horse.

Mark chuckles appreciatively as he watches the women dance. "Those two used to do this shit every weekend a few years back. Sit back and enjoy, man. Even with Clay and Mav here, those girls are gonna get rowdy, and I promise you it's funny as hell to watch. 'Course, last time they did this shit, they were both single, so who knows how rowdy it'll get tonight."

The breath stills in my lungs, his words slamming into my brain and clearing out my buzz with a sobering impact.

I turn my head and look at Mark. "She's taken?" I ask, not sure if I want to hear the answer to that.

"Huh? Oh, shit, I forgot what we were talkin' about. Yeah, gettin' married in a few weeks, I think. 'Bout damn time too," Mark slurs, still looking off toward the dance floor. He turns when I don't speak and looks at me, confused, before whatever lightbulb switched off with the first sip earlier snaps back on. "Fuck, Tate, I was talkin' 'bout Leighton. She and Maverick are gettin' hitched."

"Quinn?" I grunt harshly, not willing to have him get confused this time. My fuckin' heart can't handle it.

He laughs like I just said the funniest thing in the world and I narrow my eyes.

"You got nothin' to worry 'bout there, Tate. You fucked that girl up real good because ever since you, no man can get close enough to attempt changin' that, not that there haven't been plenty tryin'. She went through a wild stage but never had a serious relationship. Her wild hair got cut off 'bout the same time her brother got back last year."

99

I feel my body deflate, instantly eased by his words even if it churns my gut to think about what that wild stage might have meant. Makes no fuckin' sense for me to feel this overwhelmingly possessive over her, not when I ruined what we had. Logic be damned, though. There isn't anyone standin' in the way of us now and I don't care what it takes, I'm gettin' back in there.

I sit back, drinking beer after beer, and watch her move like a wet dream brought to life. Her denim miniskirt wrapped tight around the ass that's only improved with time. Her flat stomach bare, belly ring winking every now and then when the light catches it just right. I haven't the slightest clue if the plaid material covering her chest is some fancy-as-fuck bra or an actual top, but the way it's showcasing her breasts has my cock pressing hard against my jeans in a matter of seconds.

Soon, I mentally promise my throbbing cock.

Soon, I vow to the ache in my chest.

"Very fuckin' soon," I declare, mumbling the words low under my breath while I sit back, get comfortable, and enjoy the show.

8
Quinn

"80s Mercedes" by Maren Morris

— ★ —

I can't remember the last time I felt this alive.
They're playing nothing but dance music tonight at the Dam Bar. Those country hits from almost a decade ago that make you want to shake your ass, toss your head back, and rebel yell to the moon. Well, maybe not go out yellin' at the moon. I might be drunk off my ass, but I'm not *that* drunk.

I grab Leigh's hands and pull her in for a hug, laughing when she almost falls on her ass.

"—looks so hot," she yells over the music.

"Huh?"

"Don't you think?"

"What are you talkin' about?" I scream back, not understanding her.

She looks over her shoulder, in the direction that I last saw my brothers standing, and I feel her body sag slightly. Giggling, I steady her only to end up with her head resting against my shoulder and a mouthful of pink wig hair. I sputter, pulling the strands out while she reaches up, one hand landing on the top of my head, and pets my wig so hard I feel like she might pull it right off my damn head.

"Guess what," she whisper-yells in my ear.

"Chicken butt?" I snicker, laughing at my own joke.

She snorts, lifts her head, and smiles at me. Her dazed eyes aren't focusing on me all that well, but since I'm pretty sure I'm not holding two Leightons, I'm guessing mine aren't that clear either.

"I'm gonna get him home and ride him like a pony."

"Oh, gross, Leigh! That's my brother!"

She snorts again. "He has a really nice penis. It's so pretty. Like, really, really pretty. I saw a mold thingie in a magazine Jana had. You reckon he'd let me do that to him? That way I could carry his pretty penis around with me everywhere I go."

I push *that* disturbing image right outta my head and help support Leigh while walking back over to the table where we left Maverick and Clay a few hours ago.

"She's ready to go," I announce, hoping my words aren't slurring as I attempt to thrust her into Maverick's arms, Leighton slumping against me as one hand reaches out to stroke Maverick's chest.

"Pretty sure you told me earlier if I took her outta here, for any reason, before the bar closed you would take away my ability to have children. Let me tell ya, Hell-raiser, I'm not takin' any chances testin' how serious you mighta been," Maverick grumbles, taking a sip of his longneck, grabbing Leigh's hand when it gets down to his belt buckle, not letting her continue her journey.

"If you play your cards right, I'm pretty sure she's willin' to start on that tonight, not that I cared to hear about it, but I did, so can you please get her home before she tells me again how pretty your penis is?"

He chokes on the gulp of beer he was just swallowing. I can't see his eyes in the shadow his cowboy hat is casting over his face, but I feel an uncomfortable awareness when his scrutiny leaves me and settles on his fiancée.

Gross.

I feel like I'm in the middle of something I damn sure don't want to be in the middle of. Especially since Leigh won't let me go *and* still has her hand way too close to Maverick's crotch.

I register that Davis, party of two, has somehow morphed into a party of one. "Hey, where's Clay?"

"Huh?" Maverick mumbles, clearly not paying attention to me.

I snap my fingers in front of his face. "Where. Is. Our. Brother?"

"Had to head back home. Somethin' 'bout one of his new horses gettin' hurt."

"Which one?"

I wobble as Leigh's body gets heavier, almost taking both of us down, before I steady myself and her. How is she this drunk? We've been drinking the same amount and I can still stand on my own two feet.

"Major," he answers, finally reaching out to take Leigh from my arms.

I vaguely remember the stallion that Maverick is talking about, but I haven't spent much time in the stables lately, so I'm not sure which Thoroughbred he means. Clay has been busy building up his baby-making horses the last year, expanded the breeding end of the Davis ranch like he's wanted to for a while now. The only time I pay any attention to the things he's working on is when I go to take my horse, Daisy, out for a ride.

"He okay?" I ask, not sure who I'm asking about, the horse or Clay—my big, stoic brother loves those animals like they were his own babies.

"Will be, I'm sure. Clay probably didn't even have to leave, but you know how much of a control freak he is. He was out the door practically the second he saw Drew's name on his phone."

The instant he finishes talking, Leigh pounces and grabs his neck to pull his head down.

Thankfully Maverick's hat shields enough that I'm not forced to watch them make out in the middle of the bar. I roll my eyes when she bounces slightly, asking without words for my brother to pick her up, something he does instantly. Well, I guess she was done waiting for her man to pay attention to her.

"As much as I hate to point this out, you might want to put your big mitt over her crotch or this whole room is about to know what kind of panties are coverin' up her cooter," I halfway joke. I wouldn't bother, normally, but the embarrassing shit she does when she's drunk is only funny when she's aware of it. Her skirt isn't as short as mine is, but if she keeps dry-humpin' my brother it's not going to keep her covered for long. Time to get them out of here before all horny hell breaks loose.

"You two go. I'll be fine here," I yell toward the top of his head, holding my amusement in when his hand indeed goes to her ass. Generally, neither one of my brothers would ever leave me here alone, regardless of the fact that we grew up in this town and probably know every person that's in here. But with Leigh workin' her female magic on him, I know Maverick's mind is only on one thing—showin' his woman how much he loves her. Maverick waves and half-drags, half-carries a giggling Leigh out the door and into the night.

"Well, Lenore, it looks like Loretta just can't

handle us anymore," I say to myself, twisting a piece of my wig's bright purple curls around my finger. Leigh might not have staying power anymore, but I damn well do. I didn't realize how much I needed this night out until we were laughing our asses off in the middle of our dancing marathon. Not willing to lose the buzz I'm ridin' high on, I rock back on the heels of my purple cowboy boots and swing myself around, back to the dance floor. I've just started swaying my hips again to the music when I feel my phone buzz in my pocket. Pulling it out, I smile when I see Maverick's text letting me know he told Randy, the bouncer, to keep an eye on me.

Good old Maverick.

I continue to drink and dance around the floor. No one pays me any mind, the girl in the purple wig swaying to the beat all by herself. I feel eyes on me, though. I ignore them, as always, but the burn of them just grows, and it only makes me move a little more seductively to the music. I can't even remember the last time I had a good drunken one-night stand, which means it's been way too long. I stopped having them almost subconsciously when I found out the truth about my mother. Once I discovered what a whore she had been, every time I felt the urge to raise my skirt for a man, I felt equal measures irrational guilt and shame—the apple not falling far from the tree, and all that. I know it isn't the same, but

I honestly didn't even feel the pull to enjoy some meaningless mutual, mindless pleasure until just now. I think tonight is the night.

I'm not proud to admit this, even if it's just to myself, but I have to be drunk to enjoy sex. I tried sober fucking a few times, and each time ended in disaster. All I could see was the rugged, youthful face of the only person I've ever had bring me to completion. I had to shut down my mind instantly when it happened, and it just ended up being one long rutting session for the man that ended when I had enough and clenched my inner muscles so hard that he had no choice but to finally be done. Even if I wasn't the master of fakin' it, that shit got old real quick, and now I find it's better to drink myself so stupid that I lose the ability to care that I'll never feel that pleasure again.

Maybe I should take Jana up on that sex-toy shit. Lord knows it would be nice to know I'm not permanently broken.

I make a mental note to talk to her about it on Monday when I take my normal pie break at the PieHole. In the meantime, I head to the bar for another drink and let my mind drift away on the dizzy rapids of a beer-filled river.

Good God, it's bright.

I pull the covers over my head, trying to block out the harsh morning sun beating into my retinas. Everything hurts, from my tingling scalp all the way down to my toes, and I'm way too hungover to deal with the fireball in the sky this morning. I roll, trying to pull the thick blanket around me so that I can fully submerge myself in a cocoon of darkness, but I don't get far when I meet resistance.

I tug, but the blankets don't budge.

I tug harder, and still they don't obey.

Giving them one last heave, I almost roll off the bed when they're ripped out of my grasp and my body is forced forward with the momentum of the yank I didn't get to complete.

"What the hell?" I screech, blinking wildly when my eyes are assaulted by the devil rays once again before giving up and slamming my lids down in an effort to not hurl with the brightness.

I'm instantly aware of my nudeness with the loss of the blankets' warmth, the air-conditioning bathing my skin with chilly air the second I lose purchase of them.

"What the *fuckin'* hell?" I yelp, even louder, and wince when the sound hits my ears, still not able to open my eyes.

That's when I hear the male groan to my right and every inch of my body goes rock hard. Slowly, I open my eyes, giving myself enough time to adjust to the harsh lighting, but also working up the courage to actually find out where I am.

Jesus Jones, Quinn. You really went all whoreville last night, didn't you? You can't even remember leaving the Dam Bar, let alone going home with someone. God, I hope it's no one that I'll have to see daily.

The first thing I see is the tan, hairy skin of a man's naked leg. Well, I'm guessing it's naked, but I can't really tell for sure, because the blanket that was on me only moments before is now covering most of the very male body next to me. If the muscular leg is anything to go by, at least I broke my celibacy streak with someone that takes care of his body. Even though he's sleeping I can tell there is no way the rest of that body will be soft if that's the kind of power that carries it.

Not wanting to stick around and find out if I'm right, I start working my way out of the bed. I move inch by inch, holding my breath the whole time, until I'm standing next to the bed. Looking down, I see that I'm not as naked as I thought. My bright pink lace thong is still on, as is the matching bra that really doesn't do shit but look sexy, since I can see my nipples clear as day through the cups. Reaching down, I place my hand against my sex and I know the second I feel the lack of wetness that he was probably another one of those piston-hipped jerks that just keep powering through a girl's barely wet pussy. Unless he redressed me before going to sleep. Maybe he was a thoughtful one-nighter that didn't want to ruin my panties. Either way, I'm happy I don't have to do the walk of shame with wet panties.

Ignoring the lump of a man on the bed, I glance around the room, looking for my clothes from last night, but give up when I see a shirt he must have discarded last night in a ball at the end of the bed. Pulling it on, I thank my lucky stars that the hem hits my thighs low enough that I feel like I can safely make an escape now and not risk taking any longer and waking the stranger while I search. As much as I love last night's outfit, I'm not going to stick around looking for it. I see my boots tossed in the corner and pull them on, wishing I had socks to put on first, but beggars can't be choosers.

When I finish getting my boots on, I look at the bed, no longer able to ignore him anymore, and let out a relieved silent burst of air when I see his face completely covered. His hair, though, isn't and I can't say I've ever thought a man's hair was sexy until now. It's long, but in that attractive way that it looks like it needed a cut a month ago, but he keeps it that way on purpose. Seriously, there is nothing sexier than messy, intentional waves curling out from under a cowboy hat. It almost makes me wish I could remember what those strands felt like between my fingers. I bet it would be the perfect length to curl my fingers into and force his mouth

110

between my legs until *I* was ready for him to stop.

Holy shit.

My body flushes when I realize the dry panties I was so proud of only seconds before are now wet with arousal. From his hair.

I've got to get out of here.

I creep to the door, pulling it open slowly, and cringe when it squeaks loudly, echoing in the silence around me.

Come on, Quinn. I give it another slow pull, only to get the same results. Fuck. I'm never going to get out of here. A few more unsuccessful attempts later, I hear him.

"Goin' somewhere?"

The voice is thick with sleep and maybe a little bit of the same hangover fog I feel. There's no way someone has a voice that throaty and arousing naturally. It creates a slow warmth that begins to glide down my body, awaking a lascivious need deep inside of me. I'm shaking, but not with nerves. I'm literally quivering with *desire,* a feeling so unfamiliar after being gone for so long that I could cry.

"Uh," I mumble, clearing the thick need from my voice with a cough. "Um, home. I was headin' home."

"Not even plannin' on stickin' around to say good-bye? I know it's been awhile, but damn, Grease."

Breath stills in my lungs. The arousal that had been building inside of me just moments before freezes instantly from shock, recognition hitting the very core of me. "No," I gasp, dropping my forehead to the door, closing my eyes tight, and clenching my hand around the doorknob.

I hear him move, the blankets shifting before the bed makes a squeak as it loses the weight of his body.

Fear holds me immobile.

I'm not ready. I can't do this. Oh, God.

I was supposed to be prepared by the time I had to face him again. I wouldn't look like the hot mess I'm sure I resemble. I know my wig isn't on anymore, but I can only imagine what my long hair looks like after a sweaty night dancing under it. My makeup isn't applied with a practiced hand of perfection, like I had hoped it would be the first time I saw him again. I wouldn't be shocked if I look like a drowned raccoon after sleeping with the amount of makeup I had on last night. My perfect smoky eye I spent thirty minutes working on probably looks more like I was the loser of a boxing match.

"Been a long time, Quinn."

"Not long enough," I mutter under my breath, but I know he hears me, because his dark chuckle hits my ears before shooting straight between my legs, waking that needy bitch down there right up.

"Even drunk out of your mind, you're just as wild as I remembered," he whispers, closer.

Before I have a chance to move, his body is pressed against my back, and I'm pushed against the door, causing it to close with a soft boom at the swiftness of his movements. He holds his hips back, not allowing *that* part of him to touch me, but I feel him—almost all of him—and there isn't a single part of his hard body against mine that I don't remember. He feels different—bigger—but familiar nonetheless.

"You purred for me last night," he says against my ear, pulling my hair over my shoulder with one hand while the other hits my leg right under the hem of his shirt. "You purred so loud I came in my pants like a fuckin' young buck readin' his first dirty mag. Christ, Quinn, you came alive, and that was before I even got you back here."

I jerk in his hold, my spine snapping straight, and thrust my hips back to free myself. It doesn't work. His hand is at my thigh, and he's flexing and digging his fingertips into my flesh before relaxing his hold and slowly dragging it up, taking the shirt with it. Over my hip he goes, until he has his palm low on my torso, the shirt bunched around his arm. I bet I could sneeze and his fingers would be where my body wants them most. The pads of his fingertips caress my belly and I feel wetness pool between my legs moments before he uses his hold on me to pull me against his swollen erection.

"You're not drunk anymore, Quinn," he rumbles against my back, the hot air of his breath fanning against the shell of my ear. "Wanna give me that purr again?"

"In your fuckin' dreams," I respond instantly, proud of the hard edge in my voice.

"You didn't say that last night," he urges.

"I was drunk!" I yell, squirming against his deliciously hard body until he finally lets me go. "I was drunk and you took advantage of that, you stupid fuck!"

I almost fall on my ass, but eventually I get free and finally come face-to-face with Tate Montgomery after nine long-as-hell years. He left a handsome boy and came back a devilishly hot man. His body, having always been in shape, is aged to perfection. His abs are a little more defined, his pecs even larger, and his arms that would—I'm sure—feel like steel bands when they were wrapped around you. My eyes travel up his neck, over the dark stubble on his chiseled jaw, until I see the pouty fullness of lips I used to dream of every night. I almost give up there, but I keep going until his light blue eyes are boring into mine, holding me captive and immobile. I vaguely register those mouthwatering wavy locks of his, but I'm powerless to do anything else but stare up at him—the boy turned man that I spent years mourning the loss of.

Who knows how long we stare at each other, each searching with so many questions hanging in the air around us. It's almost . . . peaceful. Until he has to go and ruin it all.

"I've missed you," he whispers. "And fuck, did it feel good to have you in my arms last night. Not sure how I stayed away this long now that I remember just how good you felt against my body."

Cold water fills my veins and I slap him, hard enough to feel the burn of impact after his head jerks to the side.

"You, Tatum Montgomery, can kiss my fuckin' boots."

I don't give him another glance. I spin around and dash down the hallway. It isn't until I hit the top of the stairs that I realized I'm in Fisher Ford's house. It'll be a long walk back to the Davis ranch, but with the rage fueling my every step, I bet I'll make it quicker than Usain Bolt on the Olympic track.

I hear him yelling my name, but I don't turn. I pick up speed, running down his driveway and onto the street. Just before I'm out of sight of the old Ford place, I turn and see Tate's hulking Adonis form standing on the porch. His arms are crossed over his impressive chest, and the erection behind his black briefs is visible even from the end of the driveway.

"This isn't over, Quinn!" he bellows.

My feet stumble, but I catch myself, spinning around before I hit a stand of trees into which I can vanish. "Seriously, kiss my damn boots, Tatum Montgomery!"

Naturally, after that burst of defiance from my brain, I turn and kick up rocks in my rush to escape him, because right now I'm pretty sure I don't want anything to be over. My mind turns me toward home a second later and I'm out of his view. Without thought, having pushed the last thirty minutes from my mind, I run harder than I've ever run in my life. My sockless feet scream inside my boots for me to slow down, but nervous fear keeps my legs pumping as I sprint the three miles back to my house, Tate's stolen shirt puffing out behind me like a cape.

It isn't until I'm panting in the middle of my bedroom that I realize I was crying.

What the hell am I supposed to do now?

9

Tate

"Song for Another Time" by Old Dominion

— ★ —

"Dr. Montgomery," a hesitant voice calls through the crack in my door.

"Yes?" I ask with a harsh bite to my tone.

"I . . . uh, well, we were wonderin' if you wanted us to cancel the appointments that you have tomorrow. That is, if you, uh, need more time or anything."

I frown, leaning back in Paw's—no, my desk chair. "Carrie, is it?" I ask.

"Yes, sir," she whispers.

God, have I been that bad? "Thanks for askin', Carrie, but I'll be fine. I'm caught up on what I need to know, so no need to push things back for another day." It takes more effort than I care to admit to keep my voice calm. It isn't her fault I've been kicking my ass for the last four days since I arrived in Pine Oak.

I see one brown eye widen through the crack of my door before she sputters in shock, leaving just as quickly as she came. Goddammit. I can't have the staff here afraid of me. The last thing a woman needs when she arrives for an appointment with the one doctor she dreads going to each year is to find a staff that is afraid of the very one she's seeing.

Needless to say, my first days as the new gynecologist in Pine Oak aren't going well.

Not because of my abilities as a doctor, but because I've officially made every employee terrified of me. Okay, that might be a stretch, but these ladies have been used to my paw's gentle-giant nature and now they've got me—a grumpy-as-fuck beast snarling at everyone that even looks at me.

I'm not officially taking on any patients yet, thank God, or I reckon I wouldn't even be able to keep any with my temper sparked. The last two days since I've been here I've spent going over Paw's files, familiarizing myself with the few higher-risk pregnancies he was dealing with, and trying to get a good sense of how the staff works.

Dr. Lyons, the other doctor that worked with Paw for as long as I could remember, is the only one not paying any mind to my surly mood. Hell, he's been acting like the sun shines out of my ass, so damn happy that I'm taking over Paw's practice that he's probably blind to the fact that I'm pissin' vinegar. He had been fully prepared—albeit grudgingly—to buy out the parts of their

118

practice Paw had owned, but I let him know real quick that I wanted nothing more than take the position Paw had always hoped I would one day hold.

Leaning back in my seat, I let my mind wander to the very reason I've been in such a shitty mood since Saturday morning.

Quinn.

Or, rather, my behavior toward Quinn.

I was so wrapped up in seeing her again that I let it get the best of me. Instantly, I forgot that I should be proceeding with care and caution. Innocent mistake, since I had just woken up after having her almost completely naked body wrapped around my body all night. My mind hadn't even turned all the way on before my mouth was spewing words I was powerless to stop, my hands moving without conscious thought, only wanting to feel her close a little bit longer.

I should have told her right off that nothing happened between us the night I took her home from the bar. I could have gotten her clothes out of the dryer I stuffed them in before I crashed, having stayed up after she passed out to wash the vomit off of them. Not that they would have been any good to her, since I washed them in bleach, my drunken mind not able to actually wash them correctly, just knowing I needed to get her barf off before it ruined them. We could have had breakfast together while I explained to her the truth behind my departure. But, most importantly, I wouldn't have been able to reassure her that I wouldn't ever take advantage of her like I know she left thinking I did.

Now, not only do I have to move mountains to just get her to agree to see me again, but I have a feelin' the hurdles I need to jump to earn her heart back just got a lot higher.

On top of all that, I had to call my phone company this morning to have Ella's number blocked so she can't contact me. She just can't get a clue and honestly, I'm sick of it. I'm not taking any chances. At least this way it's fucking done with, and I pray to God things work out with Quinn and me, and that Ella will never be a fucking factor. I've got enough of the past trying to ruin things because of what I did: the last thing I want to do is add to that with a meaningless hookup making waves.

With a loud sigh, I stand from the desk and stretch my back. The tails of my flannel come untucked from my dark jeans—something I never would have been able to wear back in Georgia, but a comfort I'm afforded now that I'm back in Texas. I don't even bother to fix them: instead, I make my way out of the office and to the front desk. The office is empty now that five has hit, but the two nurses and a receptionist are still milling around. I see Carrie, the appointment and file clerk, and give her a smile. It's time to make a fresh start.

"Ladies," I greet, gaining each of their hesitant eyes. "I wanted to apologize for my mood the last two days. It wasn't my intention to have y'all's first impression of my abilities and me as a doctor be tainted with some personal issues I let carry me through the doors. Y'all have my promise that it won't happen again, and I hope we can forget this unfortunate start and move forward. I know my paw left me some mighty shoes to fill, but I'll do my damnedest to make sure I don't let his memory or y'all's trust down."

Each of them looks shocked by the time I finish talking, but just as quickly as that shock filled them, they smile. Carrie gives me a shy nod. Rebecca, one of the nurses, does the same.

"Consider it forgotten, son," Claire, the receptionist who's been here as long as the doors have been open, says while smiling up at me.

"One thing's for sure, you got your temper from Fisher," Gladys, another nurse and longtime staff member, snorts. Her laughter lightens the mood instantly.

"Reckon so, Gladys," I agree with a smile, remembering how hot my paw's temper could really get in the rare instances that he let someone get under his skin.

"I'm gonna go tell Russ to head on out. You ladies should get home, too. I'm just goin' to spend some more time goin' over the patients I have tomorrow."

"Dr. Lyons already headed out, Dr. Montgomery."

"Well, then you ladies should follow his lead and go home too. We're not likely to get any patients in the next hour we're supposed to be open, since my schedule is clear." I sigh with a smile.

They all relax visibly and start to move around the reception area. I grab the check-in clipboard and start straightening out the pens in the small coffee-bean pot while I wait for them to finish so that I can lock up behind them.

Mindlessly focused on the pamphlets I moved on to after the pens, I don't hear Gladys right away, her cold-as-hell hand reaching out to lightly grab my wrist, pulling me from my thoughts. "Uh, are you sure you didn't take an appointment and forget to put it on the books?"

I frown. "I'm sure, Gladys. Why do you ask?"

"Well, this should be interesting then," she oddly murmurs under her breath right before the front door opens so hard it slams against the wall before flinging back toward its frame, stopping when a palm smacks against it.

The pamphlets in my hand are instantly forgotten when I see who's standing just outside the front door of the old house just off Main Street that my paw converted into his practice almost fifty years ago.

"You," she growls low, lips thinned and eyes

narrowed. The hand that isn't holding the front door open is pointed at me, but other than lifting it to do so, she hasn't moved an inch.

"Quinn, honey, did you have an appointment today?" Gladys, bless her heart, questions in an attempt to extinguish some of the fire spewing from Quinn's posture alone.

Quinn snorts, clearing her expression before looking away from me, smiling sweet as sugar at Gladys. "No, ma'am, I do not."

"Did you want to make one, honey?"

"Oh, no. I definitely do *not*."

I hear Gladys moving some papers around but interrupt her before she can further question the tempting vixen in front of me. Who would have thought someone clearly wanting to murder me would be so fuckin' sexy?

"You go on home, Gladys. Quinn's not here for any appointment you'll find on the books. Reckon she's here because we've got some unfinished business to discuss," I say, smiling at Gladys while her mouth twitches, not realizing just how that sounded until I feel a sharp, poking finger on my shoulder.

A second later, that smile is wiped right off my face. I turn from Gladys, and just before my eyes connect with the heated emerald irises I only saw in my fuckin' dreams for years, Quinn's ire slams full force into me, just as powerful as a physical blow.

"Unfinished business my ass, you good-for-nothin' asshole." She checks me with her shoulder, hitting me just under my pec since she's so damn short, before stomping down the hallway and into my new office.

Rubbing my chest, I give the ladies a nod. "If you don't mind, I'll see y'all out before I go take care of the spitfire in my office."

Not having to be told twice, everyone moves a little quicker before leaving. I lock the door and take a deep, hopefully calming, breath before following the path Quinn just fumed down moments before.

I find her pacing in front of the desk. Not wanting to give her the reach to inflict any more damage, I rest my shoulder against the frame and watch her move. Her long, dark-as-night hair has some highlights dancing through the thickness that I don't remember seeing the other morning. Other than that, though, she doesn't look like she's aged at all since the summer I left. Even covered by the worn jeans she's wearing, her legs look just as long and toned as they used to be. I know from the other night that her stomach is still firm and smooth. Even though she had a bra on the other morning, I imagine her chest is just as impressive bared as it was the night she rode my body, giving me a piece of her that no man had ever had.

She's beautiful. Always had been, but now

she's got the confidence that an eighteen-year-old could never understand, let alone exude.

"Stop lookin' at me like that, Starch."

I look down my body, ignoring the very noticeable bulge of my hard-as-fuck cock, before raising a brow at Quinn. "Not sure that nickname works anymore, sweetheart. A lot's changed since my parents forced me to dress the part of perfect socialite son and private-school robot."

"Oh, really?" She sneers. "You wouldn't find a soul around here with shirts as pressed as yours. Tell me, did Daddy Dearest buy that shiny truck with his dirty oil money, or the shit he gets from being the biggest banker in East Texas?"

"Neither, Grease. I don't talk to my parents anymore, let alone let them buy shit for me. Bought the 'shiny truck' myself," I answer, calmly, even if mention of my father's "dirty oil money" is enough to fire me up. She has no idea how dangerous that man and his ill-gotten gains can be.

She snorts, the sound mocking and full of disbelief.

"I've never lied to you before, Quinn, wouldn't start now."

"No," she says low and dangerously. "Your method of bullshit is a little less untruths, a little more blatant abandonment."

"Quinn," I breathe, the word coming out nothing short of pleading.

125

"No, Tate," she interrupts. Her pacing stops and she straightens her shoulders, turning to face me with anger still swirling in her eyes. "You've been gone a long time. You can't just come back and expect there not to be consequences to your bullshit."

"Not that I don't agree with you, but I can assure you there would have been far worse consequences had I come back before now."

Her head tilts just a second before her bottom lip rolls inward, her teeth capturing it instantly. The adorable move I had forgotten about hits me right in my gut. It never failed: when she was deep in thought, she would do the same damn thing. It's easy to forget that there is the distance of stolen time between us when those memories are slamming into my brain, making the years slip away.

"Explain that," she finally demands, softly but no less pissed.

"You got that kinda time, sweetheart?"

"Seein' as the only thing that demands my attention right now is the bargainin' chip you used to get to me in the first place, I'd say yeah."

"I didn't exactly make a secret out of that."

"Anyone with a brain in their head could've fixed up Fisher's old truck. There's a reason you demanded it be me, and we both know it."

Pushing off the doorframe, I walk into the office and pull out one of the two chairs in front

126

of my desk, making a point to tip my head toward it, waiting for her to sit—with a huff, I might add—before dropping down into the one next to her. Close enough that I could reach out and take her in my arms, if I was so inclined, but also far enough away that she has space.

"I don't even know where to start with you," I tell her honestly, leaning back and running my fingers through my hair. "I should start by apologizin' for the other mornin'. Nothin' happened that night, Quinn. I was just stuck in my head, not even fully awake, not that that's an excuse. I let myself get stuck in the past, seein' you there, and I'm sorry for that."

"I figured that out on my own, Tate. Either your dick shrunk or you forgot how to work it, because had we actually hooked up, I would have felt it. And I didn't. Feel it, that is," she smarts off. It's on the tip of my tongue to reply with something crass and she doesn't miss a beat. "Shut your damn mind off, Tate."

I hold my hands up. "Do you remember anything from that night?"

"I remember Leighton and Maverick leavin' the bar. Gettin' a message from Mav that Randy would be keepin' his eye on me. Clay was gone already. Then things get a little fuzzy."

I nod. "Ran into you at the bar well after 'fuzzy,' because you couldn't even walk. You started pukin' right after that, around the same time you tossed the wig you had been wearin' into the bushes behind the bar and told who I'm assumin' is Randy to fuck off because you were goin' to ride a cowboy. I finally got you to stop pukin' long enough to get you back to Paw's place. I would have taken you home, honest to God, but you were passed out and wouldn't tell me where home was now."

"I'm still at the ranch," she whispers. "You could have just brought me to the ranch and left me on the porch," she continues, some of the anger dissipating from her earlier harsh tone.

"Yeah." I laugh without humor. "That wouldn't have ever happened."

"Doesn't explain how I got naked."

"Did you miss the part about you pukin'? Covered yourself and me. Mark's buddy got us back here, but I wasn't exactly sober, Quinn. I did the best I could with one fuckin' twisted-up head."

"Explain what you said earlier." Her change of subject makes me have to backpedal a bit, and I clearly take too much time to rewind our conversation, because she lets out a long, irritated sigh. "About consequences, Tate."

Goddammit. I knew this moment would come: it had to, if I really wanted a chance to fix the future I took away from us, but I know this isn't going to end well. I don't know if the truth will cause her to hate me more for not fighting for our chance back then or, even worse, make her understand and still hate me.

"I was blackmailed." The words burst from my lips, and with my heart about to pound out of my chest, I hurry to explain. Quinn's so still she doesn't even look like she's breathing. "The day I left, I went home and told my parents that I wanted to transfer from Emory and enroll at Baylor. Houston wouldn't have been right next door, but it would have been a helluva lot closer than Atlanta. Didn't even finish my sentence before my father was shovin' me against the wall. He told me he would cut me off if I even thought about it." I focus on the wall behind her, needing to get everything out. "It didn't matter to me. I could put school off until I came into my trust fund. It would suck, but I would have done it. I didn't want his money, but he reminded me real quick his power resides in a lot more than just money."

Unable to look away any longer, I turn my attention to her. She's so still, but her face is awash with a weird expression of understanding.

"We fought. I'm surprised the damn windows didn't explode with the volume of our screamin'. When he realized he wouldn't win by takin' away my financial stability, he hit me where he knew it would hurt the most. You."

"Me?" she squeaks. "He didn't even know me."

A puff of air leaves my chest, mixing with a

sound of pure agony that makes her jolt slightly in her seat, her fingers wrapping tight around the armrest, bracing herself, I'm sure.

"He knew about you because my mother knew about you. Paw couldn't stop talkin' about the beautiful Davis girl that stole his grandson's heart. I had no clue that they had been waitin' for me to come home to dish their bullshit out—even if I hadn't walked right in demandin' to transfer schools."

"I don't understand," she whispers. "You never mentioned that before you left here."

"I didn't want to get your hopes up. God, Quinn, there wasn't a damn thing I wouldn't do for you."

"Except fight for me. Except that."

"I couldn't fight for you, then, Quinn!" I roar, slamming my fist against the desk. "My father threatened to essentially ruin your family if I didn't go to Emory as planned. If I so much as wrote you a fuckin' postcard he was prepared to rip everything your family had built up apart. And, Quinn, he could have done it."

"I don't understand," she gasps. "How could he have done that!?"

Fuck, it kills me not to be able to touch her. The anger is long gone, and the unsteady panic settles in the more I explain.

"One of his banks owned the loan your father had taken out on not only your family land, but

130

also the auto shop. The type of loan he had, though, included a stipulation that the lender could demand repayment, in full, at any time. Your father had some money troubles about the same time I started spendin' my summers in Pine Oak. I'm not sure when he crossed paths with my father, but he did. The loan ensured he could keep providin' for y'all as he always had, but also gave him the liberty to get out of those troubles."

"The shop's paid off," she mumbles. "It's been paid off."

"It was collateral, from what I could tell. I tried everything I could, but my father's a shark. He knew what he was doin'."

"And by the time it didn't matter because my father was dead, you had already moved on," she says under her breath.

"It wasn't just you and your family that he was holdin' over my head. He had the same threat going for my gram and paw. Paw didn't do handouts, but when Gram got sick, they lost a lot of money because of her medical treatments. Insurance not coverin' shit. He took a loan out against their house and this office. A loan my father knew would probably never get repaid, but he laughed in my face, sayin' he would demand it all back and push them into the streets if I didn't bend to his will. My mother had his back, even with the threat against her own fuckin' parents."

"What's different now?" she asks, her voice

wavering. "What's different!" she screams when I don't answer right away, jumping up from her seat to pace.

I track her movements with my eyes, keeping my distance while I continue speaking. "Paw's gone. He was a proud man, Quinn, and I would have gladly paid off his loan years ago, but he refused. When he died, my father cut his losses and put the house on the market. Paw had already paid back the loan on the office and it fell to me in his will. I bought the house the second I found out they had listed it."

"And . . . my father's gone . . ." she adds, stopping midstride to look over her shoulder at me.

"And your brother knows his shit. He paid your father's debts off slowly over the years that he's been runnin' things."

"But because of your grandfather, even with that loan paid off, you stayed away." She utters my unspoken words, turning to face me completely, wetness pooling in her eyes.

"By the time you weren't being threatened directly, I had convinced myself it was too late. It had been years, Quinn. Years that I had been forced to stay away, cut off contact, all of it. I never stopped wantin' what was stolen from us, but as the years went by, my bitterness grew. I finished school, started my career, and went through the motions of my life. I didn't do serious anything. Committin' to my career only. Until the day I never thought would come cut the ties that held me back."

"And what? We're supposed to just pick up where we left off?"

"No, Quinn. You take the truth you finally know and you decide if we pick up where we are now. Get to know the adults we've become. Find out if there's still a place for what we felt as teens or if we only have a friendship now."

"We don't even know each other anymore," she argues, her claim weak, fingers twisting the front of her Davis Auto Works tank top.

A sad smile curls my lips up slightly. "Then I guess you need to decide if you want to change that or not, Quinn. Gotta let your heart talk to your mind. You know it all now. The next move is up to you."

"And you? You've spent all this time away and you're just ready to give it a go? Just like that, you've given up a life in another state, a career, and you're just ready . . . like that? You make it sound like you had no ties to where you came from at all, Tate."

I get up, walk over to where she's standing, and cup her face between my hands. My palms tingle in awareness from the touch of her alone. "I finished my time at the hospital I was workin' at. I enjoyed things there, but it wasn't even a question. I have friends back there, and me leavin' isn't gonna change that. I won't lie to you, Quinn, I never thought you would ever be standin' in front of me again. I might not have *done* serious, but sometimes the loneliness got the best of me."

She shakes her head. "You don't owe me explanations of your behavior for the last nine years, Tate. Not when it comes to . . . that."

"Maybe not, but I've spent that time keepin' things from you, Quinn. I've got nothin' but clarity when it comes to my heart communicatin' with my mind. I feel like a selfish bastard for hurtin' you, but even more so because in spite of it all I want to hold you tight and never fuckin' let you go, even if you don't want me to."

"I think . . ." she starts, but pauses to swallow thickly. "I think I need to go."

I force my hands to release the gentle hold I had on her face, my fingers trailing down her cheeks. She doesn't look away from my eyes until I give her a small nod, closing her eyes tightly while her breathing speeds up. I would give just about anything to be in her head right now. Finally, she lifts her lids and turns to leave.

"I'll walk you out," I tell her, my voice low.

She doesn't speak again. The short walk down the hall, past the patient rooms, and to the front door passes in thoughtful silence, both of our minds busy thinking, I'm sure. I stand in the threshold and watch her walk to her haphazardly parked truck before jumping slightly on her heels to pull her short body up into the cab, firing the engine up a moment later and reversing. Then she turns to look at me, something I can't place in her expression making me hold my breath while she lets the window down.

"You're only a selfish bastard if you don't fight for it now," she yells over the rumble of her truck's powerful engine.

By the time I remember to breathe again, all that's left is her taillights in the distance and the meaning of her words hanging like a thick promise in the air.

She wants me to fight.

10
Quinn

"Ain't No Mountain High Enough"
by Marvin Gaye

I call Leighton the second I speed away from
Tate.

I might have hightailed it over to his office
ready to raise some of the hell my brothers claim
I'm famous for, having spent the better part of
Monday and Tuesday taking out my frustrations
on the F1, stuck so deep in my thoughts my anger
had built up to something all-consuming. But I
left with my head spinning, and with the most
distressing thing of all—a sliver of hope that
maybe Tate and I weren't quite over, had never
really been over.

I need my bestie.

By the time I get to the diner, Leigh is already
sitting in our regular booth—in the back, away
from everyone else. I glance toward the PieHole,
seeing the lights still on, and feel a little bad for
pulling her away from her prep for tomorrow's
pies. Only a little, though.

I jump down from Ness, my old Silverado from high school, and make my way into the diner. I wave at some of the locals that *always* seem to be here.

"Thanks for comin' over. I know you're busy," I tell Leigh after I slide into the booth across from her.

"Jana's over there finishin' up. I was headed home anyway," she says around the straw of her Coke. "But if Terry makes one more damn crack about Maverick's predilection for pie eatin' at home, I'm gonna go batshit crazy."

I snort. "He's still goin' on about that?"

I glance over her shoulder and see the old man in question, Terry Long, wag his bushy brows at me.

"Gross," I mumble under my breath.

"Did he do the eyebrow dance?" Leigh questions with a smile.

"Ugh, double gross that you have a name for it."

She shrugs. "So? What's wrong?"

"I went to Tate," I tell her in a rush, needing to get it out.

Her eyes widen and she removes the straw from her mouth, pushing her drink away slowly. "You went to him?" she asks in shocked awe.

"I went to him to give him a good earful. Oh, I was fumin' too, Leigh. I'd been festerin' in that fume for the four whole days since I saw him last."

"What happened four days ago?"

Oh. Shit. I belatedly remember I didn't tell her about the morning after our night out. "About that," I hedge, gaining her narrowed eyes.

"Yes, about that. Let's start there."

"I sorta . . . well, not sorta, I definitely did, but it wasn't what I thought right away, at least . . . uh, I woke up in his bed the mornin' after we went out to the Dam Bar."

"You *what?*" she screams.

I wince and look past her again to see everyone in the room lookin' our way. I give them a wave, then point to Leigh. "Don't mind us. Just talkin' to Bridezilla here."

I get a few smiles and rolled eyes, but everyone just goes back to talking softly and eating. Thankfully, they're used to me and Leighton being crazy, and with no visible gossip-worthy things happening in front of them, they'll take our conversation to be the wedding talkfest I say it is.

"Nothing happened," I hiss, pausing when our favorite waitress, Alice, comes to take our orders. We do the usual burgers, fries, and shakes, my and Leigh's tradition. My eyes follow Alice the second she turns to go put in our orders at the kitchen window until I'm sure she can't hear anything I have to say. "He ran into me when I was past Lenore-level drunk, didn't know for sure where I lived, so when I started gettin' sick, he took me to his paw's old place—well, I guess his place now—got me cleaned up, and crashed."

"Crashed on the couch or crashed in the same bed as you?"

"Did I mention he was a little drunk too?" I say, instantly protective of his motives. I shake off the question of why I feel compelled to defend him and stare at Leigh.

"Wait a minute. You said you rushed over there today stewin' mad." Her eyes darken. "Did that bastard sleep with you when you were wasted? Is that why you were pissed?"

"Not exactly," I answer honestly.

"What the hell does *that* mean?" she blurts out, little drops of spit flying.

My lip curls up and I hold my hand over my open drink. "Gross. Say it, don't spray it."

"Quinn." She sighs impatiently, motioning for me to continue.

"He *may* have gotten a little hands-on and verbally suggestive. My hackles went up and I *may* have rushed outta there with a stolen shirt, my boots, and nothin' else."

Her eyes are as big as saucers when I stop talking. "He let you leave?"

"He *may* have tried to stop me, but he didn't get past the porch. I reckon that's because he realized he was wearin' nothin' but his tight-as-hell briefs, a devil-smile, and an erection."

If possible, her eyes bug out even farther after

I tell her that little nugget. Then, to my absolute shock and horror, she tosses her head back and laughs so loud we're once again the center of attention.

"Would you shut up?" I hiss, bending forward to use her as a shield while I reprimand her. "Seriously, Leigh. Everyone is lookin'."

Wiping her eyes to clear tears of laughter, she quiets down to a soft giggle before locking eyes with me again and snorting, then starting back up again. I lean back against the booth, cross my arms over my chest, and wait for her to stop acting like an idiot.

"Sorry." She giggles, calming down slightly, but now she's smiling at me with such a creepy expression I'm not sure if I should be worried for her sanity or not.

"No, you aren't, but I would love to know what's so dang funny." I pout.

"Remember that time I threw a pie in Mav's face, then followed him home to finish the fight we were havin'?"

Now *that* makes me smile. "You mean when you followed him home and he broke your hooha?"

"I'm not goin' to let you and Jana play together anymore if you don't stop that shit. You sound just like her," she jokes.

"Yeah, right. Anyway, get to the point."

"Weelllll." She drags out the word, and her

creepy smile grows a little larger. "Maverick told me a few months later that he got busted by Drew standin' out on the porch naked as the day he was born watchin' me leave that night. I had been stuck in my head, freakin' out about what had happened between us, I didn't even notice him chasin' after me. I just think it's pretty damn funny that you did the same thing to Tate."

"I didn't rush out of there because I was freakin' out about anything happenin' between us," I say defensively.

"Liar."

"We didn't sleep together," I whisper heatedly.

"You said he got handsy. I know you, Quinn. You would have just pushed back and played him at his own game if it was *just* a little fun. You freaked out and ran because you could never put him in some one-night-stand category."

"I could. If I really wanted to."

Alice comes back and places our plates down with a grunt, leaving just as quickly as she appeared.

"She's so sweet," I say around a mouthful of fries.

"Have you talked to Tate since that mornin' other than just now?" Leigh asks with a knowing eye.

"Today was the first time and I may have stormed into the baby-doctor office and caused a little scene in front of a few people, so I'm guessin' in a few hours the whole damn town will know too."

Her eyes widen, but she quickly calms herself.

"It wasn't that bad," I insist. "I only showed my ass for a second before we were alone and talkin' in private. Long story short, he put it all out there and I don't know what to do with the new information. Jesus Jones, Leigh, I almost understand why he vanished into thin air now."

By the time I finish telling her everything that Tate confessed earlier, our dinner is cold and forgotten about. She doesn't seem to be enjoying the conversation anymore, though, because she almost looks like she's on the verge of tears.

"What? I can tell you want to say somethin'," I deadpan, exhausted from the emotional marathon I've been on today.

"You know, I used to think that the men around here were clueless when it came to relationships. Take your brother, for instance. Maverick disappeared, for the most part, because he was runnin' from the shit y'all dealt with growin' up, but also to chase his dreams. He didn't even give me a chance to support those dreams and be there with him durin' all those years he stayed gone. He thought he was doin' the right thing pushin' me away to give me a future without him. Even if we both know now that we could have made it work, he did it all the same, because he was scared."

I start to speak, to defend Maverick's reasons for leavin', even if I never agreed with his actions in pushin' the connection he had with Leigh away. Out of the three of us, Maverick had to escape our father's reach: I knew that, even if I did miss him every day he was gone makin' a name for himself in the rodeo. It was hard to know he was doing what was best for him, the right thing for him, but that in doing so he was breaking Leigh's heart in two. Leigh just smiles sadly, her lip curling, acceptance written in her blue eyes.

"Water under the bridge, honey, I know that, but even if I was crushed at the time, I got him back anyway. Don't even get me started on Clay." She laughs, trying to lighten the mood some, but sobers instantly. "Like I said, Q, I used to think all the men around here were clueless, but I can honestly say that isn't the case with Tate. He tried to change the path he needed to travel to chase his dreams. Found a way to make a detour on his journey and keep you in the process. He did everything he could, but in the end, he didn't stand a chance. He didn't want that distance any more than you did, but in order to protect everything you, your family, and his grandparents had, he did what he was forced to do. Now he's back, Q. He's back, and from what you've told me, he didn't even waste a second in hightailin' it back here when he knew those

143

he was protectin' were no longer vulnerable to harm."

"You make it sound like the easiest thing in the whole dang world, Leigh. To just forget the past and pick back up where we left off."

A burst of air escapes her lips. "It's not. Not even close. But if you want him—if that connection is still there—then reach out and take it. Y'all still have to get to know the people that you've grown to be, and in the end, you might find what you used to feel for him is no longer there, but you also might find it's a whole lot more powerful now. Either way, you've got to jump in the saddle and take the bumpy trail together to find out."

I look away and out the window while I weigh her words. There isn't much to see, since it's just after dinnertime on a weeknight, but the darkness is easier to focus on while my head spins.

"Quinn," Leigh calls softly, breaking me from my thoughts, and I turn to look back across the table at her. "You know we had a conversation just like this when your brother came home. You sat there and supported me without question, but one thing I'll never forget you tellin' me is somethin' I reckon you've forgotten yourself now that you're stuck at the same crossroads."

Goose bumps pepper my skin and I shiver slightly when I feel the chill of déja vu making itself known.

144

"I'll never forget it, Quinn, because it was what I needed to hear in order to take that chance, and because of what you told me, I've got the man I've loved my whole life, a dream he built us, and the promise of one hell of a future. I want that for you, Quinn and I have a feelin' the man who can give it to you is the same one you're afraid to take a leap of faith on."

I bite my tongue when I feel emotion burning up my chest, something Leigh doesn't miss, because she pushes her arms across the table and grabs hold of my hands with her own, squeezing them tightly. I focus on our tightly clamped-together hands in order to tuck the heaviness I'm feeling back down before looking up to focus on her again, knowing deep down what she's about to say will be a game changer for my jumbled mind.

"It's been a year since, and I still wonder how long I would have kept pushin' had you not put it all out there with so much clarity, so now it's my turn to give those words back to you. Can you sit there and tell me that since Tate's returned you don't feel like a piece of you that's been missin' is startin' to heal? You told me when two souls are meant to be intertwined, they always find a way back to each other, Q. The difference between you and me, though, is that you know everything that kept him from you, and while he might not have come back until now, it sounds like he's been fightin' for you in some form ever since. Don't do what I did and use your pain to push him away. Allow that missin' piece to heal, and in the end, even if you decide to just be friends, at least you can finally move on with your life one way or the other and have a chance at feelin' your forever."

At some point in the middle of her speech, I lose control over my feelings. I still hold one of her hands tightly in my own, but I swipe at my face with the other, clearing the annoying tears that I was powerless to hold back. My throat is burning, a lump of pain lodged deep within it.

"Jesus Jones," I breathe, shaking my head in disbelief. "For someone who doesn't have the slightest experience in this shit, I sure did sound like I knew what I was talkin' about."

Leigh's hand tightens. "Something tells me, Q, you actually have more experience than any of us."

"I've been alone since he left, Leigh. The only relationship I've ever had was one I basically kept a secret from everyone, and when it exploded, I let the crash scar me deep enough that I never tried again. How exactly does that scream *experience?*"

"I think you've actually been waitin', to be honest. When you helped me through that rough spot with Maverick, you were speakin' from deep inside you, Q. It was advice I have a feelin' your mind was just waitin' to give you for yourself. Like you told me, two people meant to be together will always, *always* find their way back together."

"I want this chance," I whisper, fear of my desires dripping from each word. "I want it so much I can taste it, but I don't know how to forget that we lost so much. How do I ignore the fact that, while we were meant to be together, we've spent years apart and not exactly without the attention of other people durin' that time?"

"You just do," she says softly. "You just do. Now that's somethin' I can tell you from experience, honey. You said it yourself: he never thought y'all would get this chance again, and you were livin' your life thinkin' the same damn thing. You can't hold that against him, and he can't hold it against you."

"And if I do this, move forward to him and not away from him, what happens when one of us realizes there's nothin' left to have?"

"Then you have your friend back, Quinn. You guys spent a long damn time as friends before anything matured from that. There are no guarantees in this world, but at least you know, one way or the other, you have him back in your life. But, Q, that's your fear makin' you ask that question. Trust me on that."

I inhale, leaning back and pulling the air deep into my lungs for strength while I mull over her words. Is it as simple as that? Are my fears of being hurt again just creating problems that aren't even there?

"You felt the power of y'all's connection touch you from just a scribbled-down phone message written on a dirty piece of paper, Quinn. You hadn't heard his voice, seen the man he is now, or known there was a chance to have it all back, and you still felt that. All from a piece of paper, honey. Stop tryin' to think of ways that it won't work and start focusin' on the proof that it will. You're a hell-raisin' badass, remember?"

I choke on a laugh, her words warming me from the inside.

"Yeah, I *am* a hell-raisin' badass," I agree through wobbly lips.

"You betcha ass you are. Now what are ya gonna do about it?"

Well, isn't that the million-dollar question.

11
Quinn

"Burning House" by Cam

— ★ —

I stand back and study the old F1 with a critical eye. I've just finished putting everything back together, the panel fitment being the biggest pain in my ass, but after a two-day struggle, Homer is getting his first breath of fresh air after a long process of fixing imperfections, priming and painting.

Now that everything I had dismantled is put back together on the old frame and he's had his date in the paint booth, the old guy is finally aligned, symmetrical and sexy as hell, his paint gleaming in the bright shop lights. Honest to God, Homer looks even better than he probably did right off the line nearly seventy years ago.

It's taken me a whole day to get the suspension reinstalled, and with the help of Tank, Homer's new motor and transmission are back in. I just finished running the new brake and fuel lines as well as the electrical components inside Homer's sexy frame. I still have to install the exhaust system I ordered for him, one that I have no doubt will make him purr like the sexy beast he is, but I needed a break after working for almost ten hours on him alone today.

Not only that, I need to make a call I've been putting off since my dinner with Leigh a few nights ago.

The guys have long since left the shop, even if I could tell a few of them didn't want to leave me here alone. It didn't take much encouragement to get them to skedaddle out of here seeing that it's a Friday night and they've all been talkin' for days about hittin' up Coops for some beer and pool. They should be used to leaving me here alone. I've gotten lost in so many projects in the past that it's not exactly a rarity, but I think they put up a fuss for show now, knowing that I would never take them up on their offers to stick around.

I take one last look at Homer, the Lava Red paint I picked for him making me want to lay my body against the hood and just soak in the beauty. In low light, he almost looks black, but the second the light strikes his sleek metal cage, red undertones burst free, making it come to life.

It's hot.

So damn hot, I think I've fallen a little in love with the old guy.

"God, Homer, you sure are gonna turn some heads," I tell him, patting the hood with affection.

Reluctantly, I turn from the sexy beast and walk

to my office to grab a Coke, a snack, and my cell. I groan loudly when my tired body finally settles into my desk chair, taking a bite of my Pop-Tart while I stare at my phone.

Butterflies erupt in my stomach and the Pop-Tart I'm chewing on suddenly tastes more like cardboard. I'm being ridiculous right now. A big baby.

"Come on, Quinn," I tell myself sternly. "You're a hell-raisin' badass. Just pick up the phone and throw the stupid ball you've been bouncin' in your court back in Tate's."

Tossing my half-eaten snack down, I snatch my phone up and connect the call before I can give myself a second to freak out more than I already am.

"This is Tatum Montgomery," the deep, velvety voice answers.

The same voice I've been unable to stop thinking about for days. God, he sounds delicious. If that's a thing, that is. Seriously, his voice should be considered illegal. Panty-melting illegal.

"Hello?" he calls, clearly impatient, if his tone is anything to go by.

Shit, I haven't said a word. I bet I'm breathing heavy. Like a creepy stalker or something.

"Hey," I squeak, rushing the word out to quiet the panic Inner Quinn is going through.

"Quinn," he breathes. Literally. He breathes

151

my name in the most sensual way, and I feel it go straight to my gut.

"Okay, bucko, so in an effort to keep a whole full-disclosure thing goin', I'm goin' to have to ask you to not say my name like that. It makes me think thoughts that don't belong in my head at this juncture in our . . . reunion."

Deep, sexy-as-hell, lady-part-tingling grunts of laughter follow.

"Add that laugh to the list of things you can't do too," I pant. Could this get any worse?

"Anything else, Grease?"

I pause, looking out into the shop floor while I think about that one. I'm sure if I really thought about it, though, I could make a list of things that make my body burn. "I'll have to get back to you on that," I rush out, thinking that there will never be enough time in the world for me to list them.

"You do that," he chuckles.

"Maybe it's the phone," I mumble to myself. I don't remember his voice sounding this . . . erotic in person.

"What, Quinn?"

"Oh, God. Seriously, only you make me stupid. No one else does this shit to me, but you just short somethin' out in my head that doesn't work right. I'm at the shop. Do you have time to meet up and talk?"

More deep rumbles of laughter.

Kill me now.

"Just finishin' up at the office, Quinn. I've got one more patient file I need to update and then I'll head over. Sound good, darlin'?"

I squeeze my legs together, instantly regretting it when the seam of my jeans hits my swollen and very needy center. " 'Darlin' ' just got added to that list too."

"Right." He gurgles with suppressed laughter. "See ya in a bit, *Quinn*."

He disconnects the call before I have a chance to say anything else, and I replay our conversation. The second I realize I just invited him over, I freak. I didn't exactly plan this out thinking we would have this conversation face-to-face, but sure enough, that's how it came out to him. Now I need to hike up my britches and deal with it, because I no longer have the phone to hide behind.

"Holy shit, I'm gonna freak the hell out," I groan, then do exactly that.

Seventeen minutes later, after a panic session involving four more Pop-Tarts and a hell of a lot of pacing back and forth, I see him pull into the lot. I had moved to the front reception slash waiting-room area after I managed to stop yelling at myself and waving my arms in the air, figuring it would be better to have somewhere we could sit down, but then rethought my strategy. I've basically done nothing but pace since I walked up here and saw the only option is a leather love seat. I really need to replace those stupid single chairs I made Tank toss because they made this place look like a thrift store.

A sharp knock against the front glass makes me jump, scream, and spin around—stupid sugar high.

"I'm so screwed," I groan, shuffling on my booted feet to the door to unlock it and let him in. My inner voice screaming the same thing, only with a whole different meaning.

"Hey, Grease," he greets in a low, smooth voice—one that doesn't sound any less sensual off the phone.

"I'm screwed," I scream aloud. "Totally and completely screwed!" Then, because I'm clearly two seconds away from losing it, I start pacing, incoherent gibberish that I'm powerless to stop spewing from my lips. I look over my shoulder at him, only to feel my brows knit and my eyes narrow, my mind picking up right where it left off, only now the gibberish is coming out more like I'm speaking in tongues.

"Whoa," he calls out, grabbing my shoulders softly, halting me mid-stomp. "What's goin' through your mind, Quinn?" His eyes search my face as he tries to understand what's going on, and his thumbs rub soothing circles against the exposed skin.

Note to self: Wear tank tops whenever he's within touching distance.

"You scare me more than a rattlesnake about to strike," I whisper. "Right down to my marrow, Tate Montgomery."

His face softens and his eyes spark knowingly. He knows that by admitting that, I've all but signed myself over to him. Wholly and completely.

"You've got nothin' to worry about when it comes to me, darlin'."

"I think . . ." I take a deep breath. "I think that might take me some time to realize."

"Well, aren't you in luck? Seems I've recently found myself with nothin' *but* time."

I close my eyes and drop my forehead to his chest, the rapid beating of his heart hitting me the second I make contact, and I realize he's feeling this a whole lot more than his calm demeanor is letting on. For whatever reason, the knowledge that he's as deeply affected by this as I am washes over me like an instant dose of calm.

"Wanna see Homer?"

"Who?"

I laugh as I pull my head off his chest, the ice broken just like that. The second our eyes connect, my laughter stalls in my throat and I give him the truth of my heart.

"I've missed you." I reach up, pushing some wavy hair that had fallen over his forehead toward his temple. "If I didn't feel each one of those years you've been gone in my bones, I would think not a day's gone by since you were last here, this lazy man's hair fallin' into your eyes."

"It's supposed to make me look rugged yet sexy," he says keeping a straight face for a beat before his lips twitch. "I missed you too, darlin', more than I could ever explain."

I nod, feeling the air starting to shake around me with our vulnerable admissions. Not wanting to break down like a baby, I grab his hand and take him to meet Homer.

Hopefully that'll give me some time to get my mind straight and tell the man that broke my heart in two once in my life already that I'm giving him the power to do it again.

Jesus Jones.

12

Quinn

"Like I'm Gonna Lose You" by Meghan Trainor

— ★ —

"Whoa."

I smile when I hear it. The pure reaction of shock and wonder that I just *knew* Homer would incite from people. He's that perfect.

"Yeah," I breathe, lost in the trance that is Homer. "He should be ready soon. I finished up the interior wirin' earlier today; I'll install the rest of the interior finishes tomorrow, get the windows installed, and then I'll move on to the bed. I've got the most beautiful deep mahogany wood for it that will set off the red in the paint."

"You got all this done already?"

I turn to face him when I hear the disbelief in his voice, feeling the pride I take in my work inflating my ego. "Yup," I say, popping the *p*. "I kinda know my way around F1's," I smirk, and then point over my shoulder at my girl. "I've been tinkerin' with Bertha for about a year now. Took me a while because it was a side project I did in any extra time I had around the custom projects I had come in. Or I would take weeks off at a time because she's a cranky bitch that gave me a whole lot more frustrations than Homer did."

Tate whistles under his breath, looking from Bertha to Homer. He repeats the process a few times before settling those mesmerizing eyes on me. "Homer and Bertha?"

"It isn't nice to put your hands under someone's hood if you aren't at least on a first-name basis."

"Of course it isn't," he agrees, lips twitching.

"Homer's an expensive date, you know," I joke.

"I don't doubt that, Grease. Worth every fuckin' penny."

"As much as I hate havin' this talk here at the shop, I'm not sure I trust myself goin' anywhere else. For one thing, Clay's at home, I'm sure, and I would rather delay any chat he may want to have with you until I have a better understandin' of what's happenin' here. And to be completely honest, I know if we took things to your place I'm not sure you could resist this," I tell him, waving my hand down my body, in hopes of keeping things lighthearted, but I know instantly that my joke had the wrong impression on him. His eyes darken and his nostrils flare as he burns a path of awareness down my body. "So anyway, here at the shop is our only option." I rush the words out, wanting nothing more than to press my thighs together to attempt to ease the ache building between them.

"Here's got potential," he murmurs, patting the shiny hood of Homer before advancing.

"Hey now, snap outta it!" My hand meets his chest when he's just a few feet in front of me. My fingers curl, the soft material of his black button-down shirt rasping against my skin. Shit, did I just purr?

"You told me to fight for you, Quinn. You left the other night with that parting comment and I haven't heard a word from you for two fuckin' days. Do you have any idea how much restraint it's taken for me not to say the hell with it and not give you the time to sort your head?"

"Probably a good thing you didn't, Tate. I'm not sure it would have ended favorably for you had you not have given me that time."

"Yeah?" he mocks, raising one dark brow. "And now?"

"Now I think it's time I stop lettin' what happened years ago stand in the way of me livin'."

His jaw clenches and his nostrils flare. "What I did marked you."

"Marked you too, honey," I whisper, knowing the truth to my words in my gut.

"Move your hand, Quinn," he demands, pressing against my outstretched limb.

I instantly comply, and not even a breath later

his arms are wrapped tightly around my body, crushing me to him. One of his hands goes up and I feel him rip the band holding my hair back out right before his fingers push into my thick locks in an effort to hold my head against his chest. He wraps his other arm around my back, curling his fingers around my side and making it so that there isn't a part of me that isn't touching him.

His heart pounds against my ear, the rapid tattoo matching mine. Feeling him like this snaps something deep inside me, something I had thought I lost forever. I know in this moment that it would take a whole hell of a lot to make me run now.

"I'm not sure I deserve you givin' me another chance, Quinn, but fuck if I won't make sure you don't regret it."

"We still don't know each other anymore, Tate. It might not be easy and you might find you don't care for the woman I've become."

My voice is muffled, but I know he hears me, because he lets out a sound of disbelief that tickles my cheek. I take the moment to turn my head as much as I can and breathe in the scent of him, a fragrance that always made me dizzy with need anytime he was around, but that I missed like an addiction I had been cut off abruptly from.

"If I promise to resist your many, *many* . . . charms," he whispers, leaning back and causing his hand to fall from the back of my head and down my neck until I feel the heel of his hand at the top of my chest. His other arm leaves my back at the same time until he is holding the side of my chest, the heat of his hand on the side of my other breast. His eyes, though, they're devouring me and he isn't even hiding it. "Do you think we can finish this at my place?" he says to my chest.

"Tate," I warn, not sure if I want him to give our bodies what we both clearly want or follow through with his promise to deny them that.

"Haven't had you in my arms in close to a decade, Quinn, not counting the other day. While I promise nothin' will happen, I can't promise to keep my thoughts from goin' there. Make no mistake, darlin', my hands aren't goin' to be able to stay off of you when I know you're about to give me the right to put them there."

"Oh, really?" I gasp in mock shock.

Deep rumbles of his many chuckles hit my ears and I feel my face get all dreamy when he casts a lopsided grin at me. "Tell ya what," he says softly. "How about I walk you out, you let me talk you into a kiss good night, then I'll pick you up in the morning and we can start gettin' to know each other again?"

Mind stuck on that good-night kiss, I stare at him with breathy pants escaping my lips.

"I'm thinkin' I might not have to do much persuadin' for that kiss, huh, Grease?" he smarts off, winking down at me.

"I reckon not, Tate. I reckon not."

He helps me close everything down. I'm fully capable of doing it myself, but it's nice to have *him* here doing such trivial tasks—his presence alone something I'm enjoying immensely. No, that's not right. It's as if my body had been without *feeling* his presence for so long that it's feeding off being near him. I feel like I can take on the world, a burst of renewed strength and happiness making me feel almost superhuman.

The other half of me is snapping into place, regardless of the fact that we still have to get to know each other again. It doesn't matter that there is still so much unknown between us because of the years that have passed. All that matters is what I'm feeling.

Accepted. Wanted. *Whole.*

All because of him. Can I do this again? When he first came into my life, I was at that age where every little girl just wants and needs her mama, but I didn't have that. His friendship, that bond we have always shared, eased the pain her absence had created inside me, filling me up and making that void almost unnoticeable. And that had been when all I had was his friendship during the summer for years. When we finally gave into what our hearts were screaming for, that void was filled—vanishing completely.

Then he left.

He left, and with him he took all the promises

162

he'd ever whispered. He stole that piece inside me he had filled, and I hadn't found a way to fix it since.

Now he's back and promising me the chance at all those things again. All the things that it killed me to lose the last time. If losing him back then hurt me as fiercely as it did when I only wondered if he had been the one, how could I recover now as an adult that knows without a shadow of doubt that he *is* the *only* one?

"Tate," I gurgle, his name coming out in a breathy burst of panic as I let those feelings settle in and take root.

He stops, his hand on the switch that controls the lights for the whole garage floor, and looks over his shoulder at me, his expression no longer relaxed and carefree, but now tinged with unease.

"I lied. Earlier when I said that you scared me, I lied. I'm not just scared. I'm petrified, Tate. There's so much goin' on inside me right now that I'm strugglin' to make sense of it. Strugglin' to trust that I *can* make sense of it. And not all that is just because you're askin' me to take a big ol' blind leap of faith where your promises are concerned."

The strong lines of his face get soft. A melty look of pure male hotness steals over his face, making him look even more handsome, if that's possible. In all of that though, there's a certain cockiness present that makes me think he might have enough belief in this for the both of us. He levels me with an understanding gaze, accepting what he's up against instantly.

"How 'bout you let me handle all that worries you, darlin', and give your mind some time to accept what it's scared to see is real."

Just like that. Like it's the simplest of things.

"You'll get there and I'll be here every step of the way to prove you can believe, but until you do, I'll just keep waitin' for you to catch up to me."

My breath speeds up and I almost feel like I could cry. This isn't like last time. Last time we had whispered dreams and promises that we would do whatever we could to make them happen. He eased the fears my mama's abandonment placed in my heart by promising he would always be there, even if only as a friend, but that he wouldn't just leave me—and he had. But this, this is him giving me so much more with just that one sentence. He isn't leaving. He isn't telling me what I want to hear, and we aren't two kids that didn't know enough about life to build those dreams. He's vowing to help me see what we as adults know is possible. To take those steps toward what was finally our time to have.

Each other.

"Together?" I hedge.

"Always."

I nod, not trusting my words, and he gives me

his back to finally flip the lights off. We move like two people who've been doing this night after night their whole lives through the shop until he's standing behind me waiting for me to lock the doors, the silence between us comfortable, even with the lingering reminder of our need for each other whipping up the air around us.

I don't get that good-night kiss he had joked about earlier. I think we both knew it wasn't the time, and in all honesty, I'm glad. It isn't that I don't want to feel that again. Oh, I do, so much. But I feel so raw inside that I think some of the beauty of our reunion would always hold a sense of heaviness to it if we'd given in to our passions tonight.

Tomorrow. Tomorrow I have a date with my past as we start building our future.

And I can't freaking wait.

13
Tate

"The Driver" by Charles Kelley

— ★ —

The second her taillights vanished from my view, I pull my phone from my pocket and dial Mark.

"Remind me tomorrow to thank you for this call," Mark whispers before clearing his throat and talking away from the receiver. "Darlin', I'm gonna step out and talk to Tate. You gotta stop givin' me that look, though."

"If I called at a bad time, you can let me go." I laugh, not wanting to hear him and Jane fight.

"Shut your mouth," he hisses quietly.

He continues talking softly with his wife, mumbling things I wish I never heard. Knowing he's going to be a second, I make my way to my truck and climb in to crank her up, pulling out of Davis Auto Works and down Main toward home.

"Shit, man," Mark groans out a breath. "You got good timin', my friend. I swear to God, my balls are gonna fall off. Is that a thing? Can my

166

balls fall off because my wife can't stop usin' my body?"

"Your balls aren't gonna fall off, Mark," I answer with a smile.

"Well, they fuckin' might. You don't know what they've been through today alone, not to mention the last three days. Janie says it's her special time, whatever the fuck that means. All I know is my wife is startin' to make me feel like all she wants is my come, and when it doesn't work, she gets this look in her eye like she thinks she's failin'."

"How long did you say y'all been tryin'?" My doctor brain snaps into place hearing him talk about their struggle to conceive. As a doctor, I know these things take time, and it's common for many couples to try for over a year before ever conceiving. The friend in me, however, wants to do whatever I can to help them out.

"Shit, I don't know, Tate. Lost track after a year of workin' hard at it. Workin' hard turned into workin' in overdrive. She's consumed with it, and I just want to give my girl what she wants, ya know?"

"I hear ya. Tell her to call the office tomorrow and make an appointment."

"Will do," Mark says with a sigh. "She was seein' some fancy doctor an hour away, but our insurance wouldn't cover the treatments he suggested, so she stopped a few months ago."

"I'll need her to get a copy of her records from him, but we can get those after she comes in. You just worry about your balls not fallin' off."

"Thanks, man," he says, already sounding better than he did moments before. "Say, why'd ya call?"

My lips twitch. "Need someone's number from you and didn't want to spend too much time huntin' it down."

We make small talk for the rest of my drive, and as I'm putting the truck in park, Mark promises again to see me next week with his wife. I stare out the windshield after ending our call. My mind is in overdrive, but my heart feels a million pounds lighter knowing that things are as good as they're going to get at this point with where Quinn stands. Hell, they're better than I thought they would be this soon, but I know I need to do my part in making the start of our relationship as easy as possible for Quinn.

Then my text chimes with a message from Mark with the number I had requested. I don't waste a second, wanting to get this done quickly so I can plan my last first date.

"Yeah," a deep, breathless voice answers, but I hear the phone drop and some grunts before nothing but pure chaos comes through the line. Shouts to grab the lead and a whole lot of bangin' around later the phone is picked back up. "Sorry 'bout that."

"If it's a bad time, I can call back." I lean my head back against the headrest and close my eyes, hating the nervousness I feel rushing through me.

"Good a time as any," Clay Davis replies.

"It's Tate," I tell him in lieu of answering. "Tatum Montgomery."

Silence hits my ears. I know he's there because not only is the call still connected, but I can hear his heavy breathing through the line.

"I wondered when you would be makin' this call," he says, his voice calm and steady, even though I know better.

I grunt out a humorless laugh, opening my mouth to reply, but stop when he continues to speak.

"You have anything to do with my sister gettin' home just now lookin' better than she has in fuckin' weeks?"

"At the risk of soundin' like a cocky bastard, I sure hope so."

"Hmm." He hums.

"I know it's gettin' to be suppertime and all, but if you could spare some time, I feel like we have a conversation that needs to happen before I continue makin' sure your sister keeps lookin' like she did when she got home."

He hums again.

"I wouldn't even bother, Clay, but I know Quinn always did go outta her way to make sure her brothers supported her decisions. If I have any hope of winnin' her back, havin' your blessin' to do so is going to mean a whole helluva lot to her. I plan to have the same talk separately with Maverick as well, but Quinn used to look to *you* for advice and affirmation that she's doin' right, and I've got a feelin' that hasn't changed, which means you're first on my list."

"Sure you just don't want to deal with us both at the same time?"

I scuff out a low laugh. "Hell no, I don't. In all seriousness though, I know she's gonna want her brothers to stand behind her decisions, so this needs to happen."

"She's a twenty-seven-year-old woman. She doesn't need her brothers' permission to do shit."

"Just because she doesn't need it doesn't mean it's not somethin' she wants. And I think you and I both know it's a lot more than just permission she wants."

"Fuck," he says harshly under his breath. "I'll come to you." Then he disconnects the call and I'm left to the deafening silence around me, a twisting feeling in my gut.

"This shouldn't be an awkward conversation at all," I grumble to myself, getting out of the truck and going into the house to get ready for Clay.

I'm not going to find anything there to help ease my racing mind, though. It's just a shell of the house that was my grandparents' home. Aside from the layout and a few little things here and there that hadn't been lost forever after my parents almost took this place away from me for good, it's unrecognizable. The comforting scent of my paw's old pipe isn't lingering in the air. Gran isn't busy in the kitchen cooking up a storm. The old chairs that were in front of their ancient television are long gone, tossed away.

It's up to me now to create my own memories in their huge farmhouse.

I've just poured myself a cup of coffee when I hear an engine roar, announcing Clay's arrival. Not knowing if he's going to want something as caffeinated as coffee this time of evening, I walk through the living room and out to the porch, putting my mug down on the rail. He climbs down from his truck, adjusts the dark cowboy hat on his head, and then lumbers through the grass until he's standing at the bottom of the six stairs, waiting for my cue before he takes another step.

"You want a cup?" I ask, tilting my head toward the mug.

"Wouldn't mind one, but that shit will keep me up all night and I got too much shit to do in the mornin' to be losin' sleep."

"You wanna stand there or come up and have a seat?"

He looks toward me, then over to the rocking chairs before answering, "Lead the way."

Grabbing my mug, I turn and walk over to one of the chairs. I pull it away from its partner and turn it slightly so I can speak to his face and not take a coward's way out by avoiding his eyes just because he's as intimidating as it gets.

"Not to rush you, Doc, but it's been a long day and I haven't decided if I want to kick your ass or not."

"I've only been in town a week and you already want to kick my ass?"

"I've wanted to kick your ass for damn near nine years," he answers, taking his hat off to rest it in his hand before giving me his undivided attention, stoic face, and hard eyes.

"Quinn knows what happened back then, Clay. She knows *and* she understands. As much as I would love to say it isn't any of your business, I know it is. Doesn't make it any easier to admit to a man I've always respected that I was a coward before I ask him to support the relationship I hope to build with his baby sister."

With the sun low in the sky, I can see his face clearly, but still he gives nothing away. This could go two ways: he could share his sister's understanding, or he could follow through on his desire to make me pay for hurting her. While I don't doubt that he's justified in wanting that, Clay is the last man I want to go head-to-head with. He's built similar to me, but his work on the ranch puts his strength at a considerable advantage to mine, no matter how many hours I spend in the gym.

He maintains his silence as I lay out everything I told Quinn earlier this week. It's a huge blow to my male pride that I let someone keep me from the woman I loved because *I* wasn't man enough to protect her from the harm they could have so easily inflicted. It isn't an easy pill to swallow, even if I know deep down I did the right thing.

"You're kidding," he finally says when I finish my story.

"Wish to God I was. If it had been anything else, I wouldn't have kept my distance, you have to know that, Clay."

"Yeah, yeah," he mumbles, looking away and out in the distance in front of the house. "Your paw know about this?"

I nod. "I only told him enough so that he'd accept why I stayed away, but not all of it. He thought I was too busy with school and then my residency for the most part, but I told him Quinn and I just hadn't worked out, so he didn't press for more."

"Explains why you didn't come back sooner, I reckon. I paid off that loan my old man took out a year or so before he died. When I took over, that was the first thing I set to rights."

I nod, feeling the sadness of the lost years creeping back in. "Right after my inheritance was turned over to me. I know. An employee at my father's bank helped to keep an eye on those loans for me. I tried to get Paw to let me settle

173

his shit with my father when I found out, but he wouldn't budge. His pride wouldn't let him, and in all honesty, I was ashamed that I'd let my father win, so I kept my silence about why I was tryin' so hard to get him to agree and gave up a lot of my hopes in that moment."

Clay lets out a low whistle, running a hand through his dark hair. "That's one hell of a shit story, Tate. I figured I'd come over here and there wouldn't be shit you could say to make me understand you hurtin' my sister, but I gotta say, in your shoes, I'm not sure I wouldn't have done the same thing."

"I want her back. I want to give us back what was stolen from us and I know she wants that too, Clay. She's just scared, and rightfully so."

He stops studying the yard and finally looks at me. "And what do you want from me?"

I shake my head. "I wanted you to hear what happened from me. I don't care if you tell Quinn about this chat. I won't hide from her that you were here. If she wants to talk about what happened, then she has another person that can help her work through that. I need her to see me workin' hard to rebuild the bridge that was burned when I left the last time. I wanted to tell you, man-to-man, that my intentions are honest when it comes to Quinn. I don't know what the future holds for us, much as I wish I did, but your sister wants us to take some time to get to know

174

each other again, and until I know she trusts in us again, it's all up in the air until I can prove otherwise. I'm already done for. Honest to God, even if she was half the woman I loved back then, she'd still be perfect. If she gives me her trust and heart again and you want to stand in the way of us findin' the future we lost, then so be it, but you need to know an army at your back won't keep me from fightin' for that woman. No one will ever do that again."

"You sound pretty damn sure of yourself for someone that claims to be taking the time to get to know her again before you decide if she's worth it."

"I said *she* wants that time to get to know each other again, not me. I agreed to it because I'll tread as lightly as I need to to keep her from runnin' spooked."

"You need to give her more credit than that, Tate." He sighs, leaning back in the rocker. "No doubt that girl's a frightened little bunny right now, especially if you just laid all this on her, but make no mistake, that little hell-raiser is just waitin' to slap some sense into that bunny."

I laugh softly, knowing his description of his sister is spot-on. She never did let that bunny win for long.

"She's been hurt a lot, though, Tate and I have a feelin' you made the right move regardless of her normal take-charge attitude: that timid little bunny might not run away as quick as you'd like."

"I'll make it up to her," I promise, not looking away from his probing gaze.

"You know about our mama leavin', Tate, but I reckon she'll bring up what we learned about her last year soon enough since you already know most of it. Quinn's a smart girl and she'll not waste a second tellin' you, knowin' you can help her figure it out for herself. Maybe while you're makin' up your past to her you can find it in you to help heal that part of her pain, too." With that, he stands, places his hat back on his head, and walks down the stairs, turning before he steps off the last one completely. "It's good to see you here, Tate. I always did think you fit in like Pine Oak had always been your home. When you have this talk with Mav, give him more credit than whatever it was that had you thinkin' you need to split us up. He's softer than he looks. Take care of my sister, and don't make me regret hopin' like hell you win her back."

He's in his truck and pulling back on the main road not even thirty seconds later, leaving me to wonder what the hell happened last year to make her mama's abandonment worse than it was before.

14

Quinn

"Confession" by Florida Georgia Line

— ★ —

Why are you so damn hyper this morning?" Clay grumbles, cutting short the upbeat tune I had been whistling with a narrowed glare of his eyes.

I giggle and switch from my whistling to tapping out a light beat on the floorboards with my bare feet. "Can't a girl just enjoy a Saturday morning?"

He scratches his head, his hair messy from just waking up, and mutters under his breath before dragging his ass to the coffeepot. The coffeepot that, might I add, I made sure was full of strong, freshly brewed, delicious dark roast—just like he likes.

"Seriously, Hell-raiser, you drink some of those energy drinks we told you to stay away from this mornin' or somethin'?"

"Nope," I say with a smile.

"I'm not playin' twenty questions with you, no matter how much you love makin' people work for whatever it is you want them to know."

I feel my smile dim *just* a little at my brother's surly tone, but nothing can take away the excitement that hit a fever pitch around four in the morning, waking me up knowing I would be seeing Tate in just a handful of hours for our first date. Well, not our first date technically, but it might as well be. We're the same people we used to be, but also so very different.

However, just because it would be hard as hell to kill this kind of excitement I've got rushing inside me, doesn't mean I'm not nervous talking with Clay about it. I've never kept things from him before, but this seems different somehow. A lot has changed since he gave me that pep talk a few weeks ago. I went into that talk with him not knowing what would happen when I came face-to-face with Tate again after all this time. Now, well . . . now I know, and it would hurt a whole lot if I didn't have Clay's support going forward with Tate. Wouldn't stop me, but it would still hurt.

"I'm going on a date. This morning. Well, today, not this morning. Hell, I don't know. It's a date for some undisclosed time today and I'm excited about it."

His mug stills halfway to his mouth and the tired look in his eyes clears. "With Tate," he says knowingly.

"Yes, with Tate. He called last night to ask me, officially, out on a date."

"Hmm." He takes a sip—a long-as-hell sip, if

you ask me—of his coffee before arching a brow at me.

"That's it? You 'hmm' me and then just nothing? You don't have an opinion? A little pep talk for me? Some kind of big-brother motivational speech?" I huff when I finish my rapid-fire questions and plant my hands on both hips, throwing every bit of sass I have at him.

His lips twitch, but other than that, nothing.

I puff out a grunting breath and shake my head at him, encouraging him to speak. My hair drops from the messy bun I had pulled it into earlier, and some of the dark strands fall into my line of sight. I blow them away, only to have them fall back into my eyes, effectively ruining my tough-cookie act when I have to move my hands into my bird's nest of hair.

Clay starts laughing, deep belly laughs, when my ponytail holder snaps just as I'm wrapping it around my thick hair, leaving me with a stinging mark on my hand and a face full of thick, wavy strands.

"Please keep goin'. You know I love watchin' you stumble your way through tryin' to be intimidating."

"Whatever," I grumble, stomping to the junk drawer and grabbing a new hair tie, only to have that one snap too. By the time I *finally* get my hair back up and in place, Clay's still laughing his ass off. "You're such a jerk."

"How am I a jerk? Because I think it's funny as hell when that shit happens to you?" he asks, still laughing softly.

"Are you really going to give me nothin'? I tell you I'm going on a date—with Tate—and you give me nothin' at all?"

He shrugs. "What do you want me to say, sugar? I'm not gonna stand in the way of this if it's what you want. You want me to remind you I'm here if you need me, for anything? Because I will if you need to hear that, even if it goes without repeatin', Quinny. I want you happy, and if Tate is the man to help get you there, then that's good, little sister, that's real good."

"Well, I suppose that'll do," I mumble through the thickness in my throat.

He puts his cup down and opens his arms. Not needing to be told, I walk into his arms and soak up his comfort. "I knew he was makin' his play to win you back, Quinny. Talked to him myself last night, just didn't know you had a date today. I really am happy for you and will support you with whatever you need from me. Just promise me you'll listen to what your gut's tellin' you now."

I sniff and nod.

"You talked to him?"

His silent confirmation gives me pause: I'm afraid to hear how it went.

"That's all you're goin' to say?" I ask.

"It's all you need to know, sugar. Wasn't a bad talk, and all you need to take from it is that I'm happy you're takin' this chance."

My throat gets thick, and as much as I want to push him more, I can't say I'm upset about what he's willing to tell me.

"Talkin' loud now, huh?"

I look at him, confused.

"Gut, Hell-raiser. Talkin' loud?"

Smiling, remembering our talk a few weeks ago. "Been screamin' for a week now, Clay. Just gotta get rid of the big ol' scaredy-cat standin' in the way."

His chest rumbles against my ear. "Let Tate worry about that, okay?"

"Okay," I reply softly.

Clay leaves to head down to the stables shortly after our morning chat, right before the clock even ticks past six in the morning. He doesn't tell me anything else about his talk with Tate and I don't ask, but he does make sure to reiterate that he'll be supporting me all the way while Tate and I begin this new phase of our relationship. I still can't believe this is real.

I keep checking the clock, waiting. Not for Tate, seeing as it's still early as hell—according to him, I'll see him at eight and I'm to be ready for a day outside. I still have another hour and a half before he's expected to pick me up. No, I'm waiting for it not to be so dang early so I can call Leigh and fill her in.

When I got back last night, she was the first person I called, not wanting to waste a second, since I knew she was still upset that I hadn't come to her with my feelings right after the first call I made to Tate five weeks ago. She couldn't talk long, having just gotten to the movie theater with Maverick for date night, but after she squealed through the line with me, she made me promise to call first thing.

So that's what I'm doing. Standing in the middle of the living room, dusting the coffee table at six twenty-five in the morning while I wait for the next five minutes to pass.

"Oh, fuck it." I toss the rag I was dusting with down and rush to the kitchen to grab my phone off the charger.

"Hold on," Maverick answers in a surly tone that lets me know he just woke up. Oops. I forgot Leigh mentioned he was taking the morning off.

"Hello?" she says a moment later, sounding like she's actually still sleeping.

"Hi!" I rush out, my hyper excitement getting the best of me and ruining any chance I had of playing at playing it cool while she takes the time to wake up.

"Quinn? Jesus, what time is it?"

"Almost six thirty. You told me to call you in the morning," I remind her.

"Yeah, but I didn't think you would call *this* early."

I wave my hand in the air and roll my eyes. Not that it's effective, since she can't actually see me. "Tate's gonna be here in a little over an hour, Leigh. In a little over an hour I'm going on my first date with Tate Montgomery and I'm so excited, nervous, terrified, over the moon, I think my heart might stop."

I hear her say something to my brother, Maverick's deep voice coming through from a distance when he replies. A moment later, the sound of her peeing hits my ears.

"Seriously?"

"You called me two hours after I finally got to sleep, Q. Excuse me if I can't hold my piss in long enough to wait until we're off the line."

"Didn't you go before you went to bed? What the hell were you doing up at four in the morning anyway?"

"I can't answer that, because you told me I wasn't allowed to talk about your brother's beautiful penis anymore," she replies, her voice sugary sweet.

"Well," I say after a brief moment of shocked silence, my mind needing a second to purge the thought from my head. Then, like any girl that grew up with two older brothers that unfortunately didn't know how to warn someone before they walked around naked,

I detach myself from the vision of it being my brother's penis she's talking about and pretend that Maverick had a Ken-doll crotch and my best friend was ridin' someone else's manhood. "You really need to be better about usin' the restroom after sex. You don't want bacteria and shit to fester in your bits. If that happens, you're gonna end up with a nasty infection from that penis you're so fond of and an appointment to let Tate check things out."

"That . . ." She pauses. "I'm not even sure what to say to that."

"Nothin' to say. You just need to make a mental note to practice better hygiene after your late-night playdates with my brother," I sass. Then, like a lightbulb going off in my head, another thought zaps through my mind. "Unless, you two are workin' on that niece you promised me."

"Oh God, Q. Give that up, will ya?" She laughs, but it doesn't sound convincing.

"Why? Because you're already pregnant?"

She snorts, the sound unladylike. "No, Jesus. We want to have some time to enjoy each other before we start a family. You should give it up, because I can assure you there aren't going to be any nieces or—"

"Don't you say it," I warn, cutting her off.

"Nephews!" she yells. "You are way too sensitive about that. Besides the fact that we're nowhere near ready to start our family, you need

to get it through your head that there's a very real possibility that when we are, it won't be a girl!"

"You're right. We can talk about my *nieces* later. Right now, you need to help me prep for my date. My date that starts in almost an hour. Shit, oh my God, I take it back—I'm more nervous and terrified than I am over the moon and excited."

"Where are y'all going?"

"I don't know! He just said we would be outside all day. That could mean anything. Do I even bother puttin' on makeup when we're gonna roast anyway? Should I wear somethin' nice? Shit, yup . . . definitely terrified."

"Let's start with you calmin' down." She giggles. "Skip the makeup, you don't need it. Keep your hair up; just fix the mess you probably have it bound in already." She pauses, probably to see if I'll deny that she knows me so well. "Go with cutoffs, maybe a cute tank top, or maybe that flowy, blousy thing you have—the one with no sleeves. I would say flip-flops since it's gonna be hot as hell out, but you don't ever go without your boots, so that should about cover it."

I nod to myself. "Okay, I can do all that. I look great in cutoffs. That sounds perfect."

"Stop muttering to yourself, too. You're beautiful, you'll look beautiful, and even if you had a paper sack on, he's gonna think the same thing. Stop freakin' yourself out."

"What's she goin' on about?" I hear Maverick ask in the background, and my eyes widen.

"Don't you do it," I warn Leigh.

"She's going on a date with Tate Montgomery today," she answers, ignoring me, and I can hear the smile in her voice.

"What's he doing? Why can't I hear him?"

"He's getting dressed." She giggles.

"Leighton Elizabeth James," I hiss through thin lips.

"I'm kiddin'. He's callin' Clay."

"Oh, well, that's good."

"Seriously, Q. You've got this. Give yourself a break. It's okay to be nervous."

"What if I puke on it because I'm *that* nervous?"

She laughs full out at that. "Seein' as you already puked on him once and he still asked you on a date, I'm guessin' he wouldn't think twice about it."

I moan, embarrassed at the reminder of my drunken shame.

"You need to go get ready."

I nod. "Yeah. Holy shit. It's really happening."

"You got this, Hell-raiser," she hoots; then I hear the click of her disconnecting.

"I've got this," I mutter to myself, leaving the living room and walking through the big house toward my "wing." It isn't technically, but with just Clay and me in the place, the huge

186

six-bedroom house feels too large at times. His room, the master, is on the opposite side of the house from mine, and with so much square footage between us, it often feels like this side is all mine. With both of us often working long hours, we could go weeks without running into each other, because this place is so dang big.

I make quick work of pulling on a pair of short white cutoffs, grabbing the flowy black sleeveless blouse Leigh was talking about. Thankfully, I don't have to change my bra. The bloodred pushup bra being one of my favorites because it always makes me feel like an irresistible badass when I wear it, and today that is exactly what I want to feel like.

My black cowboy boots with the bright teal design stitched into the leather go on next before I walk into my bathroom and fix my unintentionally messy bun into an intentionally messy bun.

"Well, don't you look good," I tell my reflection, twisting to check out my ass.

I lean into my bedroom to look at the clock, an eruption of nervous excitement taking flight in the pit of my stomach. I hope he's feeling this too. Just the knowledge that I'm going to see him again today is all it takes to keep me awake. I feel like a child waiting for Santa to come in the morning.

One thing's for sure: with my gut communicating this kind of pure, euphoric excitement, there's no way it could be steering me wrong. It's time for me to put the fear aside and not let it stand in the way. I'll feel it, I'm sure, it won't just vanish, but I'm not going to allow it to be fed.

I close my eyes, hold my breath, and pray for all I'm worth that this date, the one I've been dreaming of for so long, is the start of something one-of-a-kind beautiful.

15

Quinn

"Don't Ya" by Brett Eldredge

— ★ —

Bite me, Tate Montgomery!" I screech, jumping when he tosses another worm at me.

"Oh, come on, Quinn. You can do it," he teases, waving another of those disgusting things at my face.

I cross my arms over my chest and give him a look that I pray screams, *If you come near me with another of those slimy fuckers you'll never see me naked.* But of course, it doesn't. He just smirks, props his fishing pole against the cooler he brought out, and advances, the worm still wiggling between his fingers.

"Tate, I swear to God and all that's holy, I will shove my boot so far up your ass you'll never find it. Don't come near me with that . . . thing."

"For such a tomboy, you would think you'd grown outta that phobia of worms by now." He laughs darkly, halting his advance and picking up my pole to murder the worm with the hook.

Dis.Gust.Ing.

"What? Just because I'm a mechanic, I'm automatically a tomboy?"

Tate rolls his eyes and hands me my pole, murdered worm included.

"Has nothin' to do with your occupation, darlin'. You're practically allergic to all things girly. And stop actin' like I meant it in a negative way. Anyway, I happen to have a preference for fresh-faced women wearing short shorts and covered in grease."

"Oh really?" I ask him in a snarky tone. "Meet many girls like that while you were in Georgia?" The second the question leaves my lips, I regret it. It's easy to convince myself that there haven't been any other women in his life—even if he has hinted at brief flings with no commitment. However, crystal-clear confirmation of his romantic entanglements over the last nine years isn't something I'm sure I want to hear.

"Quinn," Tate voices, trying to get my attention, but I just shake my head.

I quickly cast my line, looking out at the lake before me, the clouds in the sky peppering the dark water with little white dots. The spot Tate brought us to is one of the most popular fishing holes in Pine Oak, but thankfully today we're the only ones out here. I'm sure that has more to do with the storm that I can smell getting closer. There's just something about a hot summer day that carries a whopper of a storm with it. The air comes alive and there's a dangerous scent to it.

"There wouldn't ever be," he finally says after a few minutes, drawing my attention away from the dark clouds in the distance.

"There wouldn't ever be what?"

"Anyone that could ever come close to the woman you are. I'm a little rusty flirtin', it seems. I'll take care in how I say shit like that in the future."

I feel my shoulders drop, the tension leaving them. "No, I shouldn't have gotten so defensive. You don't owe me explanations like that, Tate. We weren't together, so you weren't doin' anything wrong."

"You might not think I owe you an explanation, but Quinn, I need you to know regardless. You're right, we weren't *together,* but you've owned me since I was eleven years old, comin' to Pine Oak for the first time. I never—not once—in the time that we were apart, gave any other woman what was already taken. So, at the risk of ruinin' our date right when it's gettin' started, I need you to know that. I don't want to see you lookin' at me like I might not think you're enough, Quinn."

"I didn't spend the past nine years without . . . scratchin' an itch," I tell him, embarrassed.

"And neither did I, Quinn. Get it out now, darlin', and let's move on after, sound good?"

"I'm not proud of it." My words rush out, and

I feel the shame of them. I reel my line in, check to see if the murdered worm is still attached, then cast it back into the lake. "I tried to move on, you should know that, but . . . no one was you. I haven't been with anyone in a long time, though, and even before that, it was pretty infrequent."

"Sounds like we were both in the same boat. I'll tell you whatever you wanna know, but you need to understand I don't want to know details, darlin'. You were livin' your life and I was survivin' mine. In the end, none of that matters, because we're gettin' our chance."

"My mama . . ." I pause, trying to think of a good way to explain the enormity of damage caused to my head with her shit. "She's the reason I tried to find what I felt without you around and . . . she's the reason I stopped."

I hear him reel his line in and look over to see him placing another worm on the hook. His concentration splits when he looks up from his hunched position and nods, encouraging me to keep going. The last thing I want is to be talking about this, but we're getting to know each other again, and while he might have known about my mama abandoning us—leaving me with a craving to feel loved, needed, and wanted—he has no idea about the news that came long after he left, news that brought the same feelings back, but this time riding shotgun with a whole lot of self-loathing.

"I really don't want to get into the details, but we found out she had a loose outlook on monogamy. She cheated on my father, a lot, but it wasn't until Maverick finally came home after retirin' from ridin' that he told us what he found out a few years after he joined the professional circuit." I look back at Tate before continuing. "She had run off chasin' God knows what the first time and came back pregnant with Maverick. She stuck around for a while, had me, then I guess I was the last straw for her. She left for good shortly after I was born. So, yeah . . . I'm one big jacked-up ball of abandonment issues. Without you, it got worse, and I'm not proud of the person I was. Who knows how long I would have kept dreamin' of her comin' back one day and wantin' us, but Maverick kicked those stupid thoughts to the moon and all I saw when I looked in the mirror was the whore she is staring back at me."

He grunts, rising from the ground, his newly baited fishing pole tossed carelessly next to his feet. I stand tall, not lookin' away, and wait. "I'm not even sure where to start, Quinn. It's only normal that you would want your mama, baby, but don't you ever compare yourself to her. Never met her, never want to, but even if I did it wouldn't make a difference in the truth. You aren't your mama, baby. You felt her void and everything you experienced is somethin' anyone would feel. You might struggle with the fact of her leavin', but darlin' girl, you have to know how much you're loved by the people that stayed."

He left. I push the voice in my head to the wayside. I won't let the fear come back, bringing its lies. He left, but he didn't do it because he wanted to. He could never be like my mama. He wanted to fight but couldn't, was helpless to move on in order to save everyone he loved. She didn't want any of it—the fighting, the protecting: she only cared about herself.

"I'm gettin' there. Even before you came back I was on my way there. I don't know what it's gonna take to finally make it, but I'm workin' on it."

"I wish I coulda been here for you," he says despondently.

"You're here now."

He steps closer, running his knuckles from my temple down to my chin before leaning forward and pressing a kiss to my forehead. Why that simple gesture feels so intimate, I'll never know.

"I might not have been one of those people that stayed, darlin', but I don't want you to think I wouldn't have if the situation hadn't been impossible."

"I know, Tate. I do."

"I know I told you I'd tell you anything, but can we just leave it at the knowledge that we both were livin' the best we could. You know what matters, just as I do—we mighta been livin', but there was only ever one person that would own that piece of us we kept back."

I swallow thickly, and nod. I know if I were to open my mouth right now, I would cry big, fat, ugly emotional tears, and I don't want to look back at this date—our first date as adults—and feel anything negative.

"What do ya say we try and catch us somethin' good?" He winks, and just like that, the heaviness falls away.

I'm so content in this moment with him, in comfortable silence as we cast our reels into the sparkling water, that my mind drifts away, and I'm suddenly lost in a memory of our past . . .

Twelve Years Ago

"Just jam the damn thing on, Grease!" Tate bellows from his spot a few yards away from me.

I hear some of the other kids snicker as they overhear us on their way to the watering hole and feel my face instantly flame. Why the hell did I agree to stay behind and fish, of all things? I could have gone with Leigh when she took off ten minutes ago, but nooooo—I let my stupid crush on Tate Montgomery keep me behind. I'm not even sure why I bothered. I could've been swinging off the huge rope swing into the cool water right now instead of . . . this.

I look back into the cup of worms and feel bile surging up my throat.

Oh, Jesus Jones. I'm supposed to touch them?

"Grease!" Tate yells impatiently again.

"Kiss my boots, Starch! You gross, nasty boy!"

If he was closer, I'm sure I'd see those blue eyes of his spark. It's something I've noticed a lot lately, even if I don't understand what it means. I tried to ask my brother, Clay, about it but he just looked at me like he did when I got my period for the first time a few years ago and asked him to go get me some pads. I figure it's just Tate growing sick of spending time with me. He's been pulling back this summer, and I can't understand why.

That's a lie. I know exactly why. Stupid me had to go open my big ol' mouth two days ago and tell him I didn't just want to be friends anymore. I thought he felt the same way, but he just looked at me funny and left. Now the summer is almost over and he's about to leave here with things all sort of jumbled between us.

"What was that?"

I scream, dropping the fishing pole and the cup of worms, which makes me scream again. I hear Tate's deep chuckles, even if he is trying to stifle them. Jerking my body around, I narrow my eyes at him.

"You're jumpy," he stupidly points out.

"Well, I wouldn't be if someone wasn't creepin' around sneakin' up on people."

"Only sneakin' up on *you,* Grease," he retorts, stepping closer to me and leaving a little gap between our bodies.

"Well, that was rude, Starch."

"You need me to bait your line, darlin'?" he asks, his voice vibrating through my body, making my skin come alive with chills. I shiver, and his eyes do that weird thing again—the blue swirling and becoming almost turquoise.

"N-nope," I stammer breathlessly.

"You sure about that? Got worms tryin' to make a break for it as we speak."

I gurgle a choked squeal and jump, landing against his body with my arms wrapped about his strong neck. When the softness of my chest makes contact with the hardness of his, I feel his arms move only moments before his long fingers grab my ass, urging my legs around his hips.

I feel his erection against the part of me that hasn't ever felt like it does now at the same moment a loud boom of thunder rocks through the silence around us. My shock-filled eyes bug out when he rocks himself against me. I'm not completely naïve, so I know the wetness I'm feeling is my body getting turned on, but it's so foreign . . . and obvious, I can't help but wonder if he can feel it too.

Rain pelts down from the sky. I didn't even notice the storm moving in, and now it's right on top of us. I blink, trying to see through the drops of rain running into my eyes. I'm afraid to move and have this moment broken, but the group we came with will be back soon. No one's going to stick around the watering hole when there's a thunderstorm around.

Tate lowers his head, the brim of his cowboy hat blocking the rain, and with one last slow blink, I look up at the boy that's stolen my heart.

"I don't want to lose your friendship, Quinn." His words, spoken softly, hit my ears, and, instantly aware of his intentions, I feel a burst of electricity zing from my brain.

"You couldn't never lose me, Tate." He couldn't. I'll never be anyone's but his.

"You don't know that."

I feel my head move in a weird combination of shaking and nodding. "Yes I do. Next to Leigh, you're my best friend, Tate. We've spent the past four summers getting closer and when you're back at your parents', we still email every day. There's not a second of my life that I don't think of you. I know I couldn't ever live without those seconds, either. I love you, Tate. Don't you get it?"

His shoulders are tense under my hands, the deep heaving breaths he's taking making his whole body move under my touch. Then, with another violent boom of thunder, his lips meet mine and I know without a single doubt in my mind that the boy giving me my first kiss ever will be the same one that gives me my last.

"I love you too, Quinn," he says against my lips. "Promise me I won't ever lose you?"

My mind gets muddled, his firm touch on me only making it worse.

"Quinn?"

I try to answer, but I'm so lost to him that all I want to do is feel his lips back against mine. This is it. I know he wouldn't ever have given into this if he didn't want me. He wants me. Finally. Finally, someone wants me.

"Quinn!"

Present Day

"Quinn!"

I blink, the memory fading away instantly, and look up at Tate, a much older and even handsomer Tate than the fifteen-year-old version that had just been in front of me in my mind. His strong hands hold my arms, a firey burn tingling against the skin he's touching, his gaze a little bit alarmed.

"Christ, Quinn, are you okay? You were a million miles away."

I feel my head move woodenly: I'm helpless to do anything more than just stare at him.

"What the hell just happened?" He lifts one hand off my arm to tip the black cowboy hat on his head up, giving me a clear view of his face. The movement causes me to look up as I realize that we're being soaked with fat raindrops.

"Quinn?" His hand comes back and he gives me a tiny shake when I continue to gaze up at him mutely.

My mind is still swirling with the very vivid memory of our first kiss. Having him this close to me, almost in the exact way that he had been all those years ago, makes it even harder for me to separate memory from reality.

The only thing that makes sense right now is the overpowering need to feel his mouth on mine again. To experience the silky wet rasp of his tongue against mine as I get lost in him.

His fingers flex when I move, jolting myself forward and crashing my body into his. Not expecting it, he loses his footing and lands on the wet ground, taking care to cradle me in a way that eases the fall for me. We landed with him sitting, back straight up, and me straddling his waist, my center pressed tight against the hardness in his pants. I rock my hips and he bites his bottom lip. The action so beyond sexual that I feel my body clench with need.

My lips are on his, hips rocking, right as he opens his mouth to say something, giving me instant access to deepen the kiss. A groan tumbles up his throat, vibrating my chest, and I turn my head to get more. His hands move down and grab my hips, pulling my body down and at the same time refusing to let me move, the hard pressure of his hold pressing his cock against my

200

swollen heat. This time I'm the one who groans. I'm vaguely aware of his hat falling into the dirt when I push my fingers into his hair. The thick strands feeling like heaven as they slip wetly through my fingers.

Our tongues continue to glide together, swirling and tangling with the heavy pants of our mingling breaths. I'm not even sure who is making which noise now, mewls, grunts, moans and groans combining in a chorus of ecstasy as we feast on each other.

Then he tightens his hold, my head becoming dizzy when the bite of pain registers, my panties getting even wetter. He sucks my tongue into his mouth and the coil inside me starts to wind up, tighter and tighter with each second. My hands roam through his hair, down his neck, until I'm holding his face between my palms. Just when I'm convinced my heart is going to stop—the sensations roaring through my body becoming too much—he forces my hips to roll forward, dragging against his hard length, and I rip my mouth free to cry out as an orgasm washes over my whole body.

"Holy fuckin' Christ," he whispers breathlessly, his face pink with arousal and what looks a lot like pride.

"Yeah," I pant.

I jump when he shifts his ass on the ground, the movement rubbing his hardness against my still-sensitive parts.

"I'm two seconds away from comin' in my pants, Quinn. Let me up before the front of my jeans are just as wet as my ass."

He says it with a smile, but I can't help but feel a little embarrassed about my actions. I mean, I did just virtually attack the man. I climb to my feet, with his help, and try to brush off the wet dirt clinging to my knees. When I realize it's not going anywhere, I straighten and look at Tate bashfully, embarrassed that I just knocked him to the ground and used his body to find my release—something I haven't obtained by any means other than my own hand in years.

"Don't do that," he demands, his voice hard.

"Do what?" I hedge.

"Don't you dare regret that, Quinn. That was the hottest fuckin' thing I've ever felt, and I still had my cock in my pants. Don't you *dare* regret that."

I shake my head. "I just . . . Tate, I attacked you."

He grunts out a laugh and starts picking up our stuff before speaking. "Darlin', if that's how you attack people, you're welcome to take me down any time."

"Well, I can't promise it won't happen. I didn't quite plan for us to get muddy and wet because I was stuck in a memory."

His brows arch and he stops packing up the fishing stuff. His dirty hat is now back on his head, but his head is tipped up as he looks at me, rain streaking against his face. He blinks through the drops, frozen, as he waits for me to elaborate.

"Did you bring us here for a reason?" I ask, and the instant I do, I realize there is no way he chose this location on a whim. He knows exactly where I went when I was zoned out.

"It's where we started," he answers simply. He drops the tackle box on top of the rolling cooler, then stands to his full height, making me tip my head back to maintain our connection. "It's where we first said, 'I love you'; it's where we had our first kiss; it's our place. Honest to God, darlin', I didn't plan that happenin', but I gotta say it feels pretty damn fittin' that we start bein' us in the same spot we did the first time."

"Jesus Jones," I breathe, unable to think of a better response.

His face gets soft and he leans down, pressing his kiss-swollen lips against mine.

"Let's go get dried off and wait for this storm to pass. Sound good?"

I swallow the lump of emotion that his sentimental planning caused and nod. "That sounds perfect, Tate."

16
Tate

"From the Ground Up" by Dan + Shay

— ★ —

"He's not gonna bite," Quinn jokes over her shoulder, laughing softly under her breath when Maverick's eyes narrow even more toward me.

"Not sure that his bite is what I'm worried about at the moment, Grease," I tell her, right in her ear, which makes her shiver in my arms.

We just got to her house not even five minutes ago and, after another hot-as-fuck kiss on her front porch, walked inside to find her brother staring daggers at the two of us from his position just inside. Thankfully our clothes dried off a lot on our drive back to her house—but I wouldn't mind getting this over with so we can get her changed and head to my place so I can do the same.

"You big baby," Leigh huffs in exasperation, slapping Maverick's shoulder playfully. "You're the one who told her not to fight it, remember? Actually, if I recall correctly, you said fightin' it would be pointless and what's meant to happen is gonna happen no matter what. So, Cowboy, suck it up and let it *be*."

Maverick finally looks away from where I'm standing, Quinn attempting to block me the best she can with her tiny body. Thankfully, with her standing guard the way she is, her brother can't see the raging fucking hard-on I've been sporting since the kiss outside the front door, giving me the time I needed to get control of the situation.

"Just cuz I said it doesn't mean I wanna see it."

"That holds no logic whatsoever, honey," Leigh continues, smiling up at him.

"Doesn't matter if it does or not," he mutters sullenly.

She rolls her eyes at him and gives both of us her attention, ignoring the giant daggers of anger Maverick's eyes are shooting in her direction now that she's clearly discounting his feelings.

"It's good to see you again, Tate. It's been a long damn time," she greets, playfully shooing Quinn away and wrapping her arms around me in a friendly hug.

"I'd say too long, Leigh. Feels damn fine to be back." I look at Quinn before finishing. "Like comin' home."

Quinn blushes, much to my surprise, as I'm not used to seeing her do that. I give her a wink before turning back to Leigh. "It's good to see you, too, and congratulations on y'all's engagement," I tell her earnestly.

Maverick grunts.

"Would you stop?" Leigh jokingly snaps over her shoulder before stepping away from me and whipping her head toward him. She must have mouthed something to him, because his scowl gets just a little bit harsher.

"Soooo . . ." Quinn sings. "What are y'all doin' here?"

Maverick grunts again and Leigh sighs, clearly knowing her man well enough to realize that any attempt to pacify him at this point will just fall on deaf ears. She looks back at Quinn and me and gives us a wink before walking back to his side. His arm immediately comes up and around her shoulders to pull her back against his front.

Guess he's not too big on sharing the attention of *any* female in his life.

"After your call this mornin', I couldn't keep the big guy away. He said someone needed to be here to make sure everything was all fine and dandy. With Clay busy dealin' with the vet check and the farrier down at the stables all day, he felt it was his brotherly duty and all that."

Quinn snaps her fingers. "Shoot, I forgot about that. I needed to ask him to have the farrier look at Daisy's back shoe—she's been actin' like it's botherin' her."

"Already took care of," Maverick grumbles.

"First horse Rodney looked at when he got here. Nothin' wrong with that high-maintenance princess. Trimmed her hoof wall and now she's prancin' around like the queen of the stables again."

Quinn barks out a laugh. "That's my girl." She turns and smiles up at me. "Daisy's the best horse you'll ever see. None of those high-dollar thoroughbreds of Clay's come close."

"Don't let him hear you say that." Leigh cackles. "Especially since these 'high-dollar thoroughbreds' have a pedigree that Daisy damn sure doesn't."

"Doesn't matter that she's not special on paper," Quinn huffs, immediately protective of her beloved horse. "She's still the best damn thing in the stables."

"You just say that because she's yours." Leigh laughs.

Something tells me this is a long-standing debate among the close-knit bunch. Instead of dwelling on it as another thing I don't know about Quinn because of the time we lost, I vow to make sure I can soon be one of the people *all* the Davises consider one of their own, soon enough—never missing moments that build jokes like this again.

Pushing the thought aside, I look over at Maverick and attempt to engage him in conversation. With any luck, I can get him to calm the fuck down long enough to have the same conversation I had with Clay already. I probably should have just called them both over when I talked to Clay, but if facing one of them is intimidating, together they're a menacing force if you're on the wrong side.

"How many Thoroughbreds is he workin' with these days?" I finally ask Maverick, using the topic as a bridge to broach the subject I hope to discuss but also because I'm genuinely interested to hear about the changes here at the Davis ranch since I've been gone—seeing as it means maybe all that time I forced myself to stay gone, without the woman I love in the process, I also kept them safe from my father and in turn gave them the time they needed to thrive.

"Got two mares of his own right now, but only one was inseminated in February. Savin' his breeder mare until he can find the right stallion to pair her with, which is why she's not pregnant right now. Just got a new stallion, Major, a few weeks ago, bringin' Clay's total count up to ten. With the retired ones he's rescued, though, he's really up in the twenties. You'd have to ask Clay about the stud end of things here and how many mares he accepted to breed earlier this year. Clay's focus is on the stallions with some of the most impressive pedigrees around, so I wouldn't be shocked if that number was up there due to the fact there's a high demand for his horse's lineage.

He works his boys hard, but he's selective about how many he accepts, booked full on a few quickly so he doesn't breed them irresponsibly."

Out of the corner of my eye I see the girls look at him in shock. Hell, I'm just as shocked that he answered me—at length, moreover—and that he didn't seem to mind doing so. Maybe it's because talking shop pulls his focus off the fact that his sister's getting hot and heavy with the person he knows hurt her once. Either way, I'll keep this shit going if it means his anger is distracted.

"He's still breedin' this late in the summer?" I say, pleased as fuck when some of the harshness in his face disappears.

"Stopped in June. Now he's takin' care of his stallions, the pregnant mares, and his rescues. Doesn't get any less busy for him, but at least he's not doin' the round-the-clock matin' games."

I nod, thinking about how much work is involved in running a stud farm. I can't imagine how crazy things are here for the first six months of the year.

"Look, they're getting along," Quinn whispers to Leigh, doing a shit job of keeping her voice down. Clearly, I'm not the only one that thinks so either, because the calm expression that had taken hold of Maverick while he was explaining the breeding vanishes and his eyes narrow again.

Fuck.

Well, the reprieve was nice while it lasted, at least.

"Should have kept your big mouth shut, Q," Leigh hints, doing an equally shitty job at keeping the volume of her words down.

Maverick gives me another nasty glare, and it's the tipping point for my patience.

Fuck this.

"Look, Maverick, with all due respect, I'm not really interested in wasting more of my first date with Quinn waitin' to see who blinks first. It's my first day off since startin' at the practice *and* a day that was goin' pretty damn perfect until just now. It'd probably be easier on you if you'd just get whatever it is you want to say off your chest so I can move on with my mornin'. I get that you're protective of your sister, and I respect the hell outta that, but you standin' here tryin' to intimidate me isn't somethin' I would prefer dealin' with when I'd rather be spendin' my time showin' your sister that she's not gonna regret givin' us another go. In the end, it's her opinion that matters most to me."

"That so?" he asks mockingly.

I hear Quinn make a low, distressed noise, and I break eye contact with Maverick to check on her. I don't give a flying fuck if it makes me look weak to him, breaking from our staring contest of intimidation, because she means more to me than being top dog.

"What is it?" I question.

"I don't want y'all fightin'," she mumbles.

"Who said anything about fightin', Grease?"

I try to make light of it, but to be honest, I would gladly let her brother throw some punches if it made him feel better about accepting our relationship without causing her grief. In his mind, all I am is the person who broke her heart, and as her brother he's in protection mode. I can't fault him for that. It's what I expected from Clay when we talked, and I have a feeling if Maverick knew what I had told Clay already, he wouldn't be acting like this right now. I really should have gone out of my way to talk to him before now, but taking on both of the Davis brothers at the same time was the last thing on my mind. Maverick has always been a hothead too. Bottom line, I need Clay's backing if I have a chance of getting Maverick's.

Guess I should have thought twice about that one.

"If it keeps your ass from fuckin' up again, maybe that's not a bad idea."

Quinn's eyes flash with pain and she looks visibly upset at his words, and now I'm no longer content with letting him continue his macho shit in front of her.

"Outside," I fume at her brother. If his bullshit is going to make her revert back to the girl that was almost too scared to give us a go, I'm going to make damn sure this is a fight he doesn't fucking win.

"You *guys,*" Quinn wails, but it's too late. The challenge has been issued. And no country boy worth his salt ever backs down from a challenge.

"Keep your ass inside," Maverick calls over his shoulder on the way to the door. It isn't clear which woman he's speaking to, but to be honest, I only care about one of them right now.

I let him pass, focusing on Quinn, framing her face with my hands and tipping her head up gently so she's looking at me and not her brother's departing back. "I know you don't want us to fight, baby, but I need you to trust me right now and not give me any trouble 'bout goin' out there. You have my word that I won't get physical with him, just words, Grease. As much as I hate doin' somethin' you don't want, I need to give your brother a chance to get this off his chest so he can step aside and let this happen."

She starts to shake her head, her still-wet hair falling some from the knot she's got it in on top of her head.

"Trust me," I stress.

She swallows—I feel it against the heel of my hand—and closes her eyes. I give her time, knowing that with those two words I'm asking her to do a whole lot more than just trust me to go outside and talk to her brother. If she decides she still doesn't want me to go, I won't fault her.

212

Her trust is something I have to earn back, and I'm not stupid enough to think that can be gained in just a few days.

Then she shocks the shit out of me.

"I do." She sighs. "I do trust you, Tate. What happened between us before—that's not about lack of trust anymore, now that I know the reasons behind it. I just . . . I just got both of you back, even if he's been back for longer. The two men I've dreamt about returning to me are finally where they belong, and if this ends with me having to choose between you both . . . that thought is a killer."

"I'll never ask you to make that decision, Quinn."

"You won't have to."

We both turn when Maverick speaks, standing just inside the front door.

"Love you, Hell-raiser, but let me talk to him and stop worryin' about that shit."

"Maverick," Quinn breathes. "This is goin' to happen regardless of your talk."

"Good. Then you won't mind me havin' my say."

She exhales and I bend to kiss her temple. "Go get changed. We're headin' out as soon as I finish this."

She nods, and I turn to follow her brother outside.

He moves to the end of their long front porch,

213

looking off toward the stables set a good distance away from their house. I can feel the unanswered questions vibrating off of him.

"Go ahead, Maverick. Say what you need to say and get it out, because I'm not going to have this shit come up again. Not when it hurts her like this."

He flinches, the most minute of movements, but I see it. He doesn't like hurting her, so for him to force my hand means there's no way he's touched base with Clay since I talked to him. Or . . . or maybe he has and he just doesn't give a shit.

Not waiting for him to speak, I lean my ass against the rail and look through the window in front of me to see Quinn watching us. She hasn't moved from the spot I left her in, not that I expected her to actually listen to me. I push my frustration-born anger aside and give her what I hope is the face of a confident man trying to reassure the woman he doesn't want upset.

I'm rewarded with the worry fading from her face before her shoulders move as one when she sucks in a deep breath.

I blow her a kiss, not giving one shit if anyone witnesses me acting like a lovesick fool. I am, so might as well own it.

She has just enough time to return the gesture before Leigh pulls her through the house— hopefully to get changed so we can get the fuck outta here when I finish this bullshit.

"Wasn't here that last summer," Maverick says, his gravelly voice, low and edgy. "But I heard about the depression my sister went through when you stopped takin' her calls. She thought she hid that shit well from Clay, but there wasn't shit that got past him. Each time she would email you and get an 'undeliverable address' response. When her letters to your folks' house got sent back with a nasty scribble note sayin' no one lived there by that name. Each fuckin' time, I heard about it, and there wasn't shit I could do to fix it. I was fightin' my own demons, Tate, so don't think I don't get not being ready or whatever the fuck happened between you two, but if there's even one little part of you that thinks you aren't ready now, you need to end this instant."

He doesn't waste any time getting down to the point of his anger, which I'm thankful for, even if this is the last conversation I want to be having right now.

"There wasn't ever a time I wasn't fuckin' ready for her," I force through my tight jaw.

"Sure have a funny way of showin' it, runnin' off and disappearin'."

He hasn't talked to Clay, then. "I couldn't fuckin' do anything *but* disappear!"

With a fortifying breath, I start at the beginning and tell my tale again. By the time I finish my woe-is-me recap, Maverick's looking at me like he's seeing me for the first time. The protective-

215

big-brother intimidation vibe that had been radiating off him snaps, vanishing instantly. The way he's looking at me now, though, is just as unnerving.

With pride. Pure fucking pride.

Just like Clay did. The two men that I feared would never understand why I dropped off the face of Quinn's world, giving me something I'm not sure I deserve without any hesitation at all.

Well, fuck me.

After a few minutes of silence, Maverick speaks. "You know why I left?"

I shake my head.

"The old man beat the shit out of me. Not just with his fists—he liked tearin' down a man's soul just as much as he liked hurtin' his body. Put up with that shit for too long, and all I ever wanted to do was ride. Found out he didn't support my ridin' because my real father was a pro my mama'd slept with on the side. But I ran because I couldn't face his shit anymore. It would have been him or me, but one of us would've fuckin' killed the other, and honest to fuckin' God, I'm not sure I woulda been able to go through with it. Took that woman in there—the one that owns my fuckin' heart like it's hers—and made sure I crushed her good enough she would *have* to let me go. Saw no other way and ran like a coward, not comin' back until the old man died right along with my rodeo career. And you know what?"

I cough, playing off the shock of his words. "What's that?"

"I'm not sure how long I woulda stayed gone either, if my career hadn't been shot to hell and the old man hadn't kicked it. I can tell you eventually I wouldn't have been able to resist the urge because it's fuckin' impossible to resist the kind of pull you feel when you're meant to be takin' a different path than the one you're on. Your life will always overcorrect your steps for you until you're finally on the right one."

Understanding dawning, I straighten off the porch railing and open my mouth, only Maverick beats me to it, speaking up again.

"I was wrong about you. Thought you were like me, but you're no fuckin' coward. You've been fightin' for her every step you took, even if she didn't know it. Not just her, but you fought for her family—*my family*—and that is somethin' I'll forever be indebted to you for. I wasn't here to do it, Clay was doin' his best, but you made sure a blow that would have crushed them all never came."

"You don't owe me shit. I did it because I love her, not for any other reason."

I'm not sure who's more shocked when the seriousness on his face vanishes, one big-ass smile, so like his sister's, taking its place a moment later, him or me.

"You love my sister?"

My own smile grows, and I'm sure if Quinn was watching now she would be about to shit herself with curiosity. "Accordin' to her, we're gettin' to know the adults we've become. You ask me, though, I'm just showin' the only woman I have ever loved and will ever love that we're the same people we've always been."

He bellows out a loud bark of laughter at that. "Reckon that's not gonna be a hardship for you, Tate."

"You aren't wrong," I confirm, my mouth still tipped up in a grin.

"I told her before she decided what to do with you that she wouldn't be able to resist the pull she'd feel. I said that based off what I remember of you two, young as fuck, fightin' your feelin's. Said that before I knew just how serious those feelin's got when I left. Now I'm tellin' you to enjoy the ride, because gettin' that back is the best fuckin' feelin' you'll ever experience."

He holds his hand out and I don't even think before slapping my palm against his and tightening my fingers around his grip. His hold on my hand is just as firm. His brow goes up before he gives one hell of a tug and pulls me into a backslapping hug.

"As pointless as it might be to say, I'm gonna do it anyway because it's my fuckin' duty as her brother: if you hurt her again I'll fuckin' kill you."

I laugh, but I don't say a word.

I don't say a word because not only will I do whatever I have to do in order to make sure that never happens, but also because if I'm unfortunate enough to have it actually happen . . . I hope he does.

17

Quinn

"I Like the Sound of That" by Rascal Flatts

— ★ —

What did he say?" I whine for the millionth time since he pulled me out of my house and into his truck. He just smirks, the infuriating man, ignoring me like he has for the last hour.

I haven't even been able to fully enjoy the fact that we're curled up on his cozy couch watching a movie, even though that movie is *Suicide Squad* and I've wanted to watch it since I missed it in the theater. I can't even enjoy my girl crush, Harley Quinn. Nope, none of that. All because the stupid, infuriating, stubborn-headed man next to me won't just tell me what my brother said.

He's just like Clay and Maverick, both of whom are keeping secrets about these little meeting-of-the-minds chats they've been having with my man.

Holy shit.

My man.

I look back at his profile. "Are you my man?" I

blurt, not even giving one shit that I sound loony tunes.

"What?" He laughs, turning from the TV to *finally* pay me some attention.

"Well? Are you?"

"Christ, Quinn, I thought you knew what was goin' on here."

"I do!" I yell, calming down when he looks at me like I've grown a second head. "I mean, of course I know what's going on here, but I think we've left out some important things. Are we, I don't know . . . exclusive while we get to know each other again? I mean, I know what you've said you want and all, but you've never actually said you wanted to be exclusive. So I think it's a valid question."

I snap my mouth shut, the verbal vomit just floating in the air between us, my eyes wide and freaked the hell out.

"Where is this comin' from, darlin'?" he asks, low and carefully.

"So far, in two days, you've managed to work your way back into my life all the while erasin' the pain I had held close. In that time, you've also held private meetin's with my brothers, which screams that we're a whole lot more serious than just gettin' to know each other again, Tate. That screams that you're in a place way past gettin' to know someone. You won't tell me what y'all talked about. *They* won't say anything. Meanwhile, I'm over here wonderin' if you're ever gonna grow a pair and get on with it and break my hooha!"

His eyes bug out, probably mirroring mine— only I'm guessin' his aren't wide as hell, because he isn't the one who's mortified. Nope, that's *all* me. My mouth just won't shut the hell up today, it seems.

"Uh," he mumbles, turning so that his arm isn't over my shoulders holding me close to his side. My stomach drops and my eyes fix on to the coffee table. He shifts, turning so that one leg is curled between us, allowing him to turn his body to face me. Then he grabs my hands and dips his head to force me to look at him. "Not that I really understood all of that, but you know if you do break your . . . uh, hooha, that's somethin' I feel confident that I'm able to fix, right?"

Jesus Jones. I bet my face is so bright red right now it would glow in the dark. "Can you just forget that part?"

He chuckles. "Not a fuckin' chance, Grease."

"I didn't think so," I mumble, unable to look away from him even if my mind is screaming for me to.

"Your brothers just want to look out for you, Quinn. I took the time to let them know what my father did because I felt that was somethin' they deserved to know, seein' as it had to do with them too, in a way. Trust me when I tell you that there isn't anything we're keepin' from you. The three of us, we're on the same page when it comes to you, darlin'.""

"And what page is that?"

"The one where they stop worryin' about you and I start lovin' you."

My breath stills in my throat.

"One day at a time, Quinn. One day at a time."

I still can't move. His words ricochet through my body, hitting every single nerve ending and zapping them into awareness before settling into my heart and waking it up completely after one long hibernation. Something clicks inside me in that moment, and I need to trust this between us completely. He wouldn't be going above and beyond to prove to me that he's here to stay—with and for me—if he didn't mean it.

"Get over here, let me hold you and watch the damn movie, Quinn. Let *your man* hold you and give yourself some time to really hear what your body is tellin' you when you're in my arms."

Oh. God.

Do I argue? Nope. Hell, no. That hell-raising badass inside me is already trying to lunge out of my body and curl against him, purring like a slut.

And I like it.

No. I love it.

"What?" I sleepily mumble, trying to muster up enough energy to give a damn that I'm floating, only failing.

"Hush, baby. Movie's long over. It's late and we both fell asleep. Just takin' you to bed," Tate whispers in the darkness.

" 'Kay." I curl into his embrace, knowing his strong arms will carry me without fail as I feel my body being lifted.

The only sound I hear is that of his sock-covered feet walking up the stairs and I feel myself drifting. I try to wake up, but the soothing effect of his heartbeat against my ear mingling with the slow rise of his chest as he breathes is making me slip into a powerful spell of contentment. Just like that, I'm helpless to remain conscious and I fall dead asleep with a smile on my lips.

Nine Years Ago—End of the Summer

"I don't want this summer to end," I whisper, curling into Tate's naked body. "I feel like this one just started and now I have to say good-bye to you."

His chest moves as he laughs under his breath. "Darlin', we've done it for the past seven years. What makes the end of this summer different, when I've always come back to you?"

"It's hardly the same! Every summer since we were eleven you'd leave and it would kill me inside knowin' I wouldn't see you again for ten whole months, Tate. It killed me then, and that was before I knew what it felt like to have the boy I love inside my body."

I feel my chin wobble and I bite the inside of my cheek to keep myself from crying like a child.

"Look at me, baby," he demands softly.

"I can't," I whine shamelessly.

"Now, Quinn. Look at me."

I make a big show of turning, hoping to buy myself some time to kick this vulnerable feeling out of my head. He shifts with me until we're lying face-to-face in his bed. I feel the thick velvet heat of his erection as it presses against my stomach, hard and ready even though we just finished making love not ten minutes ago. I move closer, my nipples rubbing against his smooth chest, and moan a little, making the hardness at my stomach jump.

"Stop," he says, his jaw clenching when I rub against him again.

"I can't help it. I like the way your skin feels against mine."

"So do I, obviously, but darlin' I need you to hear me."

"I hear you," I defend, lifting my leg over his hip and shifting until the part of him I want to feel back between my legs is sliding against my wet pussy.

"Fuck," he hisses, reaching one hand up and grabbing my hips to prevent me from taking him inside my body. "Don't. Move."

His chest is heaving. His handsome face is pulled tight with a frown and pinched lips. God, he's perfect.

The dark curtains in his room are pulled closed, the muted sun, high in the sky, trying to make its way into his bedroom, but only casting a low light into the space. We've practically been skin-to-skin since he called to tell me his grandparents would be gone the whole day and night and that I should figure out a way to spend that entire time with him, in his bed. He was leaving at the end of the week, and this would be one of the last times that we would have a moment like this until he came back next summer. If it was possible, I would spend every one of those moments with him inside me, imprinting the feeling in my brain so I have the memory of it to carry me until I see him again.

Finally gaining control of himself, he opens those blue eyes I love so much. "I know it's different, Quinn. Not just because we know each other in a way that no other person does. Even if we hadn't been each other's firsts, this would still mean just as much to me as I'm sure it does to you, darlin'. I'll get breaks, and I can come back here for some of them instead of goin' to my parents' house. Now you're done with school, maybe you can come out to Georgia. We're gonna make this work. I haven't gone a day without at least gettin' an email, text, or call from you in all those seven years and I'm not goin' to start now."

"It still sucks after what we shared this summer,

havin' to say good-bye." I pout, knowing he's right, but still not liking it.

"It won't ever feel right until we're at that point where school and distance don't keep us apart."

"God, Tate, you're goin' to medical school—that's a lifetime!"

He laughs, his chest moving erotically against my breasts. I try to move my hips, but he doesn't relent in his hold.

"It's not a lifetime, Quinn. Nothin' will ever keep me from you. If you love me even a sliver as much as I love you, then a few years apart will just make us stronger. There's never been anyone else for me, and darlin', there never will be."

I feel a tear roll down my cheek, falling against his forearm my head is resting on.

He lets go of my hip, lifting his fingers to my face to wipe away the rest before they all join the one that escaped. He moves until his forehead is pressed against mine, placing the lightest of kisses against the tip of my nose. My breath hitches and I stare into his eyes, soaking up everything about the boy I love, filing it away in a safe place in my mind so that I don't ever forget it.

He doesn't look away or move his head from mine, but I feel his hand slide between our bodies. He shifts his hips, and the leg I slung over them moves with him. Then I feel the thick tip of his cock press against my opening, holding still while he continues to search my eyes.

"No matter how far away I am, there will never be a day that passes that I don't wish I was here. I've never loved anyone else, Quinn, never and that's somethin' that won't ever change. Feel me and let me show you how much I love you. Feel us and let yourself remember that nothin' will ever win except this—us."

Then he's pushing his length into me, my body stretching to accommodate his thickness. I know from watching him sink into me so many times this summer that he's not even all the way in, and I already feel so beautifully full. I whine, needing more, but he just continues his slow push into me, the sensation tattooing itself into my very being.

I know his control is costing him just as much as it's costing me. Both of us are panting with need. My eyes burn with the need to blink, but I refuse to look away from his face until I see him feel me surrounding him completely. I've become addicted to the expression that crosses his face at that moment.

"God, Tate, move, honey," I gasp, the burn of him continuing to stretch me, making my vision blur, even though I'm more than wet enough.

His fingers, now at my hip, flex. The arm around my back jolts, curling up until his hand is cupping my shoulder. Then he gives one steady push and finishes entering me.

The second I feel him hit a spot deep inside of

me, I behold what I had been waiting to see. The jaw that had been locked relaxes, his full bottom lip separating from the top one with a small puff of air. His strong cheekbones are covered in a light blush. And those eyes that I could get lost in lose focus even while still looking into mine, as he seems to vanish into some other world; then his lids lower and his eyelashes flutter over his cheeks.

Pure bliss.

That's the expression I crave.

In the seconds that it took for me to get that, my center is already tightening around him just waiting for him to move. That's all it takes for me, and I'm seconds away from shooting off into space.

His eyes open again, clear now, and before he starts to move, the arm around my back yanks me into his chest and his mouth is devouring mine. Then, as if we're moving as one, he's thrusting into me as I roll my hips into his, the erotic sounds coming from both of us muffled as our tongues continue to tangle together. My hands, resting against his chest since we shifted, slide up, one going to rest against his neck and the other wrapping around his back. My nails dig into his flesh at the same time his fingers clamp down on mine. In the back of my mind, I hope to God that we're marking each other.

When our bodies start to move erratically, both

of us on the cusp of euphoric ecstasy, he pulls his head back and pants against my mouth.

"I. Love. You." He stresses each word with a slam of his cock deep into my body.

My toes curl and I explode around him, my body tightening so fiercely that I feel the sensation steal my breath.

"I love you too, Tate," I rasp through a painful deep gasp. "I love you so much."

18
Tate

"Die a Happy Man" by Thomas Rhett

— ★ —

I love you so much."
My eyes snap open in the darkness when I hear Quinn's murmured, sleep-drunk words as they dance across my neck. I know she's still passed out and just talking in her sleep, since her breathing is just as slow and steady as it was when I climbed into bed behind her ten minutes ago and instantly felt her curl into my side.

But, rational or not, those four words rush through my veins until they slam into my heart, the force of their hit stealing the breath from my lungs.

One day, when she's not lost in her dreams, I'm going to get to hear them again, and I'll fucking make sure she never goes a day without feeling like I deserve them.

I lie there with a stupid fucking grin on my face and let my mind wander. I have no idea how I managed to fight the pull I've always felt to her, not after what I felt snapping into place as I started

231

making my way back over the last two months. The day I found out about Paw, it was just a sizzle of awareness. When I turned in my resignation back in Georgia, it was a burn. The minute I heard her voice over the phone, it was a searing pain, tugging at my chest for all it was worth. Then, when I finally saw her, it was a shot of pure ecstasy to the fucking heart. I had lived without her for so long, I could have cried on the fucking spot.

Ever year the struggle to stay away became more and more overwhelming. The hot summer months in Georgia would hit and I would get the itch to just say fuck the consequences and jump in my truck and speed to her. Then I would remember everything that was at stake and I would spend the next handful of hours later in one of the biggest depressions ever.

I'll never feel that again.

Never.

Not now that I finally have her back in my life. All that's left to do now is convince her to love me again.

And if her dreams are any indication, I'd bet my Stetson at least a part of her already does.

With a smile on my face, I hold her a little closer and fall into one hell of a good night's sleep.

"Why are you lookin' at me like that?" I ask Quinn over the top of my coffee mug several hours later, finally having enough caffeine in my system to realize she really was looking at me like I'm some puzzle she can't quite figure out.

"Like what?"

"Not sure there's a polite way to describe those crazy eyes of yours you got goin' on, Grease."

Slowly, she places her mug on the counter and flips me the bird. "Kiss my boots, Starch," she says with no heat in her voice and a smile on her face.

"I would, if you had any on."

She looks down at her bare feet. I have to resist the urge to do the same, knowing that if I see her standing in my kitchen in just my discarded shirt from yesterday, with those long, tan and toned legs, bare feet with light pink polish on her toes . . . yeah, no fucking way I would be able to resist taking her on the spot.

She looks back at me, a knowing smirk on her face. "Somethin' wrong?"

"Nope," I respond, taking a long sip of my brew.

"You look like you're, what's the word . . ." She trails off, tapping her chin while she pretends to think, fucking minx. "Troubled."

"You're lookin' at me like a crazy person again," I joke, ignoring her prodding.

"Oh, Jesus Jones, Tate. I don't look crazy. I'm just tryin' to figure out how to bring up yesterday to you."

I feel my brows pull in. "What about yester-day?" I hope to fuck she isn't going to push me more about my talks with her brothers.

"You really aren't gonna bring it up? Not even mention it?"

"You've got to be clearer than that, darlin', because I haven't the slightest clue as to what you're talkin' about."

"The lake!" she laments.

Now I'm even more confused. I study her, my mind not completely awake, seein' as we just rolled out of bed ten minutes ago.

"Tate," she snaps with annoyance. "The *kiss!*"

"Ohhh." I drag the word out, a smile forming on my face that I'm powerless to stop. "That."

"I'm gonna go find my boots and kick you in the rear," she snaps. "Yes! *That!*"

"What do you want to talk about, Quinn? Want me to tell you how hard I was when you were rockin' against my cock, usin' me to get off? How about how hot it was when your thighs tightened against my legs and you fuckin' shuddered in my arms? Wanna know how all I could think about was how wet your pussy would be if I got my hands down your shorts?"

She doesn't look irritated anymore. Whatever she had thought I would say about that "kiss," it damn sure wasn't what she got. One of her dainty hands is pressed against the granite next to her, the other against her chest, which is heaving as she breathes rapidly. The mouth I can't wait to feel against mine again is hanging slack, shock written all over her face.

"Cat got your tongue, Quinn?" I question, taking another sip and lifting a brow mockingly at her.

"That wasn't fair," she gasps, coming out of her spell.

"How so? Not that I'm complainin', baby, but seems to me if you're amped up and so hot you're burnin' from the inside out, then you're in the same place I've been since you came apart in my arms by the lake."

"So this is payback because you have blue balls? Well, the joke's on you, because I won't be beggin' for more just because you've got me primed and ready to detonate by your words alone."

She must realize just how much she's given away with what I'm sure she had planned to come out as an insult, because she drops her head and mutters a sharp "shit" under her breath.

"You primed, Quinn?" The thickness in my own voice gives away just how turned on this conversation has me, my already-deep voice sounding foreign even to my ears.

"You're such a jerk." She sighs with no conviction whatsoever.

I laugh, feeling like some sort of fucking god because of the effect I have on her. When we

235

were younger—both of us with no experience and learning as we went—she came alive under my fumbling hands. It took me a while though, to find out what worked with her, and it took me even longer to get her to burn her brightest.

Now though, well . . . now I'm not a fucking boy who doesn't know his way around a woman's body. I would give anything to erase the past nine years without her, but I can't. I also can't beat myself up over the fact that I've had other women share my bed when I was stuck living a life I thought would never have Quinn in it again—just as she can't do that for herself. It happened and it will only make us stronger in the end because we know there isn't a soul out there for us except each other—well, I know it with crystal-clear clarity. Quinn's still catching up.

It's not just that the past has taught us that we'll always be connected to each other—that we'll be unable to fathom having anything but meaningless sex with others in our attempts to fill the emptiness each of us feels—but that time and loss have taught us exactly who we are.

It sucks that I know what I do now because of all the time I spent thinking I would never have her again, but it's because of that time that I won't take a single day I have her back for granted. Furthermore, it means I have more tools in my arsenal to convince her mind to believe in us again . . . to follow her heart right to me, back home where it belongs.

She's been watching me while I let my thoughts get ahead of me, and when I finally come back to myself, I realize I miscalculated. She's always been smart as a whip, but it's the twinkle in her eye—the one I hadn't seen shining while I was stuck in my head—that earned her the nickname Hell-raiser when she was growing up.

"I bet I could get you beggin' for me before you catch me fallin' on my knees pleadin' for you to fill me up with your cock, Starch."

Well, fuck me.

"Now wait just a dadgum minute, Quinn," I rush, dropping my mug to the counter and taking a large step forward to get closer to her. She moves back and I stop, placing one hand on the counter. "I wasn't issuin' a dare and you know it."

One perfectly shaped black brow goes up, and that fucking gleam in her eye all but blinds me.

I'm so fucked.

This girl has always been like a dog with a bone when it comes to dares. Doesn't matter one fucking bit that I didn't intend it to come out that way, it's how she perceived it, and by God, she'll bring me to my knees to win. I just know it.

"Quinn, whatever you're thinkin', put it outta your head right now." I try to sound firm, but she's got me right where she wants me and we both know it. The painful erection I'm sporting now is screaming that yes, yes she will get me to beg before her, at the same time my mind is telling me it would be the best fucking defeat in the world. Can't look at it as losing when either way I end up with my cock in the stranglehold of her pussy.

"I'm not doin' anything at all, handsome," she says innocently with a wicked smirk, a fucking sexy-as-hell smirk that almost has me dropping to the floor to do the begging right now.

"That's what I'm worried about," I mumble under my breath.

She giggles softly and reaches out to pat my cheek. Why that's something that makes my cock twitch in my pants, I'll never know.

"Take me home, Tate," she all but sings. "I need to take Daisy out for a ride and you should probably head out for some kneepads."

"Kneepads?"

There's that twinkle again, fucking hell.

"For when you're on your knees beggin'." She hums, breaching the gap between us and rolling up to her toes to press a kiss against my slack jaw. "Wouldn't want your knees to get sore while you're down there. If memory serves, you happened to like spendin' a lot of time down on your knees." She moves her head, mouth hovering right against my ear, and whispers, "Don't you wonder if I still taste like sugar?"

God. Damn. I reach between us and cup myself, feeling like I'm seconds away from coming in my pajama pants.

Yeah, I'm fucked. So beyond fucked I can't wait.

19
Quinn

"Fast" by Luke Bryan

— ★ —

Are you sure there isn't anything I can do for this weekend?" I ask Leigh. Her flip-flop-covered feet shuffle across the shop floor as she moves toward the F1 to peer into the open door to watch me work.

"What are you doing?" she puzzles, watching my hands as they move under the dash.

"Workin' on the last of the wirin'. Answer me. Do you need help?"

"No. Nope. No help."

I sit up and lean back against the seat I installed earlier this week, enjoying the feeling of the soft leather, and study her. She showed up about ten minutes ago looking weird as hell, but remained silent while I finished up the last of the electrical I needed to do before Homer would be officially ready to fire up. With her wedding just a few days away, I wouldn't be surprised if it's just nerves.

"What is it?"

Her eyes flit around the room, a gesture I

would normally assume means she was keeping something from me, but I have a feeling it's more to make sure there isn't anyone else around to hear her. Well, there goes the chance of this being wedding-related.

"You've been home all week."

Confused, I struggle to keep up with her distracting verbal train of thought. "Yeah," I confirm with a frown, having not the slightest clue where this is going.

"You've been home *alone* all week," she continues, her eyes getting wonky.

"No, I haven't. Clay's been there most of the time."

"God, you're so infuriating sometimes!" she yelps, slapping her hands against her denim-covered thighs.

"Unless we developed some sort of ability to read each other's minds that I wasn't aware of, you're going to have to do better than that. Spit it out, Leigh! You're makin' no damn sense."

She pouts—full-out pouts with her lip out and everything. "I can't."

"You can't *what?*" I ask sharply.

"I can't just 'spit it out,' because a certain tall, dark, and handsome cowboy made me swear I wouldn't just 'spit it out' and that I'd let you come to me if you needed anything. But, Q, serious as all get-out, I'm this close to breakin' that promise," she huffs, holding up her fingers to show a tiny gap between them. "I need you to not have me breakin' any promises to the man I'm marryin' this weekend and get a freakin' clue and pick up what I'm puttin' down!"

A lightbulb flickers on. "Are you tryin' to ask me what's goin' on with Tate and me?" I ask, getting a kick out of her frustration when she stomps her foot and growls at me. "Jesus Jones, Leigh. Calm yourself, girlfriend. You can stop your frettin', because Tate and I are great."

"You been home *alone* all week." She repeats her earlier words through her teeth, glaring at me.

"I sure have." I grin.

"You didn't have any other plans? Nothing going on since the last time I saw you *days* ago?"

"I don't know, Leigh, what other plans could I possibly have durin' the week when I've gotta be at work nice and early?" I hedge, fighting to keep my laughter in check.

"You're such a pain in the ass," she finally says after a long silence spent blatantly killing me with her eyes.

"God, you're wound tight." I laugh, tossing the empty water bottle I had sitting next to me inside the cab of the F1. "In an effort to save your sanity and help you remain an honest-ish woman before you get hitched to my brother, I can assure you that everything is fine, perfect even, with Tate and me. We've had dinner together twice since I spent the night at his place Saturday night. We've got plans to get together tonight, too. I've been home alone each night because that's my house, Leigh, and it's pretty damn normal to end up at my house to sleep."

"Oh." She sighs. "I'm so glad *you* brought Tate up, Quinn. So, you've only seen him twice since Sunday mornin'?"

I roll my eyes at her crazy ass. "Yes, Leigh, how smart of me to bring him up so we can have a girl-talk session. I have nothin' else that I should be doin' or anything. Say, you wanna run over to the corner store and get some nail polish and face masks?"

She ignores my smart-ass comment and forges on. Now that she's in the clear of not breaking any promises to Maverick on a technicality, she's not going to give up. "No more sleepovers at his house or anything? Just dinner?"

Well, I guess I might as well play this game since it's clear she isn't going to shut the hell up.

"No more sleepovers, you crazy woman. He's still gettin' to know his way around his new job, I guess is the best way to put it, so he needs his sleep. He went from a busy hospital doin' deliveries and surgeries left and right to small-town lady doctor who's suddenly booked solid with appointments. Even if the actual practice isn't a huge hospital, he's seein' patients constantly, doin' the face-to-vag consultations and stuff." I wave my hand, not really sure how to explain it. He was part of a huge hospital in Georgia, and while he didn't lack patients, the smaller-practice thing is a lot more personal than what he was doing and seems to require quite a bit more time.

"How is the small practice more exhausting? All he has to do now is make some small talk, fondle some boobies, and fiddle with some crotches."

"It's a little more demanding than that." I laugh, going to my workbench and grabbing the tools I need to finish this baby up.

"It doesn't bother you at all? That he's seeing women naked all day?"

"Why would it?" I ask, genuinely confused by the thought.

"Uh, I don't know, maybe because of all those boobies he's touchin' and the fondlin' or, more specifically, the fact that he has his hands around and in different vaginas all day."

"It's not sexual, Leigh! Jeeze, you make it sound like he's off cheatin' on me because his medical specialty happens to be gynecology."

She crosses her arms over her chest and looks at me sharply.

"What? It isn't. He's a *doctor*. Trained to see patients in a clinical manner. He doesn't show up at the office and spend the whole day coming all over himself because there's some lady pockets in his face. It's a doctor's office, not an orgy by appointment."

"So, you're tellin' me if you were his patient, it wouldn't be sexual?"

My lips pucker and I huff out a puff of air. "That is completely different and you know it, Leighton James."

"I'm not sure how it is. Look, I'm not sayin' that he's goin' to work and being some pervert. I'm just worried about you, and you not bein' with him this week had me concerned that you mighta been lookin' for ways to back away. Tryin' to find an excuse not to be with him."

"Jesus Jones, Leigh, talk about reachin' *way* up there to find somethin' to worry about in the realm of never-gonna-happen-ville."

"It wasn't that far of a reach. Most women would be insecure about their man being a gynecologist. It's a completely normal reaction, if you ask me."

I scoff at the thought. "I'm not most women, Leigh, and that's not a normal reaction in my book."

"That you aren't," she agrees, some of the worry bleeding from her face as she smiles. "Well, then tell me what *is* goin' on, then, Q. I'm just worried, you know that. You just got him back and it seemed like you both couldn't get enough of each other when we ran into you Saturday afternoon. How are you able to go almost five whole days without wantin' to be annoyingly joined at the hip with him?"

"You make it sound like we've been avoidin' each other," I protest. "Honestly, Leigh, he's busy with patients and paperwork all day. I've been busy finishin' up Homer. We're not actively lookin' for reasons to stay apart. The exact opposite. We've had dinner a few nights, sent texts back and forth all day, each day, in between, and he even came over to the ranch last night to watch a movie—somethin' I'm sure you didn't find out in all that detective work you've clearly been doin', because Clay wasn't home to know about that one."

"Five days, Q," she stresses.

"Didn't you hear? Distance makes the heart grow fonder," I deadpan.

"Oh, shut up with that shit. All you two have had is distance, and now you're tellin' me you want *more* to grow fonder of each other? You really wadin' in the thick shit now."

I snicker softly.

"We were thinkin' about going to a movie or somethin' tonight. Dependin' on how we feel after workin', though, it might just be a meal again. Tomorrow he'll be with me for family dinner, and he'll be at the weddin' on Saturday. I'm figurin' since you decided on gettin' married at ten in the mornin' we might have that sleepover you seem to be so concerned about tomorrow night. But if you really want to know why we've not been eatin', sleepin', and breathin' each other, I'll let you in on a little secret."

Her eyes light up and she claps her hands, bouncing on her stupid flip-flops.

"We have a little bet goin' on." I smirk, thinking about how close he had been to begging for it last night while we made out on the couch like teenagers. I still can't believe he pulled away right when things were about to get interesting.

"A bet?" Leigh asks, turning her head to the side to squint at me. I'm sure her mind is running a mile a minute trying to figure out what I could possibly mean.

"A bet," I confirm. "I'm not even sure how it came up, to be honest, but all I know is he said somethin' that challenged me, and you know I can't back down when someone throws a dare my way."

"Oh, shit. He's so doomed." She giggles.

"Without a doubt."

"Well, don't leave me hangin'. What's the bet?"

I wish I could see my expression, because whatever is showing on my face must be clue enough that I'm up to no good, because Leigh's eyes widen instantly.

"That he'll be on his knees beggin' for me before I'll be the one to beg him."

"You didn't," she gasps.

"Oh, I did."

"You're crazy," she says on a choked laugh. "Certifiable without a doubt."

"Probably. Lord knows if he can make my body sing from a kiss alone, he's going to stop my heart when he finally fucks me."

Her lip curls up and she groans. "Sometimes I wonder if you're really a girl."

"Would you rather I say 'make love'?" I ask in a girly-as-hell singsong voice.

She nods. "Seein' as that's what it'll be, yeah. Plus, it sounds so impersonal and meaningless when you say he'll fuck you."

I full-out belly-laugh at that. "Oh, I meant to say it just like that, Leigh. Not because it's meaningless *or* impersonal. It's been nine years since that man has been inside me. A long damn time, and while we might not have remained celibate over the years apart, we haven't had each other, and that makes all the difference in the world. It wouldn't matter if we had been with someone else months, days, or even minutes before. When we finally get that, us connectin' in the most intimate and vulnerable of ways, it's goin' to be so beyond 'makin' love.' It's gonna be hard, messy, loud, and probably a little painful—in the yummy way. You don't get your second chance with your forever often, and there's no way it won't start with a frenzied, desperation-fueled boom to it."

She fans herself. "Jesus, Q. That was uncomfortable hot to think about."

"Consider it payback for all those times you talked about my brother's little dude," I jest, pointing to my crotch while wagging my brows.

The hand waving air into her face stops and she gives me a wink. "Ginormous. And beautiful. Don't mix up the adjectives when talkin' about that work of art."

"Maybe we should sign you up for boundaries classes with Jana."

"Whatever." She giggles. "Now, enough about your brother's sexy manhood. I've got an idea. Actually a damn good one, if I do say so myself."

"I'm not sure I want to know what your mind is hatchin'," I say warily.

"Oh, trust me, you do."

I walk to the passenger side of Homer and open the door, waving toward the cab with a dramatic bow. "Well then, step into my office and tell me about this grand plan of yours."

This is the most insanely brilliant thing I've ever done.

I'm actually shocked as hell that Leigh thought of it before I did. Hell, I probably would have thought of it five days ago when I made Tate take me home after spending the night, *but* in my defense, I had been trying to talk myself out of forcing him to take me right then and there in the kitchen.

But this—*this* is insane.

Pure lunacy.

And I'm so turned on right now I'm pretty sure all it would take is me walking the wrong way, my jeans rubbing against my slick and needy sex, and *boom,* I would be crying out just like that.

Maybe this isn't a good idea, but Jesus Jones, how much longer am I supposed to deprive him of my pleasure? I laugh at my joke, the noise echoing around Ness's cab, and I jump in my seat.

Okay, so I'm a tad nervous.

It isn't like he's a stranger that I've never slept with before and that I'm not sure wants me. I *know* he wants me. It isn't even close to the quick hookups I've had over the years—the ones I was ashamed of when they made me feel like my mama. None of that is why I'm a nervous bundle of uncertainty—regardless of the plan being pretty awesome.

It doesn't matter to me how long he's been back or even how long we've officially been together. None of that bullshit about not feeling the same now that we're adults is even in the realm of possibilities, and honestly, it never was.

All it took was one day with him and I felt all that time vanish. Sure, we'll still have moments in the future where we're faced with reminders of what we missed being apart, but that's so tiny and inconsequential in relation to the bigger picture. We've got the rest of our damn lives to discover everything we missed, and at this point, I don't want to waste a second more. Those breakthrough moments when each of us discovers something about the other person that was new in the last nine years will just be a bonus in our crazy roller-coaster romance. We'll make new memories while uncovering the old.

Who wants perfect? Not me. I want *real.*

I need this. He needs this. *We* need this.

With every second that passes, the hole inside me comes closer to being full, so much so that if I jumped, I might slosh some of its contents over the edges. It's as simple as that. He's given that to me and I hope I've given him the same. Call it crazy, but when you hold that sort of connection with anyone, it will never matter how much time you're apart: your subconscious is automatically ready for you to pick up the pieces and begin your journey together again. It's as simple as that.

"You got this, Quinn," I tell my reflection in the rearview mirror. "You *so* have this. You march in there and make him end this stupid bet. Then you can both enjoy the prize."

I nod and pull my long hair from the bun I had it twisted in, thankful that it looks like purposeful waves that are meant to be there and not a crinkly mess from being up on top of my head since seven this morning.

The second my boots hit the ground, a renewed

burst of nervous bubbles starts fizzing in my gut. I ignore them, shut the door, and give Ness a pat on the side panel before walking toward the front door of the old house Fisher Ford turned his office into.

Gladys is the only one in the front waiting room, her gray head sticking up over the front-desk check-in area. She flashes me a weathered smile. Given that it's so close to business hours ending, I'm not shocked that there isn't another person waiting to be seen.

"Howdy, Quinn!" she calls with a wave. "What brings you in, sweetheart?"

"Hey, Ms. Gladys." I walk over to the little window cut into the wall and tell myself to stick to the plan. "I was wonderin' if you could get me in today. I know it's late and all, but I'm not sure I can go another night with this pain when I use the potty. It hurts mighty bad when I move around, too."

If it wasn't for the fact that she's been working this same job for as long as the practice has been open, I'm pretty sure she wouldn't have been able to catch the shock that flashes over her face as quickly as she does. There one minute, gone before you could blink. Hell, I probably would have missed it, but I'm in hyperaware mode right now.

"Uh, let me see what I can do," she answers, looking down at the old-fashioned appointment book in front of her. "Dr. Lyons is still here and hasn't had a patient for an hour now. I'm sure he could fit you in before he leaves."

I'm shaking my head before she finishes and she looks up with a frown. "It has to be Tate. I mean Dr. Montgomery."

This time she fails to hide her shock. Doesn't even try to. "Quinn, honey," she whispers, looking behind her when someone enters the front-desk area.

"Hey Claire," I greet, smiling sweetly at the receptionist.

"Hey Quinn." She's so meek and shy that I almost don't hear her. "Ms. Gladys, I'm gonna head home now," she tells the older woman, still looking at me sheepishly.

"Sure, sweet girl. I hope that headache gets better."

Claire nods, barely, and grabs her purse from a cabinet next to what I assume is her desk.

Gladys waits for Claire to leave before addressing me again. "Quinn, honey," she says hesitantly, "I know it isn't my business, but don't you think Dr. Lyons would be a better option?"

I shake my head. "Nothin' against him, Ms. Gladys, but I only want Dr. Montgomery."

"But—" She stops and checks the area around us again, lowering her voice even further as she resumes speaking. "But Quinn, honey, you don't really want him dealin' with your . . . issues, do you? It's no secret y'all are datin'. I heard about the other night at the diner when y'all were just sittin' there neckin' the whole time, not payin' any mind to your dinner once. Do you want your new beau to know your *intimate details?*"

I bite my cheek so that I don't burst out laughing and ruin this whole thing. No way I'm getting this far and having it all go to hell because I can't keep a straight face.

I lean toward the older woman. "Ms. Gladys, can you keep a secret?"

This time she doesn't look shocked. Nope, not Ms. Gladys, best friend to self-appointed town busybody Marybeth Perkins. Her face sparks with excitement and she nods instantly.

"Well, between us girls and all, I figured it should be him fixin' me up since he's most likely the reason it hurts so much . . . down there. That man." I make a dramatic show of whistling and rolling my eyes in bliss. "Well, bein' the fine doctor for ladies that he is, you would think he'd know how to *entertain* one without *bruisin'* her . . ." I pause, lean in even closer, and whisper, "Deep inside, if you know what I mean."

Gladys looks like she might faint, and this time I have to bite my cheek so hard I taste blood. If she had been anyone else, I would have thought of a better way at getting back there than giving her that kind of mental picture. However, Gladys is old as dirt, and the last thing she's going to do is use a hint about Tate working with a python in his pants to try and get with him.

"Oh, well . . . let's, uh, let's see here." She pats her hair and I can practically see the wheels turning while she composes herself. "Let's just get you back in a room. I'll let Dr. Montgomery know he has a walk-in. Don't you even fret about privacy, honey. I'll tell him it's a consultation and have him send Nurse Rebecca on home. You won't have to worry about a thing. Of course, you know I won't say a word."

I nod and smile. "Thank you, Ms. Gladys. I appreciate it. I'm not sure I could take another night of this pain. All the way to my chest sometimes, if you can believe it." Okay, so I'm laying it on a little thick now.

But Gladys must not think so, because I hear her whisper something about bettin' my ass she'd believe it before she walks toward the huge shelves of patient files and grabs the one I assume is mine.

"Come on, sweetheart. Let's get you in a room and settled before he's done with his last patient. That'll give everyone still in the office some time to clear out. Don't you worry about a thing. Let Ms. Gladys make sure you've got some privacy. Can't have such a sweet thing like you with rumors flyin' around, and if you knew which patient was in there, you'd understand. Well, you'd understand and have the whole town talkin' like you're knocked up or somethin' if she gets her eyes on ya."

It's on the tip of my tongue to say it'll probably happen anyway, seeing as Ness is parked out front. Won't make a difference to the people driving by that I could just be here for my yearly.

"You take your time and slip this on and then just sit right up there." She hands me a paper gown before rushing out of the room with a smirk on her face.

I give her five minutes before she calls Marybeth Perkins and starts that pregnancy rumor herself—only she's going to pair it with mention of Tate's huge cock getting me that way *and* bruising my insides all the way up to my ears, I'm sure.

"This better work," I grumble to myself, toeing off my boots and taking off my socks, shirt, and shorts, folding them neatly on one of the chairs next to the exam table. My white lace bra comes next, my heavy, needy breasts swaying as I bend over to pull the matching boy shorts down my legs, placing them on top of my clothes.

I pull the paper robe on, folding the ends over each other across my chest, and move to the exam table, but before my ass hits the paper on the table, I rush over to my jeans and pull my phone out of the back pocket. Without bothering to unlock it, I swipe the camera up from the bottom and check my face.

My hair is still falling around my face in natural waves, and my sun-kissed skin is flushed, but in the way that makes me look like I'm glowing, not like I'm embarrassed. It's my eyes that give me away, though. They might as well be emerald stones with a flashlight beaming through them, giving away all my secrets.

It's because of the glow emanating from deep within my soul and out through my eyes that I know Tate Montgomery is going to take one look at me and know he's lost, but *we* both won.

20
Tate

"Use Me" by Blaire Hanks

— ★ —

Fuck.

I was *this* close to getting outta here before five today.

I haven't heard from Quinn all afternoon, but knowing she's been working her ass off on Paw's truck all week, saying she's just days away from being done, I don't doubt the reason is because she's lost in her work. Something, I've discovered this week, she has a tendency to do often.

All I want to do is finish up with my last patient and go surprise her at the shop. Even though I just saw her last night, I still want more. Hell, I'll always want more. A few dinner dates and whatever the hell last night was just aren't going to cut it.

I want more.

Fuck, who am I kidding? I want it all.

I'm so close to folding on that stupid-ass dare of hers that it's not funny. If me giving in gets her naked in front of me, fucking sign me up. I'll drop to my knees now.

"Who's the walk-in, Gladys?" I ask sullenly as she's packing up her stuff for the day. "Where are you headed?"

"Oh, nowhere," she says, still rearranging shit on her desk.

"I know you sent Rebecca home, but with no one else here I'm gonna need you to stay in case I need to do an exam. You know I can't do that alone."

She waves me off. "I know. I'll be right here after the consultation for you to let me know if I can leave or if you need me."

"If Quinn calls, do me a favor and let her know I'll pick her up at the shop when I'm done for an early dinner."

Gladys nods but looks like she's about to swallow her tongue. *Strange lady,* I think with a shake of my head.

I check my watch one more time before walking down the hall. Jesus, she didn't even leave the patient's chart in the door pocket. I'll have to remind her about protocol in the morning. I rap my knuckles on the door twice and wait. After receiving a muffled confirmation that whoever's inside is ready, I turn the knob and step inside the room.

"Good evening," I say distractedly, and I shut the door and move to the sink to wash my hands.

"I'm Dr. Montgomery. You'll have to forgive me, Gladys seems to have left your chart in here. What brings you in today?"

I dry my hands and turn around.

And there's Quinn Davis. Wearing nothing but a paper gown and a smile.

"What?" I breathe.

"Hello, Doctor," she says, her grin spreading wider across her face, her hoarse, seductive rasp tingling up my spine, making me shiver.

"What?" I parrot, my mind incapable of anything more now that the only thing I can see is a fantasy I never knew I had coming to life.

"I've been a bad girl, Doc." Quinn makes a mock sad face. "I skipped my last appointment and I just realized I needed to come on in and get that done lickety-split. You see, I've got this deliciously hot boyfriend, and even though I'm sure he'll keep me safe, it's up to me to make sure I keep us both protected from any unexpected surprises and get my birth control prescription before I run out."

"You want birth control?" I ask lamely, swallowing a thick knot in my throat when she shifts her legs—uncrossing them before recrossing them, with the opposite leg over the first one, taking so much time that I know the flash of her bare pussy was intentional.

She's trying to kill me.

"Well, of course, Doc. I also should probably

get a full workup. Need to make sure everything is in tip-top shape and all." She smiles, unwavering in her patient act. I wonder if she's just as lost in the fantasy as I am.

I probably could have formed a full sentence, but when she stops talking and leans back and presses her palms against the table directly behind her, my eyes cross in pleasure.

The gown opens, flaps falling to the side, and I'm face-to-face with the most beautiful set of breasts I've ever seen. Full, more than a handful, with the suntan outline of what is obviously one tiny-as-fuck bikini. When I see her erect nipples pointing at me in the middle of perfectly symmetrical areolas, light pink against the pale skin, my mouth waters.

"Did you have time to fit me in for a workup?" she coos, balancing her weight in a way that I know isn't fucking needed, but is done to give her impressive chest a chance to jiggle.

"A workup?" I moan, my cock reminding me that he's been denied what he wants for way too long.

"Yes, Doctor, I need a full workup."

"Full workup," I repeat, stepping away from the door and advancing. Two steps into the room though, I stop, because she lifts the leg crossed over the other and widens the space between them just enough that I can see the wetness on the outside of her bare pussy.

"Well, that's up to you, Doc. . . ." She pauses, and I force my eyes to move, spending a few seconds on that hot-as-fuck chest before looking her in the eyes for the first time. "I know it's almost the end of office hours and all, so if you don't want to work me in, I understand."

"Fuck me," I hiss, finally getting some mental capabilities back when I see the truth of the reason for her visit shining bright in those green eyes I love so much.

I turn, grab the handle, and open the door enough to stick my head out. "Gladys, you head on out, you hear? No need to stick around."

"No exam?" she calls down the hall from her desk, something I know she only does when we're alone.

"Nope. We're finishing up now and Quinn's gonna stick around while I catch up on my charting for the day. I'll see you in the morning."

"You got it! See ya in the morning."

I rest my head against the doorjamb and wait to hear the front door shut and lock before turning and slamming the exam room door closed.

"You wanna win that bad, Grease?" I ask darkly.

She shakes her head, but the toothy smile she's sporting says otherwise.

"I think you're lying."

"I don't wanna win the bet," she murmurs with a needy whine to her voice. She shifts and rises off the table and places both her hands on her thighs, pushing her legs open more. "It's so much more than just the bet," she continues, dragging the tips of her fingers up her leg before spreading her sex open enough for me to see the creamy essence of her arousal.

"What's it about, then?" I ask, the last two words coming out like a growl when she pushes two fingers inside herself, pumping them slowly.

My hands are already unfastening the buttons on the short-sleeved plaid shirt I wore today, my cock pulsing behind my jeans with each thrust of her fingers into her pussy. She doesn't answer, rolling her head around on her shoulders and picking up speed with her hand just slightly. I toss my shirt blindly behind me and advance.

"What's it about?" I press. "If you don't want to win the bet, then why aren't you saying the words that'll lead to us getting what we want?"

"Because," she pants, hand moving faster.

My head drops when she doesn't speak, and the sight before me has my hands fumbling to remove my belt. I can smell her and my mouth waters. Reaching into my pants and pushing my briefs out of the way, I pull my throbbing cock free and begin stroking it. Each time her fingers come out of her pussy, they're even wetter than before.

I bring my left hand up and clamp my fingers around the base of my cock, trying to stop the come from exploding.

"Because?" I ask with a deep, gritty groan.

She doesn't answer, and I'm too close to blowing my load all over her to keep watching her touch herself like that, so I reach out and grab the wrist of the hand she's fucking herself with and pull it away from her pussy. She whines and I don't even give a fuck. I lift her wet fingers up while I bend, letting my cock free from the vise grip to stroke it again. I force her hand to move, painting my lips with the juices from her body, feeling like the most powerful man in the world when she whimpers.

I raise my brow, open my mouth, and push her fingers into my mouth up to the knuckles, my tongue swirling and licking her essence off them. The second her taste explodes on my tongue, I know she's won. I groan, my eyes rolling, and suck my cheeks hollow while I continue to swallow her one-of-a-kind flavor.

She pants breathlessly as I pop her fingers out slowly, one by one. I lean forward, letting go of my cock to rest the hand not holding her wrist captive on the table next to her hip. My cock rubs against her leg, leaving a trail of pre-come against her skin. When our faces are just inches apart, I take the hand I'm still holding and place it palm-down on her leg. Then, slowly, I drag it back up her thigh, flipping it so that my hand is on top of hers, until we've reached her soaked pussy together, her cupping herself under my hand.

"You want me to beg?" I demand in a strong voice.

She whimpers again and I press against her first two fingers, the ones I just cleaned, until the tips of our fingers are inside her together. The heat of her body almost too much to bear.

"Do you." I thrust a little deeper. "Want me." I pull out. "To beg?" I press our fingers against her clit.

A high-pitched whine escapes her lips and she nods rapidly.

"Fuckin' gladly," I grunt, pressing a light kiss to the tip of her nose before lifting my hands up and to her shoulders, forcing her back down on the exam table. She hadn't even realized she was scooting down toward me before I had the stirrups out and both feet placed in them. Then I kneel on the small step that's coming out from the table under her exposed pussy and look up her body with my mouth nearly where I want it most. "I'm on my knees for you, baby. I crave this body almost as much as I need it. Your pussy soakin' my balls while you come on my cock, takin' everything I have to give you deep inside that body. Rest of my days, I'll feel the same desperate need for you, Quinn. One day I'm gonna fill you up until my seed takes root and I'll do it again and again after that. Gonna give you that family we always talked about, but first, I'm beggin' you to give it all to me, Quinn. Give me this body I crave, but give me the heart inside it I need."

"God, yes," she cries, reaching down her body to push her fingers into my hair with both hands, pulling my face toward her pussy.

"Sit back and let the doctor work," I instruct, shaking my head to dislodge her hold. I hear her cry of protest, but the second I lick her from bottom to top, swirling my tongue around her clit, the roaring in my ears becomes too much for me to focus on anything else.

I feast on her like a madman, sucking in my cheeks with my lips spread, mouth wide and covering her whole pussy. Her wetness coats my tongue, and her cries of pleasure echo through the room.

Not wanting her to come without my cock feeling the stranglehold of it, I rip my mouth from her with a gasp, feeling the combined wetness of my spit and her pleasure all over my chin.

My knees are sore as fuck from the unforgiving perch I was kneeling on, but I ignore them and stand, kicking my foot against the step to force it into the table so I can move closer. My cock in hand, I thump it against her pussy a few times while watching her breasts shake with her rapid breathing.

"You finally know the man I am now?" I ask, lining my cock up so that the tip kisses her entrance.

"I'd know him anywhere," she breathes.

"You givin' him your forever?" I slip the thick head in, hissing when her wet heat surrounds me.

"God, yes," she moans, her heart in her eyes.

"Never, Quinn. I'll never spend another day without you in it. You hear me?"

She nods and I push an inch in, making her whine.

"I'll spend every day makin' up for the time we lost. That pain will never touch you again."

"You," she gasps when I feed another few inches of myself into her body. "You don't have to make up for it, it wasn't . . ." She moans and bows her back off the exam table, another two inches inside her. "Wasn't your fault . . . forgive you," she whispers, her whole body trembling.

"Fuck," I rumble, her words hitting me straight in the chest. Then I slam into her, the rest of my cock gliding deep until my balls are pressed tight against her ass. I reach back and grab her thighs, lifting her feet out of the stirrups and, praying to God she can see my feelings for her written all over my face, I start to power my body into hers.

The sound of our wet flesh connecting, the scent of our sex heating up in the air around us, the promise of forever confirmed in her eyes— all of this makes me feel overcome with emotion, and my thrusts falter, making my pelvis grind against her clit. That's all it takes for her to cry out, dig her nails in my forearms, and suck me deep while she comes all over my cock.

I'm not even a second behind her.

When the dregs of my release are sucked from my cock by her pulsing cunt, I collapse on top of her, our sweaty chests gliding against each other.

She looks up, a dreamy-as-fuck expression on her face, and smiles, pushing some of my sweaty hair out of my eyes, a mischievous glint in her eyes.

"Thanks for fittin' me in, Doc."

21

Quinn

"Strawberry Wine" by Deana Carter

— ★ —

Y ou look beautiful."
I feel my chin tremble and I nod in agreement, knowing I'm seconds away from turning into a blubbering mess.

"Thanks," Leigh says, turning from the mirror to look at Clay, her eyes shining. It's Leigh and Mav's wedding day, and while part of me can't believe it's already here, another part of me feels like all of us Davis clan have been waiting on this damn near forever. Waiting to call Leigh our sister and finally make it official.

"Goes without sayin', but I'm gonna say it anyway: I'm happy as hell that you're officially goin' to be a part of our family, like you've always been meant to be." His deep voice is steady even though I can tell by the tight hold he's got on his body that this moment is just as emotional for him as it is for me.

"If you make her cry, I'll kick your ass," I try to joke, but my voice comes out weak and wobbly.

"You ready, sugar?" Clay asks Leighton, and when she nods, I feel a new burst of emotion clawing up my throat.

"You're about to be my sister," I breathe, walking toward her from the wall I was leaning against.

Her chin wobbles this time, and I shut my mouth before I turn us both into sniveling messes. I wrap my arms around her, the simple lace wedding gown feeling just as perfect to the touch as it looks clinging tightly around her body. Somehow Leigh looks both comfortably casual and like she's about ready to hit the red carpet at the same time. From chest to hips, the material fits her like a glove; then it flares out to a knee-length skirt. I French-braided her hair earlier, twisting the braid so that it falls over one shoulder. Her makeup is elegant and simple except for her lips, a bright ruby red slash across her face that gives her a vibe of sophistication and drama. She looks like a princess.

"I love you," I whisper in her ear.

"I love you back, *sister*."

It takes me the whole walk to the front of her house before I'm able to successfully blink the tears completely away, avoiding ruining the mascara that I put on. I might not wear makeup often, but when I do, I want it to look perfect, dammit.

When we get to the front of Leigh and

Maverick's house, Tate is sitting in the front seat of the golf cart that'll take us to the back pasture, a place that I know means a whole helluva lot to Maverick and Leigh—it's where they first began their romance when they were just kids, and where they rekindled it as adults. Seeing Tate looking damn fine in a fresh button-down shirt and slim-fitting Wranglers is, thankfully, enough of a distraction that I'm finally able to fully compose myself.

Clay helps Leigh step up onto the back of the cart. Her teal cowboy boots, which match the ones on my feet, are so polished they gleam in the bright sunlight. Then he settles in next to her, ready to walk her down the aisle to Maverick in just a few short minutes.

I follow suit, climbing into the front seat, but nowhere near as ladylike a fashion as Leigh because in the process, I flash Tate a glimpse of my black lace panties.

"Nice," he mumbles under his breath.

"Kiss my boots, Starch," I fire back with a smile.

"Gladly." He winks.

"Knock that shit off," Clay complains, thumping Tate on the shoulder.

I spend the whole ride giggling to myself as Clay continues to groan in the back about needing to bleach his ears.

Of course, my laughter turns into one hell of a sniffle when I see my handsome brother waiting for his bride in the middle of "their pasture," his uncle standing next to him and Pastor John on the other side. Aside from Jana, waiting with the breeze blowing her curls around her face, and her man, Bart, no one else is present except for God himself, which is just how Leigh and Mav wanted it.

The day couldn't be more perfect if the weather had been ordered up. It's still hotter than hell, but a soft breeze keeps things comfortable. The wind keeps kicking up just so, turning the green valley around us into some sort of giant wave. Even the air seems to be humming, coming alive. Part of me wonders if it's the aura of Leigh's departed parents surrounding us with their love for her.

Whatever it is, it's all mixing together into one stunning cocktail.

It's perfect.

I sniffle again and Tate chuckles low under his breath. I don't even care now if I ruin my makeup, because the second I see Maverick get his first full glimpse of Leigh, I'm a goner.

Clay and Leigh stand back and wait for Tate and me to walk the distance to where everyone else is standing. I walk past Jana, giving her a watery smile, and stand where I'm supposed to. Tate nods at Mav, whose eyes are trained on Leigh like a thirsting man parched for a sip of water, before standing next to Jana and Bart. He's close enough that I could probably reach out and touch him, but not directly next to me. Leigh was clear that she only wanted her family here—Tate included—and that the only people she wanted standing up with her and Mav would be Clay, myself, and Trey.

I know my brother well enough that I can tell when he's working hard to keep control of himself, but just as it is for me, it's a futile effort for him. I look away, knowing that if I see him—the strongest man I know, except for maybe Clay—start to tear up, I'm done for. Leigh is smiling like a loon through her tears.

Unable to resist the urge any longer, my dumbass self looks at Maverick, and I turn into a big fat baby.

Unlike Clay, he clearly doesn't give two shits if he shows how much this moment means to him. His mouth is slightly open, just a tiny gap, but with each heavy breath he sucks in, his bottom lip quivers. Tears are slowly falling down his face and even though his ever-present black Stetson is on the top of his head, I don't need to see his eyes clearly to know those tears aren't going to stop any time soon.

I sniffle, loudly and pathetically, before soft, hiccupping sobs start leaving my body. I figured I was doing a good job of being quiet, but by the time Leigh is halfway toward her groom, I see an arm coming toward me and Tate's handkerchief being waved in my face.

"Th-thanks." I sob, taking it and wiping at my eyes before blowing my nose in it.

He laughs softly and shakes his head.

Clay reaches Maverick and, after giving him a huge hug—making me cry a little harder—he leans back and presses a soft kiss against Leigh's cheek. When he comes to stand next to me, both of us facing the pastor, Maverick, and Leigh, he wraps an arm around me and pulls me hard into his side. This is so much more than our brother marrying the woman he loves. Both of them came so far to get to this point—but having witnessed firsthand the pain that followed Maverick around until it pushed him to the point where he didn't come back for years and years, I know just how monumental this moment is for him.

I listen to Pastor John talk, my brother and soon-to-be sister-in-law looking at each other with so much love that it hurts to think they almost lost this. I think all of us Davis kids have all wanted, begged, and prayed for the pure and accepting love of another person: not a sibling or a best friend, but a soul mate, someone with whom we can form an unbreakable bond, who will become family. Corny as it sounds, it's the truth. There isn't a single person outside of that who will love you with such unstoppable and unbreakable force, whose whole purpose in life is to make sure you feel how much they care for you and always will. Those that will fight for you, protect you, die for you.

My brother found it with Leighton.

I hope to God Clay finds it with someone, too.

And me . . . I draw in a shuddering breath and look to my right, expecting to see Tate watching Leigh and Maverick being united, but find his eyes on me. What I see in them is powerful enough that had Clay not been holding on to me, I would have eaten dirt.

He's looking at me like *he's* the one that's found all that in me. I've spent so much time worried that even though I've fully committed myself to our reunion, he might vanish again, that I completely missed it.

I've always known that being abandoned by my mom would make me crave that pure love from someone with a ferocity that bordered on unhealthy—I was desperate for it.

I found it with Tate every summer from age eleven until eighteen; then the void of it made that desperation multiply until I knew I would only be complete with him and that no one else would do. During the time he was gone, I convinced myself that there was no way he could have felt the same and not come back.

However, not once did it occur to me he's been just as frantic for the same thing. He might have had the love of his grandparents, but there's no mistaking what's written all over his face for me to see. He's struggled, felt the searing pain, and known that void just as violently as I did. He fought for me—for all those I love, too. He protected me, my family, *and* his grandparents selflessly. And, I bet if it would have come to it, he would have died for us, too.

My God.

My eyes widen. I'm still looking at him and missing the whole ceremony in the process: I know we are right where we need to be. Where we're meant to be.

Together, forever.

He must see what I'm feeling—my love for him—because his eyes soften and he gives me a small nod before mouthing the words I've longed to hear from him for so long.

I love you.

Then, timing be damned, I give them right back, feeling that void inside of me fill up, so full it's running over the edges, causing a waterfall of pure happiness to flood my body.

I love you, too.

His eyes close as he savors this moment, and I look back at my brother and best friend just in time to see them kiss for the first time as husband and wife.

When we walk into the Dam Bar later that night, after our group and the wonderful pastor enjoy a big wedding lunch at Leigh and Mav's, the whole place goes nuts. I smile at my brother when he takes his wife and dips her low, laying a huge wet kiss on her mouth, commanding attention.

Looking around, it seems like the whole damn town came out tonight to celebrate, which makes sense seeing how everyone's been waiting for this moment a long time.

"You want a drink?"

I look away from the happy couple and smile at Tate, nodding and leaning up to kiss his jaw before he walks toward the bar.

Maverick and Leigh walk farther into the bar but are stopped and surrounded by well-wishers before they can get too far. They knew this would happen and gladly welcome it, seeing as we purposely chose to go out to celebrate instead of them hiding away.

"You look happy," Clay observes, bending so he can say it low enough that I can hear him over the music.

"My brother just married my best friend. If I look happy it's because I am, big brother."

"It was a beautiful day, but I meant a little more than the weddin', sugar."

My eyes travel from Mav and Leigh to where Tate is standing, hip against the bar, smiling at the new couple.

"I feel whole, Clay," I tell him, still not looking away from Tate. "So completely full that there isn't a part of me that remembers what it felt like to *not* feel this way. I thought . . . I thought I wouldn't get this, even with things bein' perfect with Tate, I figured there would always be somethin' lackin'."

"What do you mean?"

I turn, face Clay, and nod my head toward the front door. When we came in earlier, there wasn't a soul outside, so I know we'll have complete privacy there, and it'll be easier to talk to him without the pounding music around us.

I look over at Tate one more time, seeing his eyes on me, and point between him, my brother, and myself before pointing to the door. He nods in understanding and holds up a finger. I grab Clay's hand and walk us outside, knowing that Tate won't be far behind. I'm not sure why I feel he needs to hear this too, but something inside me knows that it's just as important for him to hear as it is for Clay. I can fill Maverick in another time: I don't want to bring this up on his wedding night.

"We waitin' for Tate before you tell me what's goin' on?" he asks unnecessarily as he takes a seat on one of the chairs lining the outside of the bar, pulling out his phone to keep himself occupied.

"Didn't want to waste time repeatin' myself for him later when I could enjoy other things instead."

"God, Quinn, could ya not?"

I laugh. "What's wrong? I'm sure the guys

around the ranch talk about sex all the time," I continue, knowing which buttons to push.

"They aren't my fuckin' baby sister," he grumbles. "Stop tryin' to get me all riled up."

I hold my hands up in surrender, my shoulders shaking with suppressed laughter. "But it's so much fun to see you break free of all that seriousness you carry around all the time. Come on, big brother, promise you'll live it up tonight?"

He snorts but doesn't deny me. When Tate comes out, the noise of the bar wafting out the door around him, Clay rises and pushes his phone back in his pocket before taking the beer Tate offers him and taking his seat on the rail again.

"Where's mine?" I ask, pointing to the beer in his hand.

"What's going on?" Tate questions, ignoring me and taking a sip of his beer while looking between us, handing it to me when he's done so I can have a drink.

"I've been thinkin'," I tell them both, my smile growing when they both get a worried look in their eyes. "Nothin' bad, give me a little credit." I hand the beer back to Tate while they both mutter something under their breath.

"Give you too much credit, Hell-raiser and you'll run with it," Clay grumbles.

Tate laughs under his breath, and I roll my eyes, knowing it's pointless to argue, since Clay's not exactly lying.

"Anyway," I tell them, not taking the bait Clay's trying to lay out, "I know you and Maverick have been wonderin' if I would bring up goin' out to see Mama again, and honestly, Clay, it's been on my mind. I felt like maybe I would find something other than the hurt I felt when Maverick told us why she really left, but . . ." I take a deep breath and look over at Tate, reaching out for his hand. He instantly offers it to me and I give it a squeeze. "Now, I'm positive there isn't anything I *need* from her, but I'd like to see if maybe Maverick can arrange a visit with her. I have some things I would like to get off my chest and I'm finally at the place that I'm ready to do it. So, while I might not need anything from her any longer, I need some closure so I can well and truly move on."

Clay looks at me like I've just sprouted a second head. "You wanna visit that . . . woman?"

"Our mama, yeah." I shuffle my feet, waiting for him to process my request.

"What could you possibly need to say to that bitch?"

I don't flinch, his hatred toward her something she damn well earned. "I know you don't want anything to do with her, Clay, but I need this so I can put her out of my mind forever. So I can no longer think about the woman who birthed me and wonder if she might actually want me, love me. Part of me still can't believe what I know is the truth without seein' it with my own eyes. I thought I needed *her,* but I know now that she isn't what I need to feel whole. What I need is to let go, Clay. I need to let go and move on so I can finally have what they found," I voice, pointing toward the door, knowing he's going to understand just what I'm referring to. Or whom, I should say.

Tate's hand tightens around mine, telling me without words that he gets what I'm saying.

Clay continues to look up at me, his expression unreadable, and for a split second I worry that he's disappointed in me for needing this.

Then he nods once and stands. "If that's somethin' you need, then we'll make it happen. I've got nothin' to say to her, but I'll do whatever it is you need to help you through this. I'll even go there with you if you want. I might not understand you needin' this, but I'll support your wishes."

I bite my cheeks and lift my free hand to rub against Clay's stubbled cheek. "You're a damn good man, Clayton Davis, and I'm one lucky girl to have you as my big brother. I know you're only doin' this for me, and I want you to know I appreciate that more than you could ever know."

"For a long time I know you looked up to me like one of the only few men that would move mountains for you, Quinny," he says in a gruff voice. "You took Maverick leavin' hard, and that made you look at me as the *only* man that would fight for you, protect you, love you. I think we both know that's not the truth anymore." He looks over my head toward Tate with a nod before giving me his eyes again. "You got three men who would do anything for you now, sugar, and even though I know I ain't that top man anymore, I would do anythin' in my power to give you a piece of what Maverick has with Leigh."

I try to speak, but he just shakes his head with a ghost of a smile on his lips. He walks toward the door, turns to Tate, and proves to me just how good a man he is.

"Think you'll find, Tate, you've finally won that war you been fightin' for way too long. You protected her while sacrificing your own happiness and now you're savin' her just by lovin' her. Don't think I haven't put it together and seen just where her confidence to confront this kinda pain with our mama is comin' from. Owe you my life for givin' that to her."

He doesn't wait for a response but turns and walks into the crowded bar. Neither Tate nor I move for the longest time until a strangled sob rips from my lips and he quickly wraps me in his strong arms.

Saving me, just like Clay said. Just by loving me.

22

Quinn

"It All Started with a Beer" by Frankie Ballard

— ★ —

"You're so pretty, sister!" I scream over the music at Leigh as she twirls around the dance floor at the Dam Bar, the two of us in our own little circle as we continue to dance the night away.

Her hands whip above her head and she starts to shake them to the Luke Bryan song playing, her blond hair long since having fallen from the braid I had worked so hard to make now in her face as she puffs out her cheeks and blows over and over to get it out of her eyes. Reaching out—being the great friend that I am—I start to pat it away but end up hitting her softly a few times and only making it worse.

"You got butter hands." She giggles, laughing even harder when I start shaking both my hands in the air.

"You're my sister!" I scream, remembering why I'm so happy.

"Yay!" she shouts, and we start flailing about the room.

"Can I have my niece now?!" I yell and turn to sneer at Savannah West when she bumps into me. I never did like that tramp.

"Depends if I can get mine," Leigh calls back, still shaking her hips to the music. I can't believe she didn't even see the way that Savannah Stupid Slut West just looked at us. Whatever. Wait a minute. What did she just say?

"What did you say?" I gasp, trying to help my brain swim through all the beer I've consumed tonight so that I can understand her.

"You want a niece, well so do I." She confirms what I thought I heard.

"You're crazy! I'm not gettin' knocked up, no matter how much I love Tate's huge, sexy penis."

"You're not supposed to call it a penis," Leigh scolds, her giggles ruining her attempt at being serious.

"Why? That's what it is."

She comes closer, wobbling, wraps both arms over my shoulders, and pulls me so close our noses are touching. Her eyes as wide as mine feel as she tries to focus on me from up close.

"Because they like you to call it a cock so they feel all big and badass man about it."

"Ahhhh," I say, agreeing with her completely. "Wait, I'm still not gonna use it to get knocked up, you crazy woman!"

"I will if you will," she singsongs in a childish voice.

"Did you just . . . dare me to get knocked up?" I gasp, feeling the normal undeniable urge when it comes to dares being issued.

"So what if I did?" she mocks.

"You're gonna pay for that," I fume. "I bet you get big and fat when my brother knocks you up."

"Don't care. Even if I'm big and fat, I'll still get to play rodeo queen and ride his big, beautiful cock." She smiles hugely and almost takes us both down when she starts to swerve.

"You're so gross."

"I'm drunk."

"I wanna play rodeo queen with Tate. I don't think I can, though. He already almost doesn't fit in there. I start bouncin' on him like he's a bull, I'm likely to really break my hooha," I worry out loud.

"S'long as he gets that baby in there, doesn't matter if the hooha works." She nods her head as she talks.

"Shut up about babies, you freak!" I pull on her hair and laugh when she starts wobbling even more. "Oh, slow song! Switch up!"

"Maverick!" I scream across the dance floor. "Your *wife* wants to dance on your love rod!"

His eyes widen, but he blindly hands his beer off to a laughing Clay as I spin from Leigh and start marching over to where he was, leaving Tate and Clay standing there watching us with smiles on their faces.

"Let's go, Starch," I demand, trying to get my hands to stay on my hips, but they just keep sliding down the stupid dress I'm wearing. I look down at the offending material and start to gather up the skirt of it to tuck it into my panties, but Tate moves into my space quickly and bats my hands down.

"Stop tryin' to get naked, darlin'," he snaps, but with unmistakable amusement in his voice.

"I hate this stupid thing." I yank at the dumb dress Leigh made me wear again before looking up at Tate.

"You might not like wearin' it, but trust me when I say I'll make it up to you when I get you alone."

"Oh yeah? How's that?"

His eyes get hooded and he quirks up one side of his mouth. His lips look so delicious right now. I wonder what he would do if I licked them right here on the dance floor, in front of half the town.

"You wanna find out right now, keep lookin' at me like that," he says heatedly.

"I can feel your cock on my belly," I say in answer, reaching between us and cupping his hard length through his pants. Prying eyes be damned. "I don't even care if I can't play with your bull rider."

"What the hell?"

"Hey, can I give you some head?"

We never do make it to the dance floor after

286

that. I'm not even sure if he tells anyone we're leaving. One second I'm trying to figure out the best way to get all of him into my mouth and the next he's tossing me over his shoulder, holding my dress down with his hand and storming toward the door of the bar.

Oh, his ass is really pretty.

I reach down, my head bobbing with his steps, and grab two huge handfuls of muscled, tight butt.

"That's my sister!" I hear Leigh bellowing over the slow tune.

Using my hold on the hard, denim-covered butt cheeks, I lift myself up and shake the hair from my eyes and look for her through the laughing crowd.

"Have fun, rodeo queen!" I yell back, not knowing if she can hear me, but not really caring because hello, perfect ass.

God, that feels good.

I move my head around, feeling the softness of sheets under it, and try to remember what felt so good just a moment before. God, my head feels like a giant mess of confusion. How the hell did I even get into a bed? The last thing I remember was toasting, again, with the whole bar to Leigh and Mav. Then a whole lot of broken bits and pieces that don't make a whole lot of sense.

"You awake?" I hear Tate drawl, and I instantly

feel all my senses coming back online when his hot breath hits a very needy part of me.

"Jesus Jones, do that again," I whine, reaching out blindly to find what I need, smiling when I feel the silky-smooth thickness of his hair, grabbing a fistful somewhat gently and pushing him where I want him. He goes willingly, laughing against my core before giving me a long lick and swirl of his tongue. "God, yes," I moan.

He grabs my thighs and forces them apart, no longer content to let me make a sandwich out of his head to try and keep his mouth on me. I squirm, loving the feel of him ravishing my needy sex with his mouth. When he bites down on my clit and sucks it between his teeth, my eyes pop open and I yelp into the darkness, feeling myself get even wetter.

"Please, Tate," I beg, pulling at the hair between my fingers to try and get him to move.

"Please what, Grease," he asks, voice vibrating against my pussy, and I hear myself make a pathetically needy whine.

"Get your cock inside me!" I yell, trying to pull his hair again. He laughs and shakes his head until I let go, and he climbs up my body until I feel the cock I'm so desperate for pressing against my pussy—resting against it instead of pushing inside, dammit.

"How do you want it, Quinn?" he asks, thrusting his hips so that his cock is pushing through the wetness, but not penetrating me just yet. Each time he bumps against my clit, I gasp and feel like my eyes are crossing. "Thought you wanted to play rodeo queen, Grease? Don't tell me you've changed your mind."

Blinking the pleasure from my vision, I look up at him with a question on the tip of my tongue. What the hell is he goin' on about? Then I remember and groan. "Fuckin' Leigh. Swear to God, I'll never be able to think about that position ever again."

Tate laughs, his body still moving against mine, the delicious friction consuming my mind.

"Bet I can make you forget," he vows, lifting his ass in the air and pulling his hard, thick heat away. His bottom lip rolls in and he bites his teeth on top of it. God, that's so sexy. He looks down our bodies, and I'm still so stuck on why biting his lip was enough to cause a new rush of wetness between my legs that I don't notice him moving until he's pushing his thickness deep inside me with one long, powerful thrust.

I scream out his name, slap my hands against his strong back, and dig my nails in. My legs go up, toes curling, and I would swear to anyone that asked, angels sung in that moment.

He flexes his ass and goes even deeper.

"I can feel you everywhere," I gasp. My gasp turns into a high-pitched yelp when he rolls— keeping us connected—and from his position, now with his back to the bed, gives a thrust of his hips, causing me to feel him so deep I'm thinking I might actually have to make a real appointment with Gladys to get some internal organs checked out for bruising.

He slaps my ass playfully and smirks at me from the pillow. "Show me what you got, cowgirl."

Oh, God. I clench involuntarily, so turned on it isn't even funny.

My palms go to his chest, and I flex my fingers, scraping my nails against his skin. He lets out a hiss when I drag them across his nipples.

Then I dig my knees into the bed and start riding.

"Fuck yeah," he grunts, using his hands on my hips to help me move when my legs start shaking, till hitting a part so deep inside me I feel like I'm being split into two glorious pieces. "Squeeze my cock, Quinn. Show me how much you love it."

"I do," I pant. "I do love it."

Crack. His hand against my ass makes me yelp. "Reach down and get yourself there, Quinn. Not gonna make it much longer with you grippin' me so tight with your pussy. Get yourself there so I can fill you up, baby."

His gravelly voice sets my body on fire almost as much as the part of him I'm riding. I pick up my speed, move one hand to my clit, and start rocking against him. It only takes me a few thrusts against his body before I'm tossing my head back and screaming his name into the darkness.

"God, Tate! So good." I fall on top of him, completely worthless to do anything more.

"Arghh, Quinn," he breathes, and I feel the hot splash of him inside me while he twitches under my body.

Long moments later, when both of our breathing has returned to normal and my head feels better, he shifts. I feel him brush my hair aside: I guess he just spent the last few minutes breathing through a face full of it. He kisses my temple, and I hear him breathe me in.

"Remind me to take you dancin' more often."

I giggle, which makes him moan. I feel his still-hard cock twitch inside me.

"Thank you for today," I whisper, lifting up to look down at him, my hands on the mattress on either side of his face. He looks adorably confused, so I smile and continue. "For givin' me your support while I talked to Clay. You didn't even say a word, but all it took was your hand in mine and I felt it. I wasn't even sure I would be able to get all that out with him until I felt that, and I just want you to know that it means a lot."

"That's not somethin' you need to thank me for, darlin'. Any battle you go into, even if it's just a mental one, is one I'm gonna be by your side for."

"Then how about this," I start. "Thank you for comin' back to me."

He jolts under me and slides from my body. I whimper when I lose that fullness, and he twists us so that we're both on our sides and wraps his arms around me, pulling me against his chest. His heart pounds against my ear.

"God, baby, you damn sure don't need to thank me for that. You've given me another chance, when I thought I'd lost it forever. You let me in and gave me back the only thing that ever felt like home to me—*you*—you give me all that, and *you're* thankin' *me*?" he questions in disbelief.

I snuggle into his tight embrace and smile against his warm skin.

Home.

That night, with his arms never leaving me, I fall asleep dreaming of waterfalls and a home built with pure love that nothing in the whole world could ever tear down.

I'd always thought home was a place, but he's right: our home is right here, in each other's arms.

23

Tate

"Here Comes the Sun" by the Beatles

— ★ —

"What's got you so quiet over there?" I ask Quinn, looking over from the passenger seat of Paw's old F1.

Quinn's eyes have a faraway look to them, her face more downcast than usual. "I'm just a little sad about startin' him up. It seems like forever ago you called about him and that's all it took to throw my whole world for a loop. I'm not sure I'm ready to say good-bye to the beast that helped bring us back together. Every time I walk into the shop and see him sittin' there, waitin' for me to come crawl under him and mess with his body, I get a sense of pride in not just him—but because really, he's kind of . . . us."

"I find it oddly sexy when you talk about workin' on trucks like that," I drawl, twirling a long piece of her hair around my finger.

She rolls her eyes and looks over at me. "I'm serious."

"I know, Grease. I wasn't tryin' to devalue your

feelin's. Bad timin' to bring it up. How do you figure this old thing is us?"

Her face grows serious, and I'm not sure if I should brace myself for what she has to say or not.

"Think about it, Tate. You had this thing delivered to me a broken, rusty, sad shell of the beauty he used to be. Everyone would have counted him out and taken one look at him, immediately assumin' that he would never be set to rights again. That he was a lost cause or somethin'. All he needed, though, was the right touch and someone determined to get him back to what he used to be. With a little hard work, sweat, tears, and maybe a little blood—he's lookin' better than he probably ever did, even when he was first made. He's . . . us."

I blow out a breath and study her face, her words tumbling around in my mind, making a whole lot of sense when she puts it that way.

"No one woulda thought we would get a second chance, Tate. Not even us. That's how much of a lost cause we were," she continues, her voice lower as she shifts in her seat to look at me better. "Even though we both would have given anything to have each other back, there were just too many broken pieces, rusty unused parts, and the broken shell of what we were. Situations changed and you—thank God—were determined even without knowin' for sure what you'd get when you got back to Pine Oak. Together, we had the right things drivin' us toward bein' a better version of what we once were. You and me, we're Homer and Bertha. The two wouldn't be what they are now without the other."

"Bertha?" I ask thickly, her explanation rocking me to my core.

She points over my shoulder and I look over to the other F1 I vaguely remember her talking about weeks ago. I had been so desperate for anything from her, that conversation was a test to my abilities of focusing. I try to remember exactly what she said, but the only thing I can remember is that Quinn had used the engine in that truck for mine.

What she said finally registers completely and I feel my heart skip a beat. "Wait a minute, how are we these two trucks when that one," I say, pointing to the one she keeps calling Bertha, "doesn't have an engine anymore. Are you sayin' you're still broken, baby?"

God, I fucking hope not. I thought, after the wedding and her talk with her brother that night, that we were past this. I figured we were finally in the right spot—that place where nothing would stand in our way again.

Her serious expression breaks and a sly, content smile tips up her lips. "No, honey," she breathes, reaching out to caress the side of my face, stopping when she reaches my jaw to cup it lovingly. It's pathetic how addicted to her touch I am. I fucking crave her hands on me. I turn my head to nuzzle into her so I can smell the perfume on her wrist better.

"Bertha's a good girl, Tate. She's patient when it comes to her man and wants to give him what he needs to be whole. I'm sayin' you came back and gave me Homer to fix *and* in turn offered me somethin' I never imagined I would get another chance at again. They both got the same thing in the end. Homer got Bertha's engine—her heart, the part of her that is the most vulnerable and important—and you . . . you got mine."

"Fuckin' hell," I mumble in awe, feeling like my heart is about to pound out of my fucking chest over what she's just said *and* what it means to our relationship.

"What d'you say we fire this bad boy up?" she asks, giving me the moment of recovery I need to get my shit together.

Too overcome by her words to speak right then, I give her a nod and try not to cry like a fucking baby.

The second she turns the key and the truck roars, vibrations shooting through my whole body, she tosses her head back and laughs—pure elation shooting from her, just from starting up a truck. She shakes her head, pressing on the gas a few times to rev the engine, the whole time bouncing in her seat like a kid on a sugar high.

She's fucking eating this up. Seeing her like this, in her element, is a joy.

When she looks over, her dark hair running over the skin of my forearm that's still resting on the back of the seat, goose bumps shoot over my body. I just stare at her, at the streak of grease just above the line of her chin, at her eyes wild and bright with excitement, and I'm not sure that she's ever looked more beautiful.

"You wanna drive?" she asks, her green eyes sparkling and cheeks flushed. No fucking way I would take the chance to do so away from her, not when she looks like she was just handed the world by turning the key.

"Figure with what you just said, darlin', the only person that should be drivin' the truck that represents *me* is *you*."

She leans her head back and sighs with contentment, still bouncing slightly as her hands grip the wheel.

"Show me what you got, darlin'," I say with a smile.

I know she gets what I'm saying—that she reads between the words spoken to find the deeper meaning—because her whole face gets even softer, love shining so fucking bright in her eyes that it would bring a lesser man to his knees. It's that expression, paired with the rumble of Homer as she pulls him out of Davis Auto Works and starts tearing up the streets of Pine Oak, that confirms to me that she is giving me *exactly* what I was requesting.

She continues to race through the whole damn town, laughing and giggling. She switches gears, the window down and her hair flying wildly around her face, the truck under her control coming powerfully back to life with her hands on him now that she's fixed every single thing that had rotted.

If I live to be a hundred, I'll never forget this ride.

I rub my stomach when it rumbles again, the scent of the food Quinn's gotten out of the fridge reminding me just how hungry I was. We just spent another afternoon after work in Homer's cab, riding around like we've been doing the past few days. It's become a routine of sorts: bump around in the revamped truck until eventually, the high dims enough that Quinn wants to head back to either my house or hers. I'm sure there are a million other things I could be doing, but this time with her is so fucking perfect there isn't anywhere else I would rather be.

It's been a few days since our first ride—a full week since her brother's wedding. Until today, she's been acting fine. Her smile rarely dropped, and she's even gone out of her way to come have lunch in my office with me every day. Other than when we were both at work, we haven't spent a moment apart in seven days. But right now, she seems different. Not even when she was feeling bummed about being done with the truck was she this quiet and almost fretful, like she is now.

The truck I can't stop referring to as Homer is now parked in the garage behind my house— back in his old spot, only now he doesn't stay locked up. Quinn's taken him to the shop every day since with the excuse that she just wants to keep an eye on him to make sure nothing is going wrong, but I can see through her bullshit. She's as attached to the truck as she is to the man she claims he represents.

"When do the newlyweds get back from their honeymoon?" I call to Quinn from my spot in the middle of the couch.

Up until a little while ago, she had been in this spot with me, warming my body with hers while we did more listening to the TV than watching it, seeing as we haven't been doing much focusing lately other than on each other's bodies. I'm pretty sure she would still be in my arms, letting me run my hands all over her body, if we both hadn't gotten hungry.

"Two days," Quinn mumbles, looking up briefly from the sandwiches she's making before looking away.

Her sudden shift in mood makes me pause, lowering the remote that I had been holding up to shift through the channels, waiting until she was done so we could start a movie. She was bouncing around the kitchen like she was full of happy, bubbly energy not even five minutes ago. What the hell could have happened in the time it took her to pull out sandwich shit and start putting a meal together?

"You okay?"

"Mm-hmm." She hums, nodding her head.

"You're a shit liar, darlin'. What's wrong?"

She shakes her head and continues to move around my kitchen, looking like she feels at home here in my house—exactly how I want her to feel, since I hope one day she'll be living here with me. I give her some time to work through her thoughts. If she hasn't figured out how to let me know what's bothering her by the time she sits down, I'll have to think of a more creative way to get her to speak up.

When she drops down on the couch, handing me my sandwich before leaning into my body and placing her own on her lap, she still doesn't speak.

"Quinn," I prod, trying to get her to tell me what's bothering her because she wants to, and not because I'm pulling it out of her.

A long exhale answers me back, and she tears at the corners of the paper towel she's using as a plate for her sandwich. My heart pounds while I wait her out. I can't think of a single thing that's happened this past week that would have made her look this . . . despondent.

"Maverick gets back home in two days," she whispers, still not looking at me, picking at her sandwich.

I frown. "I know, Grease, you just told me that."

Her back moves against my side as she breathes deeply and because she's so close to my body, I know that deep inhale was held tight before she blew her breath out slowly. Almost like she was using those few extra seconds to work up the courage to finish talking. Jesus, where is she going with this?

"He . . . Well, with him comin' back from their honeymoon and all, I couldn't help but remember the talk I had with Clay at the bar, and I started thinkin' about goin' out to California again. To see my mama. Him comin' home just reminded me of that."

The fog of confusion that was hanging heavily in the air between us is sliced in half instantly, giving me a clear path of certainty as I realize where her head is at.

She's nervous about talking to Maverick.

And . . . more than that, she's scared.

Not because of anything between her and me—thank God. She hasn't spoken to Maverick about this yet, not wanting to dampen the mood around his wedding, so his arrival back home after taking his new wife to some tropical beach for their honeymoon is rightfully making her nervous. This woman loves her brothers so much, respects their feelings, the last thing she wants to do is upset them. Even though she knows that Clay is on her side with this, Maverick is still an unknown, and there's nothing wrong with being nervous about how he'll react. After all, I can remember all too vividly how Maverick responded to me at first, when I was a piece of news he didn't seem to want to hear.

However, I have a feeling the majority of the fear floating around in her head is because, even with her wanting and needing this so she can move on completely, she's been weaving a fantasy for twenty-seven years around this woman and she's about to face the fact that the fantasy is really a nightmare. Going to see her mama is basically her admitting that those dreams are just that—dreams, fantasy, unreal.

If there was anything I could do to make this right in her mind and heart, I would do it in an instant, but this is a fight I can't take on for her. All I can do is stand at her side and help her forge through the battlefield.

"What if I can't do it?" she finally asks, looking up at me with desperation in her pleading eyes. "What if Maverick doesn't want me to, or maybe, even worse, if askin' him to let me go hurts him? What if I get out there and I can't even function, seein' her only tearin' me up again instead of helpin' me move on?"

"God, Quinn," I breathe, leaning forward to put the plate of food she's handed me onto the coffee table before pulling her into my lap, her back against the armrest and feet on the couch. "You're the strongest woman I know, Quinn Davis, but even the strongest people need help sometimes. There's not a damn thing wrong with that. Everything you're feelin' is normal, darlin', but I promise you, your brother is gonna support you every step of the way. That's not somethin' he's gonna do for any other reason other than because he loves you. The only thing that's gonna hurt him in all this is knowin' you seein' her will be hard on *you*. That's nothin' you can prevent, darlin', because he loves you and that's somethin' he will always feel when it comes to you feelin' heartache. If y'all get out there and you can't go through with it, then that won't make you less of a person. You makin' this decision alone shows your strength, regardless of whether you can take those final steps. It makes you human, Quinn. And anyone would struggle with this. No matter what happens, nothin' will ever touch you with the power to tear you up. Not one damn thing. Not when I'm here to make sure you stay whole."

She blinks a few times, clearing from her eyes the moisture that had formed while I spoke. "I don't want my brothers to go with me," she breathes.

I frown, and she brings up a hand to rub at the

space between my eyebrows until I feel my face relax and the frown fall away.

"You want to go out there alone?"

She shakes her head, looking unsure again.

"I only want you there," she mutters, looking down and fiddling with the end of her shirt. "You brought me back, Tate. You made me believe again, and when I think about how bad it could get there for me—there's only one person who could bring me back from that, if that's the case."

I feel the tension rush out of my body and gather her closer to me, my arms wrapped around her. I have to bite back a grunt of pain when her ass shifts awkwardly in my lap. Since we're in for the night, both of us are in loungewear, so the basketball shorts she just yanked on aren't offering much protection. Still—I pull her even tighter, pain be damned.

"Is that what you've worked yourself up worryin' about? That I wouldn't want to be there with you or somethin'?" I ask softly.

She nods. "Kinda. I think bein' scared about talkin' to Mav on top of worryin' about askin' you to come with me and not them just got the best of me. I didn't know how to tell you I needed you when it would pull you away from here. I didn't want you to feel torn after just startin' at the practice and all, but also put you in a position that you didn't exactly sign up for, Tate. Mama issues are messy, and I didn't want to burden you with that kinda stink when you've been so happy."

I kiss her temple and she shifts so that she's curled up in my lap, head against my chest as she looks up at me, one hand moving up my naked torso until she stops and rests her palm there— something I've noticed she does a lot lately—her thumb tapping softly with the beat of my heart.

"No matter what, and no matter how far, I'll follow, Quinn. Don't ever be scared to tell me you need me when that's somethin' I've spent the past nine years prayin' to God you'd feel about me again. I struggled for years knowin' me disappearin' like I did would stir up the painful memories of your mama doin' the same, Quinn. Comin' back and findin' out that you felt that pain over and over again while I was gone slashed me through the gut, but you were usin' all that— what I did, what she did, my unspoken truths and her lies—to convince yourself you were just like her when that couldn't be further from the truth, that was a knife to the heart. It would be just as excruciatin' stayin' back knowin' you would be facin' these demons again and I wouldn't be there again to slay them if you needed me to. But more than that, I want to be there because when you realize you're nothin' like her and finally see the beautiful strength inside you it's goin' to be somethin' that steals your breath, it's so powerful."

She looks up and I pull my head back just in time to miss her colliding with my chin.

"You say that like you know from experience what it'll feel like," she gasps, eyes wide with a hesitant hopefulness.

"That's because I do, baby," I answer. "The day I knew there wasn't shit keepin' me from you any longer, I called my parents—FaceTimed them, so they wouldn't be able to have a sliver of doubt as to how serious I was, bein' able to see me—and even though I knew I'd still have to fight to convince you to give us another chance, they had to know where I stood."

"And . . . where was that?"

"With you, Quinn. The same place I stood for nine years, helplessly on the sidelines miles away. I told them both that, while they might have been the reason I was alive—havin' made me and all—they wouldn't keep me from the person that keeps me breathin' one day longer. My father actually laughed at me, and I swear to God, it didn't even touch me, because I knew I had won. Not them. When I found out what had motivated my father to keep his son away from the woman he loved, I let the security of my win over his bullshit cushion the blow, and in that moment, I knew he might have cost us a lot, but in the end, we would be the ones to gain from his efforts. He finally taught me the difference between a coward and a fighter—somethin' I

306

couldn't keep from mixin' up the whole time I was away from you and powerless to change the course of my life—but in that one phone call, he at least gave me that."

"Why did he do it?" she hesitantly questions.

Knowing this moment would come eventually and having to actually go through with it are two different things. She deserves to learn what motivated him, but I also don't want her to think poorly of herself just because the man who fathered me is a spineless, misogynistic prick. My fear that she will is what kept me from telling her this weeks ago, when I explained why I stayed gone.

"He thought what he wanted was more important than what I wanted—that our family would gain something they couldn't if I was attached to a family that didn't have the bullshit social pull ours did. He had some bullshit plan that I would become a successful doctor and he could then use me as a pawn to collect more power players in his life, marry me off to someone whose family he could use to fulfill his need for supremacy. All my father saw was that I was begging him to let me be the man *I* wanted to be, not the one he tried to force me to be."

Quinn whistles slowly in disbelief. "All of this because I wasn't good enough? Everything we lost was because my family wasn't important enough for him to use?"

I shake my head, praying she understands me. "No, all of this was because he never felt like what *he* had was good enough. He craves status and wanted to use me to get him more of it. It wasn't even about you, in the long run, but about him securing a future through me that he could exploit for his own gain."

"What would have happened if he had forced you further in his game? Tried to hurt more people in order to get you to agree to be his pawn fully?"

"Never would've happened. I'm not proud of it, but he was close to pushing me to the point of no return as it was. If fate hadn't stepped in, I'm not sure I would be walkin' the earth a free man. I did what he asked. I sacrificed my happiness to keep those he threatened safe, but I still had my pride. I would have killed him or been killed before I let him have that. I didn't have you, and baby, death would have been a far less painful fate at that point."

She gasps.

"I'm not my father," I tell her, holding her gaze, speaking the words for my benefit just as much as hers.

She jolts in my arms. "I would never think you were, Tate. Does what you said shock me? Damn right it does. But I won't ever hold what he did to you—to us—against you. I know you did what you had to do and that you would have done anything to get back to me if there had been another way. The only thing I hold you accountable for, Tate, is protectin' those that you care about."

"I would die for you." I say the words softly, but there's a desperation to the truth in them.

"I know, honey," she breathes, pressing her lips against mine. "That's why I need you with me. Every step, not just to help me deal with movin' on from what my mama did. I need you with me to help me finally let go so I can give you all of me without the fear lingerin' in the back. I also want you with me so I can prove to you that I'm worthy of you after the sacrifices you made. I'm nervous beyond belief, but I'm like you—I can't let what her leavin' did to me win over the future we have before us."

God, this woman brings me to my knees. If only she knew how strong she was already just by admitting this.

"Trust me when I tell you, you're gonna feel the nerves of knowin' you're about to face somethin' that's stood in your path in some form your whole life, even with me there to shield you the best I can. Your mama might not have stood in the way like my father did, but her leavin' put a shadow on you that I think you're just now startin' to see fade. We'll go talk to your brother this weekend. If you want me there while y'all talk, I'll be there, or if you want to do that alone, I'll wait close by for that to happen. Either way, you won't be without me. We'll figure out when to go out there, get things settled at the practice and the shop, and I'll make the travel arrangements for us to go see her. However you want this to play out, I'll move mountains to make sure it happens, as long as you know that through all that, I will never let your step falter, and in the end, I'll be with you when you see the sun shinin' and that shadow around you vanish completely."

She nods, and I feel her body relax in my arms.

It won't be easy, but I meant everything I said to her. Our sandwiches lie forgotten a moment later when I rise from the couch with her in my arms and carry her to my bedroom.

Words aren't needed when I lay her down on the bed, worship her body, and show her with every part of my body just how loved she is—as we come together.

I know she's still worried about facing the last thing holding her back from moving on with her life completely. She might not be as nervous after our talk, but I have a feeling that's because she's distracted by the truth of my father's motivations. She's got a forgiving heart, thank God, but even if she does understand the reasons that kept us apart and doesn't hold that against me, when you factor in that her mama's abandonment has compounded everything she's lost over the years until she was terrified to believe she could move on without it happening again, I know this visit to her mama is even more important to her and our future than she realizes, because with her finally letting that part of her past go, there will be no stopping our future.

24

Quinn

"It Don't Hurt Like It Used To"
by Billy Currington

— ★ —

I narrow my eyes and give Barrett another
heated glare through the front window of
Davis Auto Works. He just shakes his head and
laughs at me, ignoring what I am *so* sure is one
hell of an intimidating expression. He should be
quaking in his damn boots knowing the boss is
pissed at him, but nope, not him.

I turn in a huff and look around Main Street,
not even really believing I just got kicked out of
my own damn shop. It's not even lunchtime yet
and I was such a nervous mess all morning that I
kept screwing things up. I should be thankful that
Barrett finally had enough and made me leave—
after, of course, he made sure that I wasn't upset
about anything having to do with Tate. I swear,
he was more concerned about the status of our
relationship than he was over the wiring I had
just done incorrectly on the electrical system for
the Tahoe I was working on.

I laugh to myself and kick another rock. When it almost hits Homer, I give up my pity party and acknowledge that there's only one way to get over some of these nerves. As much as I would love to run to Tate and use his strength, I need to show him I can do some of this on my own. More important, I need him to see that I believe in *myself* so that he will never doubt that I believe in *us*.

While I can admit without shame that I need him to come with me on the trip to see my mama—his adoration and strength being something I'm not willing to go without when facing her—I don't need to be afraid of my brothers, and in using Tate as a shield with them I'd set a precedent I don't want to, given that I want Tate to be around the rest of my life and all.

I think a lot of the reason I want to do this without him is because of what he confessed to me the other night. I want to prove to myself that I'm stronger than I give myself credit for. All I've ever done was hide from the things that caused me pain. I used my smile as a shield and pretended like I wasn't missing part of myself. I didn't spend years sacrificing myself for someone else like he did. I'm ready to let go and move on so that I can feel this beautiful life with no more pain from the past touching it. With Tate by my side, that will happen, I just know it. But I need to take this next step by myself. Part of me can't wait to taste the victory that Tate spoke of in awe, but just a small fraction. The bigger part of me wants to get past this on my own so I can play an active role in taking my life back, gain that for myself so that I can hopefully give him the same fulfillment that him fighting for us gave him in the end.

I'm not living with my mistakes, my mama's, or Tate's father's.

Not anymore.

I'm taking my life back, grabbing the man I love, and I will spend the rest of my days learning from my past while I create the most beautiful forever anyone has ever seen.

With that thought in mind, I climb into Homer and send a quick text to my brothers asking them to meet me at home in fifteen.

Then I call Leighton.

"This better be good," she barks after picking up. "I just had a whole dadgum bag of flour explode all over me and the kitchen. It looks like the North Pole in here!"

I snicker and wait for her to stop grumbling under her breath before I speak.

"You done?"

"I might be," she fumes. "But I also might just throw in the towel and demand my husband take me back to that stress-free, blissful island in the middle of the tropics. No one feels stress in the tropics."

"That good, huh?"

She's silent for a beat before she speaks again, her frustration gone. "Am I allowed to tell you just how *good* it was?"

"Uh, nope. No, I definitely don't want to hear about just how good it was."

"That's a shame, Q. It was sooo good. He did this thing with his—"

"Leighton, shut the hell up! Jesus Jones, we should have thought out this whole you-lovin'-my-brother thing better."

She laughs so hard she ends up snorting. "Ack! I just shot flour up my nose!"

"Serves you right, you hag! That's instant karma right there! Feel the burn, Leigh. Feel. The. Burn."

"Good heavens, who are you? A Bernie Sanders cheerleader? Hurry up and tell me why you called so I can go get this shit show in order and get outta here. I miss my husband."

I roll my eyes but smile huge, so happy for her and Maverick. "Speakin' of that husband of yours—he's the reason I called, actually."

"For the last time, I'm not going to be an accomplice so you can get him drunk and get my name tattooed on his ass."

"Hey, you actually considered that one!"

"Because I was just as drunk as you wanted to get him!" she defends.

"Well, that might be true."

"Q! Focus. What's up?"

"Oh, that. I don't want you to freak out or get all mother hen, okay?"

"No one starts a conversation like that expecting the other person to actually stay calm, you know that, right, Q?"

"I'm on my way home and I asked Mav and Clay to meet me there," I rush out.

Leigh pauses. "Ohhhkay, and why would that make me freak out?"

"I'm gonna ask Mav to arrange for me to go see Mama." If I wasn't driving down the street, this would be when I clamp my eyes shut and wait for my words to register.

"You what?!"

"It's not that big a deal, I just wanted you to know just in case he was in a mood or somethin' later. That way you would know what happened and you could, I don't know, proceed with caution?"

"Are you kiddin' me with this, Quinn Everly Davis? You wanted me to know in case he's in a mood? Have you lost your ever-lovin' mind?" She's practically screeching into the phone.

I shake my head and thump my thumb against the steering wheel. "I don't think so. I think I finally found it."

"That makes no damn sense."

I love Leigh like she's my own sister, but I don't need to explain how I feel about this to her, or to

316

anyone. Me knowing what I need to get done has to be enough now. "You don't have to understand it, Leigh. I just wanted you to be aware so you could be there for Maverick if he needs you."

"It's not Maverick that I'm freakin' worried about, Q! Maverick is the last person I'm worried about. He's done his time frettin' about that shit, and all he's done for a year is prepare himself for when this moment would come. It's *you* I'm freakin' out about. What does Clay think about this?"

"I already talked to Clay. He's supportin' me on this, Leigh. It's somethin' I need to do."

"It's somethin' you need to do?" she repeats in disbelief. "And Tate? Does he support this as well?"

My shoulders relax at the mention of Tate and I feel the worry leaving my face, my lips tipping up into a small smile. "Tate would support me if I wanted to drive to the moon."

She scoffs. "Well, that's ridiculous, you can't even drive to the . . . Oh." With the wind taken right out of her sails, she stops talking.

I laugh gently. "I love you, Leighton. You're my best friend, my sister, my strength through some hard shit, but I need you to not worry about me. You'll always be the first two, but it's time I learn how to be my own source of strength—somethin' I'm findin' isn't as dauntin' as I believed it to be."

She sniffles and I feel my nose burning, my own emotions getting wonky.

"That being said, you know how much I love you, Leigh, but when I'm done talkin' to them you're not gonna be the first person I run to. Don't spend the rest of the afternoon freakin' out, but I need to get this done alone, and when I do, it's gonna be Tate I run to after. I suspect you aren't gonna be left wonderin' what's goin' on in your snowy flour kingdom for long, though. You might think my brother's done his time frettin' about our mama, but he's still gonna fret over his sister, and you need to give him what you woulda given me when he comes to you, and we both know *you're* gonna be *his* first stop."

She lets a choked sob out, and I know if I continue this conversation I'll lose it, and I need to have my wits about me for this talk with Maverick.

"I love you and I'll call you tomorrow, 'kay?"

" 'Kay," she agrees on a final sob.

It damn near kills me, but I end the call and toss the phone in the passenger seat, just in time to downshift and pull Homer down the drive toward home. Both Clay and Maverick are sitting on the front porch, booted feet up against the rail while they move their rocking chairs slowly, appearing relaxed even thought I know it's all for show. I can see, even from my spot parked in front of the house, that Clay knows why I asked both of them here. He's holding himself in a tense way that makes me think he's bracing for Maverick not taking it well. He should give Mav more credit.

"Damn," I hear Maverick call from the porch when I climb out of Homer and shut his door with care. "This Tate's paw's old truck?"

I look up at Maverick and smile with pride. "Maverick, meet Homer."

He lets out a few deep chuckles and ambles down the steps toward me, throwing an arm over my shoulder and pulling me into his ridiculously tall body, my head smacking against his chest with a groan of protest when I feel his sweaty pit on my shoulder. I tip my head back and look up from my position under his arm and smile at him, then reach up and twist his nipple.

"What the fuck, Hell-raiser?" he grumps.

"What have I told you about puttin' your pits on me!"

He tosses his hands up in exasperation. "I hadn't even been workin' long enough for my shirt to get wet, Quinn!"

"You took a step outside and that's all you need, you big brute."

He lifts his arm and tilts his head to look at the offending pit I'm talking about, and sure enough, the material of his shirt is wet all around it and emanating a distinct odor that ain't none too pleasant. Gross, man.

I turn to see Clay standing stock-still on the top step of the porch. "Hey, big brother," I call up to him.

"You all right, Quinny?" he questions, his eyes searching mine.

"Just wanted to talk to Maverick about somethin'."

"Huh?" Maverick asks, dropping his arm and looking at me apprehensively.

"Where's Tate?" Clay asks. Getting the lay of the land, I'm sure.

"I would reckon at work, seein' as he's got patients all day," I reply smartly.

"He didn't want to come along?"

"Not sure, Clayton, I didn't tell him I was comin', but even if I had told him, he wouldn't have jumped in, knowin' I want to do this alone. For me."

"What the hell are you two goin' on about?" Maverick barks, stepping in between us while looking from Clay to me and back again.

"I'm guessin', Mav, that our big brother is just tryin' to make sure I know what I'm doing—which I do, thank you—before we go talk."

"Talk about what?"

I ignore Maverick's question and move up onto the porch, placing my hands on Clay's shoulders and pulling him down while I lift up on the toes of my boots. I kiss his jaw and lean back to look him in the eye. "I'm okay and I know what I'm doin'. I need to do this part by myself, Clay."

His throat works as he takes a big swallow, but he gives me a nod. I walk around him and into the house, waiting for them to follow me into the living room while I pace in front of the fireplace, my thoughts starting to line up in order with the soothing, repetitive movement.

I stop, turn, and face my brothers, both of whom are standing on the other side of the couch, making no move to actually sit down. Knowing it will be pointless to try and get them to sit and relax, I figure I might as well just go for broke.

"I want you to arrange for me to visit Mama at the facility that you've got her at." I hold Maverick's gaze, my chest heaving while I wait for my request to finish taking root and the shock to clear from his body.

Clay claps him on the back, encouraging him, and gives me another nod to let me know I should keep going.

"I need to let her go, Mav. I need to let myself see that she isn't the fantasy I spent my life dreamin' she would be. I need to tell her I forgive her for bein' selfish and that I'll spend my life makin' sure the man I love always knows I choose him, that I'll never abandon him or us even when things get difficult. I want to look in her eyes, even if she can't hear or understand me, and let her know that when I'm blessed with children one day, not even God himself could tear me away from them. I need to do this so I can take all the pain she made me feel over the years and drop it off with her, where it belongs."

I can see how hard he's working to keep himself in check. His whole body is coiled in an unnaturally tight way that tells me he's about to lose the hold he has on his control.

"And I need you to make those arrangements and then let me go do this without you," I add in a strong voice.

His head drops and I can't see his expression. I shoot my gaze over to Clay, and his impassive face tells me nothing. We stand like this for what feels like forever while Maverick works through what I just told him. I keep looking between Clay and the top of Mav's cowboy hat, my heart in my throat.

I'm about to start panicking that I hurt my brother by asking him to let me do this alone, and then Clay clears his throat.

"Look at me, brother," he tells Maverick, his voice hard but full of respect as he keeps his eyes on me when he says it. When Maverick lifts his head and looks at Clay, only then does Clay look away from me and focus completely on Mav. "You spent a long time keepin' this to yourself, thinkin' you had to in order to keep us from feelin' that pain. You did the right thing by not holdin' that in, no matter how much knowin' why Mama left us stung, but you also gave both of us a chance to move on and heal with that truth. You knew this day would come, but I need you to fight against what's inside you tellin' you to protect Quinn. She's got a damn good man who's doin' that for us now. We'll always be there just in case, but you gotta let her do this. Don't deny her knowin' she's gotta let go of that hurt in order to move on and find what you got with Leigh."

I can't hold in my emotions now. I know I'm seconds away from breaking out into an ugly cry.

"Fuck!" Maverick bellows, making me jump. A sob escapes my throat, and I hate it for betraying what his silence is making me feel. His eyes shift to me, focusing with a steely force that makes me rock from side to side while I wait under his probing gaze. "You really don't want us there?" he finally asks, and I feel the meaning behind his question right in my heart.

His hushed, defeated tone spurs me into motion, and I breach the distance between us instantly, walking around the couch to stand in front of both my brothers. They normally keep this part of themselves hidden—the vulnerable side that we all share from the bond built among us during our tornadic upbringing. I gaze up at

323

them, hoping that they can stop seeing me as the little sister that they have to guard from pain and set me free—not only by helping me move past what Mama did, but also to build a life with the man that's taken the top spot in my heart.

"I love you both more than you'll ever know, but yes, I need you to let me do this without you. Mav, you've spent enough time cleanin' up her mess, and you don't need to go back to that. Clay'll figure her out on his own time and I know his comin' along would force his hand in dealin' with her before he's ready. And," I sigh and shrug, feeling the power of Tate's love slam into me right when I need it the most, filling me with the words I need to use to make Maverick see. "Tate's here now, and with him I've got my heart back, Mav. He spent a long time missin' that part of me too. You don't live without that for all those years and not want to protect it the best you can. He'll be there to pick me up if I stumble, help heal me if I feel pain, but it's up to *me* to take this last step and solidify that protection myself. I want to do this for him just as much as I do for myself, so I can move on without her pullin' me back, but I *need* to do this for me so I can finally let go."

He rocks forward and wraps his arms around me, pulling me into his chest, where I feel his heart pounding under my head. Clay moves in next, wrapping his strong arms around both of us. I feel my knees buckle when I remember all the times over the years that we would find ourselves in a similar huddle. When we would feel the absence of our mama, not knowing why she didn't love us; when our father would start spewing his hate; or any other time we just needed to draw strength off each other. It was times like this that would make me believe that no matter what life threw at us, the Davis kids *always* had this. That will never change: even when, years from now, we've built our own families, the core of us will always be here.

"I'll make the call tonight," Maverick mumbles into my hair, still holding me tight.

"Thank you," I tell him, my words muffled against his chest. Pulling the arm smooshed between Clay's stomach at my side, I wrap it around him and hold both my brothers a little tighter. "I love you guys. Thank you for lettin' me go."

Maverick guffaws. "We ain't lettin' you go, Quinny, we're not ever gonna do that, but we'll stand by and let another man—the *right* man—keep you safe while we support you from the side."

And there go the tears again.

I don't leave for another hour, the three of us not doing any talkin' but piled on the old couch and lettin' a television show be the excuse we give for the delay, when all three of us know we just want to be near each other a little longer.

When I head out, waving out the window of Homer, there's only one place I want to go, and that's into the arms of the man that's helped me get to this place of healing.

The man I love.

25

Tate

"What Ifs" by Kane Brown

— ★ —

W"hat can I do?" I ask Quinn for the tenth time since we walked into the long-term facility that her mama's been staying at for the past few years.

It's a nice place, to be sure, and for anyone else it would probably scream *welcoming* and *comforting,* letting family and friends know that their loved ones are being cared for in an environment they can visually trust.

To me, it feels like hell.

Not because of anything they're doing, but because I can see the nervous fear on Quinn's face as her eyes swing around the room. She's been doing this since the nurse Maverick arranged to meet with us left to go make sure her mama's been moved to a private room where visitors can have a moment with the people they care about without being stuck in a hospital room.

I've got to hand it to the place—from a doctor's standpoint, it's a top-notch facility. It's evident they encourage visitors, seeing that they go to great lengths to ensure a level of comfort in those visits that most long-term care places just aren't financially able to. It tells me that Maverick, despite everything this woman did to her children, didn't spare a single expense when it came to her care.

I'm not sure I would do the same thing if my own mama needed something like this. I haven't spoken to my parents in months, and that will never change. To me, they died nine years ago.

"Do you think I'll recognize her?" she asks, not looking away from the family of four that looks to be sharing a quiet, happy moment on the other side of the waiting room. A young mother with her three small children, in fact. What are the odds?

"I'm not sure, darlin'," I answer honestly, reaching over to take her hand in mine. "There's nothin' wrong with not recognizin' her, Quinn, so stop worryin' yourself over it. You were too young when she left to have a clear picture of her like your brothers do, and you can't fault yourself for not havin' pictures to remember her by."

She looks up, the fear in her eyes making them look murky. "Shouldn't a daughter be able to feel a connection to the woman who birthed her? What if I don't have that?"

I squeeze her hand. "Then you don't, baby. That's not on you. Would you be able to pick your brothers out in a crowd?"

"I could find them with my eyes closed," she confirms breathily.

"Then, Grease, your heart knows what's important."

She nods, looks back at the young family in the corner, and nods again to herself. I leave her to her thoughts and pray that what happens this afternoon doesn't hurt her more than heal.

A week ago, she showed up at the office just after lunch. I was in an examination room with a patient, but Gladys pulled me aside when I stepped out for the woman to get undressed and told me that Quinn was waiting in my office. I could tell by looking at Gladys that whatever brought Quinn here was unusual. Gladys looked troubled and concerned.

I don't think I've ever finished a yearly exam quicker. Even my nurse, Rebecca, looked at me like I was insane.

I found Quinn smiling through her tears in my office, and after I frantically tried to get out of her what was going on, she said she went to see Maverick and that he was on board with her seeing their mama and would set things up.

By the next day, I'd rescheduled my patients and made all the travel arrangements. Quinn hadn't wanted to wait, but I purposely set up a weeklong gap between her talk with Maverick and us getting to California so that she'd have time to really make sure this was what she wanted. I didn't do it to talk her out of it, but to give her a safety net if she wanted it.

Clearly she didn't, because we're sitting in the middle of a Los Angeles facility for the mentally ill and those medically incapable of caring for themselves.

"Ms. Davis?" the nurse calls, pulling me from my thoughts, and I stand quickly as Quinn scrambles nervously to her feet. She reaches behind her, blindly searching for my hand, and I instantly grab hold and tighten my grip. "We've got your mother ready in the green room. It's one of the favorites amongst our patients. Nice and soothing, with a tropical theme."

Quinn hums in acknowledgment but doesn't speak. I can feel a slight tremble in her hand, and I know I need to do something to ease her mind before she walks into the unknown.

"I don't know how much your brother told you about your mother's health. I've been here for about two years and I wish I could say things were better, but she's gotten a lot weaker lately. She won't be able to talk to you, but I assure you that she can hear what you're saying. She's quite the fighter, that one," the nurse recites in a monotone, as though she's rehearsed this speech a thousand times before.

I don't roll my eyes, but inside I'm ashamed that this woman can't at least act like she isn't reading a manual on how to deal with patients' families. I know just how bad off Quinn's mother is, because I had Maverick get her medical history sent to me. Her liver and kidneys are failing. Her heart is weak. Her lungs keep filling with fluid. She's on dialysis and taking heavy narcotics for the constant pain she feels, and her last checkup showed signs of dementia.

She is, in simple terms, a mess.

"Can we have a moment please?" I ask the nurse when she brings us to a stop in front of the green door.

"Of course," she says with a fake-as-hell smile, not looking me in the eye. "When you're ready, just head in. If you need anything, let us know. I do need to make you aware that sometimes Mrs. Davis gets . . . agitated. Don't be alarmed if that happens. Just press the red button directly next to the bathroom door and we'll be right there."

"We've got it covered," I tell her impatiently.

I wait for her to walk to the nurses' station five doors down, giving us her back while she talks to some of the other nurses seated behind the desk. Then I turn to Quinn and wish I could erase this whole visit from her mind.

"I want you to listen to me, Grease." I search her eyes and hold both her hands in my own. "Whatever happens in there, I want you to remember that the family that matters to you is waitin' for you back in Pine Oak. Your brothers and Leigh, they care about you so much there isn't anything they wouldn't do for you. Their unconditional love, understandin', and support will always be there for you. And baby, you've got me. There's nothin' in the world I wouldn't do for you. You didn't need that woman in there to mold you into the bright, compassionate, and lovin' woman that you are today, and when you walk out that door later, you damn sure aren't gonna need her then. Don't forget that. You're loved, baby, more than you could ever imagine."

Her shoulders relax and she closes her eyes and drops her forehead to my chest, mumbling something I can't quite hear.

"What's that, Grease?"

She does it again and I smile.

"You're gonna have to speak to me and not my chest, darlin'."

When she looks up, the anxiety that hasn't left her since we landed four hours ago is gone and she finally looks like *my* Quinn again. I lift my hand and push her loose hair behind her ear, resting my hand against her neck, and I smile down at her. Her eyes drop to my mouth and I get the first grin beaming from her since last night.

Her luminous green eyes jump back to mine. "I love you."

My fucking God.

It's the first time she's initiated it, said it out

loud, clear as day. She's mouthed it. She's hinted at it. But this is the first time I've gotten from her those words I've ached so long to hear.

"I love you more than ever. I owe you for makin' me realize what really matters."

"God, Quinn." I exhale. "I love you too, darlin'. You ready?"

"Yeah, Tate . . . I think I am."

I press a kiss against her lips and wait for her to open the door. She takes a fortifying breath, turns the knob, and walks inside.

I'm not sure what I expected to see when I saw her mama for the first time. Medically, I knew she wouldn't look good, but seeing a woman that looks so much like Quinn on her deathbed knocks me for a loop so hard I struggle to breathe.

"Jesus Jones," Quinn whispers, her eyes not leaving the woman who's staring at the door.

I can see the alarm in the older woman's eyes—the bright green eyes that mirror those of the woman I love. Her raven-black hair that appears to be as thick and lustrous as Quinn's, only streaked with tiny hints of gray.

"She looks just like me." Quinn steps forward and I let the door shut behind us, not willing to stay far from her. "In all the years I imagined what she would look like, it was never like me."

Her mama starts to shake her head, the heart monitor showing an increase in speed. I don't want to rush Quinn, but if her mama continues to get agitated, I don't think Quinn is going to be allowed to come back anytime soon.

"You know who I am," Quinn tells her mama in a clear, halting voice. "I used to dream about you, you know. I would conjure up these beautiful stories where you would speed back into town and grab your children in a warm hug and tell us how much you missed us, but you had somethin' so important to do and you got back as soon as you could. Spent *years and years* dreamin' that, thinkin' I needed you to be complete." She stops talking and points over her shoulder. Her mama's eyes follow her movement. I don't relax the expression of harsh judgment on my face and she flinches. "That man filled me right up and completed every single jagged piece your abandonment created inside me. One day I'm gonna beg him to marry me, then I'm gonna give him babies, and then, *Mama,* I'm gonna love him and those babies until the day I die and there won't be a soul on earth that could tear me away from them. I forgive you for being selfish enough to love yourself more than your family, and I even thank you for runnin' off, since your actions gave Clay and me our brother. Even with a mama that only loved herself, my brothers and me know how to love others, and we definitely can't thank you for that."

Done with her speech, Quinn turns and looks up at me with shining eyes. I look away to see her mama wide-eyed and starting to get even more upset. I glance at the screen showing her vital signs before looking back down at Quinn.

"You got everything you need to say out?" I mutter to her.

"I did." She nods and takes a breath. "It's over."

"Make sure you got nothin' left, baby."

She looks back at her mama, seein' the distress in the woman's face. "I hope you find the peace you need, even if it isn't until after you've left this earth. Good-bye, Mama."

I watch the monitors while Quinn talks, and the second she finishes speaking, I reach up and press the red button the nurse told us to hit when we were done. We're out of the room and down the hall before the nursing staff has even left their station to settle Mrs. Davis.

"You okay?" I ask Quinn, pulling her under my arm and tight to my side.

She glances up, nods, and finally smiles back at me. "I'm perfect."

26
Quinn

"Circles" by Jana Kramer

— ★ —

D o you want to call your brothers?"
I turn from the window I've been gazing
out of since we got back, focusing on nothing,
just staring down at the busy street below us
while my mind wandered, and look at Tate. He's
sitting up in the middle of the bed, pillows all
around him, looking like some sort of sex god.

We returned to the hotel about thirty minutes
ago, and the first thing both of us did was kick
off our boots. He went a step further and yanked
off the button-down he was wearing, leaving
him in just a plain white undershirt and his dark
denim jeans. His crossed legs were the only thing
I could see reflected in the window and before he
spoke, I was trying to figure out why I thought
his feet were so damn sexy.

"I can think of a million other things I would
rather do right now than call them."

"They're gonna worry about you, darlin'.
They know what time we were goin' to be there

for our appointment, and they're not gonna wait much longer for you to let them know you're okay."

I roll my eyes, but I know he's right. I'm shocked that they actually haven't called yet, to be honest. "Do you know where my phone is?"

He nods and points to the other side of our suite, where the small living room area is. I walk over, see my phone, and nab it off the coffee table, dialing Clay quickly before I can let myself avoid making the call any longer. It isn't that I don't want to call them—I'm just still processing everything. But Tate's right; knowing my brothers, it's taking everything in them not to hop a plane right now and come after me as it is, so I owe them an update.

"Are you okay?" Clay says rapidly in lieu of a greeting, the phone not even ringing once before I hear him coming through the line.

"Hello, Clayton, how are you?" I smile, glancing at Tate with a roll of my eyes.

"Quinn, fuckin' swear to God," he fumes under his breath, his worrying getting the best of his normally calm and cool demeanor.

"Chill, Clay. I'm okay, big brother. More than okay, actually. I feel like a rock I didn't know was attached to my leg, weighin' me down with each step, has finally been cut off."

A loud exhale comes through the line. Hearing that noise, I realize how wound up he's been about all this and I'm glad that Tate pressed me to call sooner than later.

"One day, when you're ready, you'll come for yourself and see what I mean, Clay."

Clay's tone hardens. "That day'll never come, Quinny. Don't set your heart on that shit. I don't need that and I never will. You'll only end up disappointed if you're waiting for it to happen."

"Clay—"

"Not now, sugar. A fight for another day, okay? I won't bend, but you're welcome to go at it until you're blue in the face if it makes you feel better. You promise me, Quinny, you're really okay?"

I continue to hold Tate's gaze across the suite, him still watching me intently, and smile. "I'm not feelin' like I'm missin' her anymore, Clay. I've got everything I've ever wanted right here in front of me. I've moved on from the fantasy of her I held onto, and I've got my heart back. I'm a little sad, but I've let somethin' go today that needed to be let go so I can finally move on with my life and get nothin' except beauty for the rest of my days."

Clay clicks his tongue before humming a low sound of agreement.

"I'm gonna call Mav now and tell him the same thing, big brother."

"He's right here, sugar, so not necessary. He's probably breathin' a whole helluva lot easier now that he's finally heard your voice, though."

"When I get home, we'll sit down and talk so you guys can see for yourselves that I'm fine, but right now, I've got a doctor that needs a checkup."

I hear two groans coming from the other end of the line, and I feel my smile amp up a few more notches closer to insane happy levels. They make it too easy.

"I love you guys," I tell them, putting them out of their misery, still smiling like a loon.

"Love you back, Quinny," they say in unison.

"I'll come over when we get home tomorrow, okay?"

They agree, and we disconnect without any more fanfare. I can talk to them about Mama when I get back, but I wasn't kidding when I said that right now, I would rather decompress with my man and not my brothers.

I toss the phone onto the couch and walk toward Tate. He drops the room-service menu he was reading before I've even taken a few steps and uncrosses his legs, giving me silent confirmation that he knows what I'm after.

"You want somethin', Grease?" he asks with a knowing smirk as I start to climb onto the bed.

From my position, legs spread, with my knees digging into the mattress, hands on either side of his hips and my face directly above his crotch—I give him a sly smile and arch one brow without speaking. He laughs deeply, his chest rumbling

339

with a titillating sound that shoots through my body in one delicious wave.

"Pretty sure you know what I want," I answer in a hushed tone.

"That so?"

He leans farther back into the pillows and lifts his arms to rest his hands behind his head. I feel his legs shift, the top of his knee whispering against the material covering my crotch.

"You did that on purpose," I accuse with a shiver of awareness.

His brow quirks. "Did what?"

I narrow my eyes. Well, if that's how he wants to play it.

Leaning back, I sit my ass on his legs and reach forward to his belt. Some of the cocky arrogance falls from his face when he sees my intention. He might think he can't make me drunk off the need I feel for him—which probably isn't too far off the mark—but after today, I feel like I could take on the world and win . . . starting with Tate Montgomery. He won't gain the upper hand in the bedroom this evening.

The sound of his belt releasing echoes around the room. I give a tug, indicating for him to lift without words and the second his ass is off the bed I give the belt a yank, pulling it from the loops on his jeans. It hits the floor, the sound a loud *thwack!* in the silence, and I jump, so completely lost in him that I can't focus on my task, my fumbling hands undoing the fastenings on his pants. The whole time, my eyes don't leave his, so I'm rewarded with witnessing the color of his arousal as it heats his cheeks. I tap his hips at the sides and he lifts again, giving me enough room to pull his jeans down far enough that I can get to what I want with nothing hindering me.

I place my palm on top of his erection as I roll my body forward, the heat from him radiating through his black briefs as I lean over him, stroking him. When my face gets level to his, I turn before giving his lips the kiss they're after and press my lips against his chin. I pepper kisses slowly, along his jaw, to the spot under his ear that drives him insane. Then I lean back slightly to take his earlobe between my lips, giving him a nip with my teeth.

He grunts, and then an animalistic vibration shoots from his mouth in a low rumble, making me throb between my legs. I suck in a harsh breath as I shift my body back down, my jeans rubbing against me again, the pull of air carrying a strong scent of his cologne. They work together to create a dizzying feeling that rushes through all my senses. My head spins as I feel instantly drunk off him.

No longer able to wait, I reach into the gap in his briefs and pull out his long, thick erection. He hisses, and as much as I would love to see his face, I'm a girl on a mission. The wet drop of his arousal beading at the tip of his cock calls to me, the pull so strong that I moan before opening my mouth, bending over, and enveloping him in my mouth.

I feel him move until his abs are touching the top of my head, and out of the corner of my eyes I see him fisting the comforter on both sides of his body. In my head, I picture his face contorted in pleasure as he hunches over me, overcome by the feelings my mouth on his cock brings forth. As much as I love seeing his expression when he's this close to losing control, I'm not stopping now. My cheeks pull inward as I suck even harder, the sound of my suction vibrating through the gap on the side of my mouth where the air pulls through against his cock. My mouth waters when I feel a tiny burst of his come escape. Somehow, he still holds himself back, but that small taste is all it takes for me to become mad with need.

"Fuckin' Christ," he hisses when my hand reaches down between us and rolls his balls gently, the cotton of his briefs holding the hot skin from my touch, but not hindering the pleasure I know he feels from this.

I could spend hours moving my mouth on his steely length, but I know he's close to snapping when he releases his fists holding the bedding and gathers my loose hair into a ponytail before he starts feeding me his cock—his hold on my hair moving me down while his hips lift up off the mattress—taking control over how much and how fast I suck him. I breathe through my nose and relax the back of my throat the best I can, taking him so deep I gag on him.

That sound, me gagging on his huge cock, seems to be enough to make the hold he has over his control shatter. I squeal when suddenly, his cock isn't in my mouth anymore and *I'm* the one lying against the mattress with him now kneeling between my spread legs. His chest is heaving, his wet cock pressed against his cotton-covered stomach looking almost painfully hard. No words are spoken between us as he lifts both my legs at the same time, his hands on my ankles, and puts each against one of his thick shoulders. His hands go to my waist to undo the denim, his deft fingers moving quickly; then he hooks his hands in the waistband and yanks my jeans and panties down. He drags the material upward until it's bunched at the ankles resting against his shoulders, then pauses.

What I see in his face is nothing short of pure payback. My eyes widen at the same time one of his arms wraps around my bound legs—holding it even more captive than my jeans and panties are—before he bends slightly and reaches down. The dark glint of desire flaming brighter in his eyes is the only warning I get before he's filling me instantly with two thick fingers, the knuckles pressing against the wet entrance when he's gotten them as deep as possible.

"Tate!" My head thrashes back and forth, the pleasure mixing with the slight pain of him stretching me overwhelming my senses.

"You like teasin' me, darlin'?" he questions, pulling his fingers out before thrusting them deep and holding them there again. "Answer me."

I nod. "Love it." Swallowing the lump in my throat, I whimper when he twists his wrist and hooks his fingers in a come-hither motion. I swear, my eyes cross in that moment, him touching something deep inside of me that makes my heart start pounding violently in my chest.

"You drive me insane. It's maddening how much I crave this pussy." His nostrils flare, and again, I hear myself whine. "Fuck, Quinn, I'll never get enough of you."

He pulls his fingers from my body, sucking them deep in his mouth while his other hand finishes pulling my jeans and panties the rest of the way off. He moves and shuffles down the bed, dropping my legs with a bounce against the mattress as he pushes to stand, his jeans falling from his knees to the ground. I watch dizzily as he pulls his shirt off and steps out of his pants. When I see his toned, naked body, it sparks me into moving, and I lift up to yank my own shirt and bra off. His gaze goes right to my heavy, needy breasts when they fall free from my bra with a bounce.

I watch him as his eyes roam over my chest and shiver when he licks his lips. My boobs jiggle and he doesn't miss the movement, raising his glance to mine again. We stare at each other, both of us breathing heavy, chests heaving, each just as needy for the other.

The air around us seems to come alive the moment our eyes connect. The urgency dims and something changes what's driving us. A giant and beautiful sense of calm falls over me, something I see mirrored in his own expression. The frantic need we both felt just moments before is knocked to the side as I feel the love I have for him meeting the love he has for me in space and time, crashing between us and falling against our naked bodies with a sprinkling of goose bumps.

He doesn't rush.

I don't want him to.

He reaches his hands out and I immediately put mine in his. He tugs ever so softly and I follow his silent demand until I'm standing before him. His hands drop from mine and I shiver when he places both palms on my hips, dragging them painfully, slowly up until they've reached the sides of my breasts. His eyes never leave mine as he cups both heavy globes and thumbs my nipples, his fingers flexing against my flesh as I grow wetter between my legs.

Sensation shoots through my body and zaps my clit. I moan and shift on my feet. Not looking away, he lowers his head and ravishes each nipple with his flat tongue. One lick, and the wetness makes the cool air of the room feel like ice. I lose his hands when he straightens until he's grabbing me right under my ass and lifting my body into the air, pulling me against his. My legs wrap around his hips, hooking at the ankles, and my arms go around his neck.

Our mouths collide, slowly at first, but then he starts thrusting his hardness against my pussy. I can smell the scent of my arousal as the motion pushes it up between us. I know he notices too when he pulls in a harsh breath and deepens the kiss.

His tongue rubs against mine and he lifts me away with the hold he has under my ass, my hands lifting to tangle in the hair at the back of his head. I feel the blunt tip of his cock tapping against my entrance twice before he slowly feeds himself into my body. Unable to handle the fullness of him going so deep, his hold on me opening my body in a way that I haven't experienced with him before, I gasp and pull from his mouth, my lips feeling swollen and bruised from our kiss. My nipples rub against his chest, his thrusts slow and so deep I know I'll feel him long after he's left my body.

It isn't the delicious feel of his thickness hitting me deeper than ever before that makes me inhale sharply, though. It's the love shining brighter than anything I've ever seen in his ocean-blue eyes. They're alight with feeling. He's open, completely and beautifully open, pushing his emotions forward so they're projected straight into my soul.

I hiccup, a soft sob rippling up and out of my throat.

He seats himself deep inside me and holds my body against him, his sweat-slicked forehead pressing against mine as he continues to gaze into the darkest parts of my soul.

"I've loved you since I was eleven, Quinn Davis, and I'll love you until I'm one hundred and eleven. You have no idea how proud I am to call you mine, and after today, you showin' me just how strong you are, baby, that pride is somethin' that brings me to my knees." His fingers flex and he pulls me closer, going even deeper. "There will never be a day you aren't feelin' my love for you, baby. I'll spend the rest of my life makin' sure you never, ever, regret givin' us this again."

My eyes close as he tightens his arms, holding me to him, pressing me closer to him as he brushes his lips against my cheeks, catching each of my tears as they slowly fall from my eyes.

"I love you, Grease."

I shudder a breath. "I love you, Starch."

27
Tate

"Brace for Impact (Live a Little)"
by Sturgill Simpson

— ★ —

I shut the door of the truck that Quinn just jumped down from and turn to follow her up the walk to her house, some lingering exhaustion still clinging to me even with the long nap we had when we got back to my house from the airport. Even though we were only in California for a short time, it was enough for the trip to drain us both.

My cell vibrates when I reach Quinn's side, and I pull it out of my pocket to see the word *unknown* on the display.

"How do your patients expect you to call them back if they're callin' from an unknown number?"

"No clue," I mumble, putting my cell back in my back pocket and pulling Quinn into my body with one arm over her shoulder as we continue to walk up to the porch.

"Did they leave a message this time?"

"No message. Must not be an emergency." Even as I say the words, I don't completely believe them. "I need to talk to Russ about gettin' us hooked up with an answerin' service. They could filter out the calls that need to reach me and avoid leavin' me worryin' that someone needs medical care."

Quinn hums and leans into my side. "That would beat you handin' out your private number to each one of those floozies that come into your practice."

I snort out a laugh and look down at her, careful as we steer our way up the porch steps of her and Clay's house. "You make it sound like they got pregnant just to get my number, Grease."

"Well, if you weren't my man I'm pretty sure I would be desperate to get that number myself."

I shake my head but smile at her crazy logic.

When we got home earlier this morning, I called her brothers to let them know we would be over later. As much as I knew they wanted to see her, her emotions were in overload territory and it was my job to help carry that load for her. They didn't like it, but they gave us the time we needed. It was a good thing too, seeing that she could hardly hold her body up to just walk through the airport, falling asleep the second she buckled up in my truck before we even pulled out of the parking spot.

I drove us back to my house and carried her

to my bed. She didn't wake up once during all that until about an hour ago. While we were sleeping, I got an abnormal number of missed calls, though, and it's been nagging at me ever since. The majority were from her brothers, three from the office, two unknown numbers . . . and one from my parents' number.

It was that last call from my parents that was making me the most uneasy. They know better than to call. I made sure the last time I spoke to them that they knew never to contact me. It's kind of hard to argue with someone when they say they want you to forget they were ever born—that they should consider you dead to them forever.

They had never given me a single hint that they actually had hearts residing inside of the two of them, so I doubt they're calling to set up a reunion. No, something forced them to make that call. I'm just not sure I ever want to find out what it was.

"Hey!" Quinn calls out into the house after opening the front door and walking inside. I trail in after her, my mind still a million miles away. "I figured they would at least be around since they knew we were on the way," she huffs while her eyes roam through the parts of the house she can see from where she's standing just inside the entryway.

I shut the door and walk up behind her, not

wanting her far from my touch with the unsettled nerves twisting my thoughts. Right before I reach out, my thoughts shift from her to the phone vibrating in my back pocket again.

"Hey," Maverick says with a deep grunt, coming out of the kitchen and hugging his sister. "I just called you," he says to me, holding his phone up and shaking it.

"Felt it, but we were walkin' up so figured I would check it later. My phone's been going off since we got back." I didn't realize I had been holding myself so tensely until he said he was the one that made my phone go off just now.

"Everything okay?"

"Gladys called a few times, but it was just some patients with questions. Other than that, yeah, nothin' I need to deal with at the moment."

He nods, brushing me off, but not in a rude way. He's worried about his sister and that's taking precedence in his mind right now. "And you? You okay?" he asks Quinn, his green eyes searching her face for clues as to how she's feeling.

I look down and watch her lips, feeling my chest get tight when she smiles up at her brother. I'll never get sick of seeing that smile.

"I told you yesterday on the phone that I'm fine, Mav. Honestly, I am."

I hear Clay stomping into the room, but I don't look away from her.

"You sure about that, sugar?"

She looks over at Clay when she hears his voice, and I lose sight of her smile. She doesn't answer right away, moving away from me to give Maverick a hug before stepping in front of Clay.

"Positive." She turns, the braid she pulled her hair into before we left swinging in an arc, and beams that heart-stopping smile at me. "Plus I had one hell of a support system with me."

I feel my face get soft as I smile at her. She winks before looking away and giving Clay a hug.

"Where's Leigh?" Quinn asks as she steps back and into my side.

"She's at the PieHole dealing with some prep for tomorrow or somethin', I don't know. Said she wanted to have her mornin' clear for some girl time with you, but I think she really just got sick of dealin' with his broodin'," Clay says with a gruff laugh, pointing at a scowling Maverick.

"Ask," Quinn says to Maverick, sighing and ignoring her brother's joke.

He frowns, giving her his back as he walks toward the kitchen. Taking it as a hint, we all follow, and she grabs my hand before we step into the room.

"I'm just worried about you," Maverick says, holding the back of his neck as he leans against the counter. "Seein' her wasn't easy for me, Quinny, but I hadn't been thinkin' she was some kind of fairy-tale mama. It couldn't have been that easy on you, darlin'."

Quinn walks over to the island directly across from him and hops onto it. I stand next to her with my hip against the counter and let her run the show. I look up, seeing her studying Maverick with a reserved look of love and acceptance—no pain—before glancing back at him.

"What do you want to hear? That it sucked seein' her? It did, but probably not because of what you're thinkin'. Mav, I felt nothin'. Not one thing gave me a connection to her other than the fact that I clearly favor her in looks. I walked in there and it was like lookin' in a freakin' mirror. I think that shocked me at first, but after that, nothin'. It was like everything I had ever thought I would feel if I saw her vanished. The things I thought I needed from her didn't matter anymore. All I felt was pity for her."

"Pity? You felt sorry for her?" Clay asks, a hard, bitter tone to his voice.

She turns, looks at me, and takes a deep breath. I can't tell what's she's thinking, but I know what she's telling her brothers, what they want to believe, is true. She really is okay. I press a ghost of a kiss against her lips and she pulls back, rolling her forehead against mine on her way to look back at her brothers as they lean against the counter in front of her.

"Yeah," she breathes, then clears her throat

353

before finishing. "I felt sorry for her because she left. She left and because of that, she's missed this," she says, lifting her hand and pointing between the three of them. "She'll never know what a strong man her eldest son is, how he protects us and worries about us like a parent and not a brother. She won't get a chance to know the proud and courageous man her middle son is. How he beat all the odds to take back the life he wanted. And, well . . . she won't know me. So yeah, I feel bad, because in my book, we have the whole world together and she's got nothin'."

"Christ," Maverick whispers under his breath.

"Fuckin' hell," Clay hisses.

I give the hand I had been holding a squeeze and let go when her brothers both push off the counter and step toward her. I want them to have this moment with her, alone.

"I'll be outside, darlin'."

She leans over and gives me a kiss before I turn and walk out of the Davis house with a full fucking heart knowing that I'm one lucky son of a bitch and the woman that I love with all my damn heart doesn't have a single fucking ghost clouding her eyes when she looks at me anymore.

Fuck, does it feel good.

When I got back to Pine Oak six weeks ago, I was too afraid to believe that I would actually win my fight for Quinn. I was determined, that's for sure, but fuck, was I nervous. Now here I am, her love given to me freely and her trust earned.

I glance over the pasture to the stables, seeing everyone down there busy at work. It's getting to be the end of a long workday and I bet they're ready to get home.

I take a deep breath and look up at the cloudless sky. The sun is shining and there isn't a single thing about the day around me that isn't perfect—except for the feeling crawling up my back. There's something in the air, and even with everything in my life sailing smoothly, I feel a storm rolling in.

"Shit," I hiss under my breath.

28

Quinn

"Ain't Always Pretty" by Logan Mize

— ★ —

You ready to head out, Starch?" Tate jumps when I step out on the porch, and I stifle my laugh. "Whoa there, cowboy. What's got you so jumpy?"

His eyes flash at my joke, but just as quickly as it comes, it's gone, a neutral expression in its place. I frown but write it off as him just being overwhelmed and exhausted from our trip. Even though the trip was tough for me, the quick back-and-forth must have taken its toll on him, too.

"Just tired, darlin'," he answers, confirming my thoughts. "You sure you don't want to stay here tonight?"

I smile and wrap my arms around his stomach, looking up at him as I hug myself to him. "As much as I appreciate you makin' sure I don't want to be with my brothers right now, my place is with you, honey. Mav is about to head home and Clay's headed over to Coal Creek tonight to meet up with some friends of his. They know where I want to be, so they didn't make plans to be here tonight."

His lips hit my forehead and I close my eyes in contentment, his arms tightening slightly around my shoulders.

"That's what I like to hear."

"Well, then take me to bed or lose me forever, Starch." I giggle, trying to keep a straight face.

He starts to smile, but when I feel the vibration of his phone under my clasped hands resting on top of his belt, he frowns, lines of stress forming between his eyes as his lips thin.

He doesn't move.

"What is it?" I ask apprehensively.

"This time? Not sure."

"Then what has you holdin' yourself so tense?"

I feel his heartbeat pounding against my chest, and a slight ripple of unease twists through my body.

"Someone called from my parents' number a few hours ago."

A flash of cold slams through my senses before I can prevent it. I know what he's said about his parents, and that alone makes me feel panic. I know he meant what he said about never letting them control us again, but still . . . They probably aren't calling to get a status update on our relationship and ask when the damn wedding is.

"And?"

"I'm not sure what to do with it, to be honest."

"Do they know about us?" I ask, trying to push back the worry.

He nods. "They know I was set on gettin' back what they stole from us. I doubt they know that I've been successful, though."

I take a deep breath and calm my roaring heart. I didn't get this far just to let someone else come between us again. "Well, honey, let's get in the truck and call them back on the way to your house. No sense in letting them darken our day any longer," I tell him with a deadly calm tone. His body deflates slightly at my words and I roll up to my toes to press a kiss against his jaw. "I love you, Tate. One battle at a time. We're almost at the finish line of the past and it's time we take those final strides so we can finally start our new life together."

Some of the harshness in his face softens and he takes a deep breath. "I love you."

I wink. "I know."

His chest moves as he laughs, and I feel my own worry wash away when he seems to return to his normal, confident self. I get a deep kiss from him after I climb into the passenger seat of his truck before he shuts the door and walks around the hood. He climbs in a moment later and starts the truck, turning and driving to the end of the long driveway.

When he reaches the turnoff, he pulls his phone out, looking down at the screen before glancing over at me. "You mind if I call them before we pull out of here? No offense to your family place and all, but I hope one day my house will be yours too, and I don't really want to bring my parents near there . . . even if it is with just a phone call."

Jesus Jones, if my heart could get any bigger, my love for this man just continues to grow. I shake my head and relax in my seat, letting him know I'm good. He nods and looks back to his phone, his fingers moving over the screen. It's only a short few minutes' drive to his house, but still, I'm glad he's making this call before we get there.

Tate presses the call-back button and puts the phone on speaker.

"Too busy in that backwoods town to answer the phone, Tatum?"

I jump when a nasal, high-pitched male voice answers. The man I assume is Tate's father sounds just as spineless as I know him to be. Good Lord, I'm glad his son didn't get his voice.

"What do you want?" Tate asks, voice harsh and tense.

I scoot as close as I can, with the center console in the way, and see his fingers tense around the steering wheel, his knuckles turning white with the pressure. I place my hand on his thigh, giving him a gentle squeeze so he knows I'm here if he needs me. He looks down and the second my touch registers, he rips one of his hands free and wraps it around mine.

"What do I want?" The man laughs and I suppress a shudder when the mirthless, vile sound echoes around the cab. Tate's hold on my hand jerks. "A few months ago, my good-for-nothin' son told me he was runnin' back to the trash in Fisher's old town. You made it clear then that any association between us was to be severed. What *I* want is to know why your bullshit is floatin' up to darken my doorstep again."

I don't flinch at the implication that I'm the trash Tate was returning to. His father's words don't hurt me. They might have two months ago, before Tate and I made it to the solid ground we're on now, but not anymore. Tate looks over, eyes searching, and I give him a small smile and a shake of my head, reaching over to hold his hand between both of mine. I hope he realizes that I'm not affected by his father's hateful words.

"You hear me, Tatum?"

"I heard you, but I also heard you insultin' my woman. Don't make that mistake again."

His father grunts. "The last thing I want to do is think about that woman you've run back to despite all attempts at me trying to get you to see your error in judgment. What could you possibly see in a mechanic, of all things?" He spits out *mechanic* like other people would say *hooker*.

Tate's eyes spark with ire and I try to soothe his

temper by shaking my head and rubbing my hand over his arm. I can feel his rage growing to be a palpable thing and I'm helpless but to witness the effect his father has on him. I can't imagine what it was like dealing with the man while he held the upper hand for so long.

"She is so much more than that, you son of a bitch," Tate practically growls. "She's everything that you will never find and would have never found in those idiotic women you had such high hopes of me ending up with."

"Oh, you stupid boy. Tell me, son, if she's all that you claim, care to tell me why I had to deal with one of those so-called idiotic women early this morning?"

I frown at the same time Tate does.

"Excuse me?" he asks in a calm voice that I know is just for show.

"Even when left to your own devices, you can't even find one that isn't fucked-up. Could've seen it with the hick, at least she was a looker with some great tits, Tatum. This girl that showed up, though, not sure you understood what I was tryin' to get you to go after if that's the side piece you're attemptin'. Want them mute and compliant, not mouthy and fuckin' crazy, goin' on about how you two are meant to be together and wantin' to see if you were around."

I feel a tremor of fear shake through my hands, something Tate doesn't miss, because his other hand drops from the wheel to hold mine tight. Confusion is still written all over his face, but, even not understanding what his father is saying, he's pleading with me to believe in him—in us.

Jesus Jones—can I do that, faced with something that has the potential to gut me deep, carving out a hole in the part inside me that had finally healed?

"I don't know what game you're playin'," Tate fumes through clenched teeth, and I pray for the strength to calm my breathing. "I don't give a shit if the goddamn president shows up lookin' for me next—you lose my number and forget that I was ever alive. I'm not your son. If in some unfortunate event we're to cross paths, look through me like I will you and pretend that we're strangers. I have a good life started here and I'm not going to let you rip it away again."

That evil-as-hell laugh booms through the line even before Tate has finished speaking.

Then, a ball of doom is thrown into our court.

"Well, I gave your crazy little bitch directions to Fisher's, so she should be well on her way. Have fun cleanin' up that mess, Tatum."

The phone disconnects and all that's left is silence between us.

"Tate?" I ask, my voice shaking as fear gets the best of me.

"Fuck!" he bellows, slapping his palm against the wheel.

"Tate?" I try again, feeling my throat get heavy with emotion, making my voice sound weak.

"I swear to fuckin' God, Quinn, I don't know what he's talkin' about. There isn't anyone else, goddammit!" He ends this declaration with a roar so loud my ears ring.

I swallow thickly, my eyes stuck on the man I love with all my heart. All logic is gone when it comes to my feelings for him. This scared me nine years ago when I was too young to realize just how powerful things were between us, but now that I know what it feels like to lose him, that fear is multiplied tenfold.

I gave him my heart again. I took the promise of his affection because I know he meant it. The man next to me now is lost in the madness of his anger, but it isn't the fear of a cheating man caught in the act that I see. When his eyes flash on mine, anger and just as much fear as I'm feeling burning bright in them, I know he wouldn't have come back if there was even a chance that what we have could be snatched away from us.

He fought for *us* when that wasn't even something he had anymore. Sure, he might have lived his life during that time, but he did it with half a heart—just like I did—because we each held the missing part of the other's. He fought for my family. He fought for his grandparents. All the man I love has done for nine long and lonely years is fight for something he didn't know if he would ever have back. No one does that, endures that kind of debilitating pain, without meaning it. No man strives so hard to obtain a second chance at something without being sure that's what he wants.

I close my eyes and take a deep breath.

A sense of calm that I can't believe I'm feeling envelops me, giving me the strength I need. The strength he can't find through his raw anger. All the weapons I need to mentally take onto a battlefield to fight for him.

To fight for him.

To fight for us.

To protect *him* with my love and unwavering support.

To win.

"Whatever it is, we handle it together, Tate. I won't lie and tell you that what he said doesn't freak me out, but I'm here, and you're not fightin' for us alone anymore."

"Fuckin' Christ," he hisses, closing his eyes as my words take root. His chest is still heaving when he opens them again, but I feel better seeing some of his anger dissipate. "There's no one else, Quinn. You have to believe me."

I smile, trying to give him courage even where I feel none. "I know, Tate. One step at a time. Just start drivin'."

I wish I could say more, but right now I have so much swirling in my mind that I don't know what to say to make him understand my thoughts. I know what he's saying is true. I honestly do, but I also know that there were a lot of years when we weren't together and we've both admitted that we didn't spend all that time alone. I can't fault him for what he did while we were apart, because I know how overwhelming the loneliness got.

Had I not just spent the past two days banishing fears that I held onto for so long, I might have looked at this moment and run far away, but I'm not that person anymore. I'm stronger, and I've gained that strength because of the man behind the wheel now. With every turn of the tires, I feel his uncertain fear growing. He looks over every half mile or so, begging me without words not to run.

He's been working to win me back for over two months. He's spent every second leading up to his return to Pine Oak gearing himself up to give us both back what we've been missing— not stopping once. He's been open, honest, and truthful since day one. He's not had a single moment of having someone else lessen his burdens in years, not had someone willing to take on the world for those that he loves, and it kills me to see the panic in his eyes that all that work has been for nothing.

I might not know what's going on with this unknown woman, but I know the man I love, and it's time I show him that he's not the only one willing to fight the hounds of hell to win the life he wants.

Not when he's got a hell-raising badass on his side.

29
Tate

"For Her" by Chris Lane

— ★ —

I look over at Quinn, feeling like my chest is about to split open. My fingers ache with the harsh grip I have on the steering wheel, fear like I've never known eating at me. I knew something was coming, felt it deep inside me earlier, but I didn't expect this.

Everything is out of my control now. I've done all I can to prove to Quinn that I want her—I need her—but if she still holds just a sliver of doubt, this could rip her away forever. I won't survive losing her. I can't go through another hour, let alone more years, without feeling the power of her love. I tighten my grip, my knuckles screaming in protest. I won't let this be it. I can't.

"Tate," she says and I almost don't hear her over the roar of my frantic heartbeat rushing through my body. I glance over at the same second I see my mailbox come into view. "I love you and I trust you."

367

Her words make the breath shudder in my lungs.

"It's time you let someone else fight for us, honey."

She speaks at the same time we turn into my driveway. I park next to an unfamiliar sedan waiting there and look out my window toward the house when I see the car is empty. I might not recognize that car, but I can't say the same of the woman sitting on my porch. What are the odds that in the hour we've been gone that she would show up? I guess it's a blessing and a curse that I've had time to prepare us both for this shit.

"You've got to be fuckin' kiddin' me." I see her stand, adjusting her sunglasses. "You have got to be *fuckin'* jokin'!" I shout. I know she can't see into my truck because of the dark-tinted windows, but that doesn't stop her from smiling and waving at me like some fucking beauty queen.

"I take it you know her?" Quinn asks in a venomous tone. I crank my head to look at her, expecting that anger to be directed toward me, but she's not even paying me a lick of attention. She's staring straight at the porch, shooting daggers with her eyes at the very unwelcome visitor.

I look back over to see Ella's frantically happy waves start to slow down when I don't open my truck door immediately, but she still stands there smiling. I shake my head, hating that I have to even explain her to Quinn.

"I knew the moment that I would be reminded of the time we lost would come eventually," Quinn continues in the face of my silence. "I figured it would have been you runnin' into someone I . . . spent time with, though, and not the other way around. Didn't expect it to be your old girlfriend I would run into seein' as you were in Georgia and not here. Here, I would understand. It's not easy to escape the things that happened in the town you live in. That bein' said, I understand you had a life without me, Tate, and like I've been sayin', I'm not gonna hold that against you. You didn't make it across that battlefield you were fightin' on only to step on a land mine now. Just tell me and I swear it's the only time I'll need to ask." She pauses and holds my gaze. Something in her eyes makes me sit a little straighter and the fear dim. "That woman there isn't someone you'd want here even if we hadn't gotten back together, right?"

"Fuck no," I spit out without even a millisecond of thought.

"Does she know that?"

"Quinn, the first day I heard your voice through the phone almost three months ago was the same day I had a conversation that needed to be had with that woman. She was a coworker at the hospital I worked at who, yes, I unfortunately crossed the line with almost a year ago, but it had ended long before that talk and she knew it. I only wanted to attempt to make the last month I worked with her go smoother and even told her about the woman I was hoping to win back when I finally went home to Texas. Trust me when I tell you she didn't have a single doubt as to where I stood."

Quinn flinches when I mention crossing the line with Ella, but other than that, she doesn't give me a clue as to what she's thinking.

"And now?"

"I had her number blocked through my carrier almost two months ago, the same day you showed up at my office pissed as hell at me after wakin' up in my bed hungover. I did that because she wouldn't stop harassin' me, Quinn. But I did it well before you finally gave me back your love."

She nods and looks away from me to narrow her eyes at Ella again. I don't look away, my concern only being for Quinn. Because of that, I'm rewarded with one hell of a sight. She shakes her arms out and rolls her head, the braid in her hair moving like a wild rope being shaken from one end. When she looks back at me, there isn't anything reflecting on her face at me except the devious expression she normally only gets when she and Leigh are plotting something together, the two little devils. One corner of her full lips is tipped up, and even in the middle of some serious fucked-up shit, she looks happy as fucking hell.

"You're gonna let me lead, Tate. Wanna know why?"

I shake my head, not trusting myself to speak without swallowing my tongue. Fucking hell, I shouldn't be this turned on after feeling like I was about to have a panic-driven heart attack just a few minutes ago, but the sight of the confident woman I love overcoming the fear I saw in her eyes during my father's call is inspiring. The woman before me giving testament to just how far Quinn has come in overcoming what had gripped her tight for so long.

"You're gonna let me lead because your woman is a hell-raisin' badass, and no one messes with her man."

"Goddamn," I breathe, my heartbeat not roaring in my ears anymore—nope, it's rushed south now.

"Give me a kiss, Starch, and sit back and enjoy. You might not be able to hit a woman, but I can."

Then, without waiting for me to actually give her the kiss she demanded, she leans over the console and gives me a hell of a smooch, one that sets my already painfully hard cock throbbing.

When I open my eyes, I see her door open and just her long braid licking up in the air as she jumps from the truck. "Shit," I hiss, unsnapping my seat belt and rushing to get down from the truck myself.

"Who the hell are you?" I hear her yell at Ella.

Ella actually has the decency to look alarmed. Whatever fucked-up thought convinced her coming here would be a good idea isn't looking so good now, I'm guessing.

"Uh," she starts before clearing her throat, "I'm his girlfriend, and who might you be?"

Quinn throws her head back and laughs. A breeze picking up around us makes the material of her sleeveless top dance around her tiny frame. It's nothing fancy, just some sheer blue material that's about as dressy as it gets for a normal day with Quinn. Her boots are dirty and scuffed from long wear. The frayed edges of her shorts stand out against her tan skin. Right now, she's the most beautiful woman I've ever seen.

"Oh, bless your heart," Quinn says sweetly. She turns back toward the truck and calls out to me. "Tate, honey, did you forget somethin' back in Georgia?"

I cough to cover up my laugh, walking the rest of the way from my truck to the bottom of the porch steps where Quinn is standing and placing my arm over her shoulder. She wraps her body around mine instantly, one arm around my back and the other around my gut, her front pressed tight to my side as she looks up at me. I shake my head just enough, loving this woman even more than I thought possible.

"Got everything I ever wanted right here, darlin'. Nothin' forgotten now that I got this back."

"You hear that?" Quinn calls, smiling brightly up at me.

"I'm sorry, who are you?" Ella asks snottily, apparently unwilling to admit defeat.

Quinn's eyes sparkle, fucking twinkle like a goddamn kaleidoscope. I soak that shit up before she looks away, stepping out from my body and on to the bottom step. Never in the sixteen years that I've known her have I seen something so beautifully confident and strong in her eyes.

Until today.

When she learned how to fight.

"Well, honey, don't you know? I'm his future wife. Reckon you didn't count on that when your ass went off the rails on the crazy train to try and get a man that doesn't want you." I can't see Quinn's expression, but judging by the way Ella blanches, there's something powerful there. "Now, I won't hold it against you and all, especially since I know just how magical he can be, if you know what I mean. We had a little gap in our relationship that was unfortunately unpreventable, but just because I know how addictive he is doesn't mean you get to keep on tryin' to get a taste. Sweetheart, he's off the market and he will *never* be back on it. You got me?"

Ella's eyes narrow, and that mask of beauty she wears slips, the sneer on her face transforming her into something troll-like. "His future wife?" She throws her head back and laughs. "You expect me to believe that after he's only been here for seven weeks?"

"Actually, he's been here for almost eight, but who's counting?"

"Fine, two months. In two months, he's gone from the playboy who's allergic to relationships to engaged?"

Quinn snorts. "Him? Allergic to relationships?" She looks over her shoulder at me, that scheming glint still shining in her eyes. "Honey, the only thing this man is allergic to is peanuts, bees, and dirty psycho skanks who don't know how to take a hint."

"What did you just say?"

Quinn straightens, appearing taller than she really is, with her boots braced apart and her hands on her hips. "You heard me. Let me be clear so that maybe, God willin', you get this through your head. Tate Montgomery is my man. He was my man when he stomped down Main Street at eleven convinced there wasn't a damn thing to do in this town. When he was fifteen and gave me my first kiss in the middle of a rainstorm on the edge of the lake with some worms between us, there was no doubt. When I gave him me and he gave me him at eighteen, the same held true. Might have lost some time with him, but that is one truth that never wavered. He wasn't allergic to relationships; he was allergic to givin' up hope that he wouldn't get the woman that held his damn heart back. And sweetheart, that woman is me. So with that said, you wanna rethink what you claim is the reason behind this ridiculous visit?"

Unable to stand there anymore, I stomp the three feet keeping me from Quinn, grab her hand, and spin her around. I don't give a single thought to Ella standing there as I lower my head and give Quinn a deep, hungry kiss. It's short but sweet, and when I pull back with a single lick against her lips, I feel the last of the fear my father's call instilled in me vanish.

I look up at Ella, my eyes hardening, at the same time I whisper in Quinn's ear. "I'm going to fuck you so hard when she gets off my fuckin' property."

She shivers in my hold and then addresses herself to Ella. "You've got two seconds to get your ass outta here before I show you just how friendly us Texans can get with a shotgun. Shoot-first state, honey."

I see Ella jump in her high-ass heels before tottering down the porch steps. She almost breaks her neck trying to avoid getting near Quinn.

The next thing I hear is the door of her sedan slamming and the heavy acceleration as she spins tires out of here. Who knows what absurd notion brought that woman to Pine Oak, but I have no doubt that Quinn's show just now will ensure her never returning.

Quinn shades her eyes with her hand as she watches Ella's car disappear in the distance, then turns toward me. "Jesus Jones, Tate. You sure know how to pick 'em. She wasn't even very pretty when her face went all *Bride of Chucky*, Tate," she says with a laugh.

"Goddamn, I love you."

She loops her hands over my neck and leans into my body. "I love you too."

"I'm sorry for that," I whisper against her lips.

Quinn shakes her head. "You didn't make her come here, Tate. I meant what I said—you're not the only one fighting for us now."

I close my eyes and lean my forehead against hers. "I haven't felt fear that great in my life, Quinn. Not even when I realized what my father had against us did I feel it. Not when the years kept passing that kept us apart. When I heard him earlier, the only thing I felt was a desperation that I might lose you because of this bullshit. I can't live without you, Quinn. I knew that before now, but fuck, darlin', if the last half hour didn't just stab me deep when I felt that panic drowning me."

I finally open my eyes when I finish talking, swallowing thickly when I see how much love is written within her emerald irises, shining bright as hell like gemstones.

"Been workin' toward this moment for weeks now, Tate. You came back when I never thought I would see you again. You mended what was broken when you left, then healed the pain that was there long before we had even met. *You* are the reason that I've found myself whole after a lifetime of knowin' somethin' was missin'. You will never know a day without me showin' you just how thankful I am to have you back in my life, Tate. That bein' said, if another tramp from Georgia shows up, I'm gonna make sure I bring up that shotgun first."

"Noted," I say with a smile, feeling my throat get thick from her words.

"It's our time now, Tate," she whispers, her eyes watering and one tear falling. I reach up and wipe it off and smile even though I feel my own eyes getting misty. "And anyone dumb enough to try and stand in our way can just kiss my damn boots."

Epilogue
Quinn

"Huntin', Fishin' and Lovin' Every Day"
by Luke Bryan

— ★ —

W hy do you look like that?"
I look up, blow some of my hair out of my
eyes, and huff at Leigh. It's chillier than normal
out today, but even if it was summer still and not
winter, I would be freezing my ass off. I've been
like this the past few weeks, and nothing aside
from using Tate's body as a human heating pad
seems to help.

I've been clicking my teeth together with my
shivers for the past hour while Leigh and I move
the rest of my stuff out of my childhood home
and over to Tate's. Lord knows how we made it
the past six months without moving in together
officially. There wasn't a night we spent apart but
it wasn't until he finally sat down with Clay and
asked for my hand in marriage that we decided
to stop putting it off. Thank God, because I was
sick of running out of things at one or the other
house. My belongings had been basically split

378

into two groups with some there and some here, the things I needed never in the right place at the right time.

"Look like what?" I ask, pulling my sweater tighter around my body and straightening the pile of shirts I had ready to cart down to my truck.

"Like you're starving but also might hurl. Kinda like that time that you wanted to ride that big roller coaster even though you know you get that weird motion-sickness thing when you ride them."

I scrunch my nose up. "You're insane, Leighton. That makes no sense."

She continues to stare at me unnervingly and I just barely resist the urge to look away.

"You've been the one actin' insane, you weirdo."

"You really are makin' no damn sense. Are you gonna grab the pile of shorts or do I need to come get those later?"

She huffs and bends to pick up the last stack of clothing that I have left to bring to Tate—no, Tate's and my house.

"Lemme ask you somethin'," Leigh commands, her voice muffled by the clothes in her arms that are covering her face.

I turn and start walking down the hall to the stairs before answering. "What now, Leighton?" I deadpan.

"When was your last period?"

I stop walking, halfway down the stairs, and stare down them with wide eyes.

"Christ!" Leigh screeches out as she bumps into me, falling back onto her butt on the step behind her. "Just stop in the middle of the stairs, Q. That's really safe. We should try runnin' down them before jumpin' and tryin' to fly next."

"Repeat that last question," I breathe, my eyes feeling dry from being bugged out for so long, reminding me to blink.

"What question? Oh, about your lady time?"

"Yes, that one."

"I'm thinkin' you don't need me repeatin' it."

I drop the shirts in my arms, seeing them fall down around the stairs, and turn, my hands frantically uncovering her face while flinging the clothes she was holding all around us.

"Oh my God, you've really lost it," she gasps, wide-eyed, looking at the clothes all over the stairs. "I'm not pickin' that shit up." She leans back on her elbows and looks up at me.

"Why would you ask that?"

She smirks and shrugs. "Told you, you've been actin' weird."

"I have not."

"You're the only one that looks like she's ready to break out a turtleneck when it's not even that cold, Q. Not to mention the whole lookin'-seasick-even-while-smilin'-like-a-freak

380

thing. And"—she reaches out to poke my boob, making me yelp—"your boobs are bigger and— thanks for confirming, by the way—sore."

"No way." I pant.

"Oh, yes way."

"You could be wrong. I'm pretty sure I just had my period recently, Leigh."

She looks smug at that. "You didn't."

"How do you know?" I all but yell.

"I know because you were supposed to have it last week. The same week *I* was supposed to have mine."

Even through the shock of her words, I don't miss that. "Wait a minute. . . ."

She winks. "Surprise!" Her excited word comes out just a whisper and I see her chin wobble.

"Jesus Jones! You're pregnant?" I ask feeling my own chin start to tremble. "I'm so happy for you."

She smiles, her eyes shining. "Thanks, Q. I'm still comin' to grips with the whole thing, but you're the only one that knows aside from Mav. Waitin' to get a little further along before we start spreadin' the news. Anyway, I'm bettin' you are too, sister, so I'm happy right back at ya."

I shake my head. "You're gonna have my niece?"

She raises one perfectly arched brow. "You gonna have mine?"

"Holy shit," I wheeze, dropping to sit in the

pile of clothes around us. The silence continues, and even though I'm over-the-moon happy for her and Maverick, I can't deny there could be some truth to her words. "Holy fuckin' shit!" I yell, turning to look at her. "What the hell am I supposed to do? My fiancé is a damn gyno, Leigh! I can't hide this from him while I find out if you're right."

She taps her chin and thinks it over. "Hey!" she exclaims. "I have an idea!"

Oh boy. Famous last words.

Unlike the last time I came here unannounced, the parking lot at Tate's practice is a lot fuller, seeing as it's the middle of the day and not the end of it. Leigh's bright idea was to basically seduce him at work again. It has merit, seeing as it worked so well last time, but I want the moment Tate finds out he's going to be a daddy to be something we can tell our future grandchildren about and me ending up naked and stuffed with his cock doesn't need to be part of that.

I step down from Homer, smiling as I shut the door to the beast that helped bring Tate and me together. It's his turn in the rotation, Bertha's being last week, and I still get a different kind of thrill when I'm driving him than I get from any other truck. He's always going to be the most special out of every one I own just because of what he represents in the Tate-and-me story.

When I enter the office this time, the waiting room is full, and Gladys is in her normal spot. I walk over and lean in to get some privacy in the crowded room.

"Quinn?" Gladys questions as my face gets closer. "You okay, sweet girl?"

I smile. "I would give you a big long excuse about why I need to get in there without an appointment when I'm sure all these nice ladies have been waitin' and all, but that pain's back, Ms. Gladys, and it was everything I could do to get here. He's a naughty man, you know. I just need a quick walk-in appointment so he can get a good look at what he's done to me this time."

Her eyes are huge as I whisper my plight to her, not actually lying this time. Tate really does need to get a good look at what he's done.

"Oh my," she breathes. "You just come on around, honey. We'll get you in real quick."

"Thanks, Ms. Gladys. I owe you huge."

"Don't even think about it. Why I remember back in my day, a youngin' like you, what it felt like after enjoyin' your young fella's attentions a little too much. Nothin' like havin' that fella bein' a doc and all, seein' as you won't end up sittin' with an ice pack between your legs for hours. Lucky girl you are, Quinn."

I pray my tongue doesn't actually fall down my throat in shock at her words and mumble what I think is some kind of thanks.

"Just wait in here and I'll send Dr. Montgomery on in."

I walk into the exam room, not removing my clothes this time, and stare at the sea of baby pictures pinned to the board in the center of the wall. Jesus Jones, will our little one be up there soon? I press my hands against my flat stomach and hope that Leigh wasn't wrong. Now that the thought that I could be pregnant has taken root, I can't handle the excitement I feel, praying that it's true.

I sit against the table, resting my body back with my palms against the paper-covered surface. So much like the same position I used to my advantage the last time I surprised Tate at work with the plan of seducing him to win our bet.

I hear knuckles rasp against the wooden door and I straighten, placing my hands in my lap.

He walks in, frowning at me, his blue eyes meeting mine instantly. Gladys must have told him I was waiting this time.

"Hey darlin'," he says, walking over and kissing me lightly. "You aren't feeling well?"

"I'm feelin' fine, Tate."

He clears his throat, shifting on his booted feet. "Quinn, it's the middle of the day. I can't give you a quickie no matter how much I would love to when I'm slammed with appointments."

"Not here for a quickie, Starch."

He looks confused. "Then what are you here

for? You just had your checkup two months ago with Russ, darlin'. I could have written a scrip if you're low on your birth control at home." He steps closer and trails his finger down my cheek. "You know I love playin' doctor, Quinn, but you're gonna have to wait until the patients aren't fillin' the buildin'."

"Not here for any of that either."

His brows pull in even more.

"Need a checkup, Tate. One only you can give me. Figure the rest out."

"Darlin', it's been a long mornin'. I just got done doin' a checkup house call at Mark and Janie's since she's on bed rest until she delivers the triplets. Before that, it was patient after patient since Russ is out today with a stomach bug. My mind just isn't firin' on all cylinders at the moment."

Taking pity on him, I rise from the exam table and stand, looking up at his handsome face. I bring my hand up, my diamond engagement ring winking at me as it catches light, and rub my palm against his cheek. Seeing that ring, the one I only wear when I'm not working at the shop, just makes my emotions amp up until I'm looking at him through blurry, tear-filled eyes.

"Give me a pregnancy test, Starch."

His eyes widen, and had it not been something he could do on muscle memory alone, I'm not sure he would have been able to figure it out. He stands stock-still as I slip out of the exam room and into the bathroom across the hall to get a urine sample. He's in the same position when I walk back in and place the cup on the counter. His hands move in slow, practiced movements as he collects a small amount and drops it into the test window of the pregnancy kit he must have gotten out while I was gone.

His harsh breathing is the only thing that I hear as we both stand, waiting for the test to tell us if I am, in fact, carrying our child. It feels like a lifetime, but when I see the two lines indicating a positive result, my heart feels near full to bursting. I look up at him to see him still staring down at the test, his cheeks wet and his jaw slack.

"I love you, Daddy," I whisper, leaning up to kiss his jaw, tasting the salt of his tears.

I grab the purse I had tossed in the chair before walking out of the room. I smile at Gladys and thank her for fitting me in before walking on what feels like air to Homer. I don't stick around because he wasn't wrong when he said the exam room wasn't the place to get in a quickie and if I know my man, he's going to want to celebrate when the shocked happiness I left him experiencing wears off.

I make it home just twenty minutes before I hear the familiar sound of his steps on the porch. I had been standing in the middle of the living room, waiting, that confident that he wasn't far behind me, so when he throws open the front door in a rush I've got a front-row seat.

"You just left me like that?" he whispers hoarsely. His eyes are red and I know he probably didn't stop those tears from falling until well after I left.

"I knew you wouldn't be far behind me, honey."

He closes the distance between us. "Oh you did?"

I nod. "You wouldn't have wanted to celebrate with an office full of patients, Starch. Just lookin' out for my baby daddy and all." I smirk, feeling my chin start to tremble. "You're gonna be a daddy," I breathe, his hands framing my face as his thumbs wipe away the tears that finally escape my eyes.

"You're gonna be a mama."

"God, Tate," I choke out with a sob, smiling through the happy tears. "I love you so much I feel like I could burst."

He presses his forehead against mine, pulling me closer. "Always knew it would be a wild and unpredictable ride with you, Grease. Not sure I could love you more than I do right now, knowin' you're givin' me somethin' as beautiful as our first child."

The tears continue to fall down my face as he presses his lips against mine, stripping us both down before carrying me to the bedroom and showing me just how happy he is that we've created a life with the love we feel for each other.

It was a long road, us getting here, but when I have him holding me in his arms—skin-to-skin—and his large palm resting low on my stomach, protective over the space that will grow as our child does, I know I feel it down to my bones, that full feeling of being complete inside me tipping over the edge even more.

This, this moment right here, makes every single second that it took for us to get here worth it. We're building our forever now, and there isn't a damn thing that could take this from us.

I've got everything.

And it's freaking beautiful.

Books are
produced in the
United States
using U.S.-based
materials

Books are printed
using a revolutionary
new process called
THINKtech™ that
lowers energy usage
by 70% and increases
overall quality

Books are
durable and
flexible
because of
Smyth-sewing

Paper is
sourced using
environmentally
responsible
foresting methods
and the
paper is acid-free

Center Point Large Print
600 Brooks Road / PO Box 1
Thorndike, ME 04986-0001 USA

(207) 568-3717

US & Canada:
1 800 929-9108
www.centerpointlargeprint.com